I0662703

AIR

by

Nicki Greenwood

The Elemental Series,
Volume Three

This is a work of fiction. Names, characters, places, and incidents are either the product of the author's imagination or are used fictitiously, and any resemblance to actual persons living or dead, business establishments, events, or locales, is entirely coincidental.

AIR

Cover Art by *Kim Mendoza*

The Wild Rose Press, Inc.
PO Box 708
Adams Basin, NY 14410-0708
Visit us at www.thewildrosepress.com

Publishing History
First Fantasy Edition, 2015
Print ISBN 978-1-62830-814-3
Digital ISBN 978-1-62830-815-0

The Elemental Series, Volume Three
Published in the United States of America

Dedication

To Hank Schyma,
storm chaser and incredible photographer—
who, by utter coincidence,
happens to share a name with the hero of this book.

Author's Foreword

Every year, the United States faces more than a thousand tornadoes, and still more severe storms. The damage from severe weather can be disastrous. My heart goes out to the families who suffer the loss of their family members, friends, or homes, and yet find a way to rebuild. I can't imagine the courage it takes to do that.

It is partly the admiration of that courage that drove me to write this book. In my mind, Elsa personifies the indomitable spirit of the people who face such disasters and refuse to be beaten by them. That's true heroism.

I consulted various sources in the writing of this book, including storm chasers, meteorologists, and the usual suspects of library and Internet research. Alas, I'm still human. Any errata are entirely my own. Thanks for reading, and stay safe out there. ~ Nicki

Chapter One

"Elsa Pemberley, you hike your rear end back here this instant!" shouted Nina Parnow.

Elsa ignored her teammate's call and went right on running at the tornado. Her hair whipped her cheeks in the wind. Her power crackled along her skin, even now gathering the force needed to punch it. She had one shot at this. The base of the twister was narrow and angled, and for the last ten minutes had been zigzagging its way through the farmland. An unpredictable one, even for her.

Which, Elsa considered as the funnel switched direction and began driving toward her, eating up clods of earth, was exactly why Nina was now screaming bloody murder.

The tornado hopped a ditch and tore a few boards off a lonely tractor bridge at the edge of the field across the road. Watching the lumber fling itself up into the whirling monster, Elsa held out her hands. She'd better kill this one before it hit that barn and house at the end of the field. Lord knew if the family living there had found the time to evacuate its livestock, or themselves. They might be hiding in their basement, praying, right now.

"Elsa! Doll, this ain't one you wanna tackle!" hollered Brian Wozinsky. He hooked an arm around her middle and hauled her backward while she protested. A piece of lumber hurtled past the spot where her head had been a second before.

"I can do this if you just shut up and stop distracting me!" she said, struggling against his grip. "Woz, come on! Let me go!" She begged him with her eyes. "Please? There's a house over there...probably with people in it!"

"El, honey, there's *always* a house probably with people in it!" Woz shouted back over the fitful jet-engine roar of the tornado.

She gave him Puppy Eyes. Woz was a sucker for Puppy Eyes.

Her lanky teammate crumbled. "All right, but if that thing gets much closer, you run for the truck!" He backed away and hurried for The Beast, the first vehicle in their convoy. Her team had built the ground-hugging, welded-steel monster to face the storms of Tornado Alley. He launched himself into the vehicle. Nina slammed the door shut, and two pairs of worried eyes peered through the bulletproof glass of the passenger window at her. Elsa couldn't see the rest of her team, who'd paused a safe distance behind in the weather van and Elsa's old crossover wagon.

She turned back to the tornado eating up the field. Five hundred yards away and closing fast. Four hundred. Three hundred. No sweat.

Spreading her hands, she recalled her power. It snapped and popped, as fitful as the wind. Illumination coursed along her skin, and fused together until her whole body glowed wherever bare flesh showed. Then she punched it.

Light exploded outward from her skin. No sound, just a blinding glare that forced her to shut her eyes against it. And in its wake, the growling rush of the wind stopped. Between the settling gusts came the thump of debris hitting the ground.

"Watch it, El!" shouted Rory Grant, their weather expert.

Elsa opened her eyes in time to see one of the boards from the tractor bridge falling toward her. She bolted out of the way just as it slammed down. When all was quiet, she started breathing again.

Seth Loughlin, their youngest team member, leaped out of their weather van. "Woo-hoo! Elsa, that was awesome!" He rushed toward her with an enormous grin.

A grin Nina clearly didn't share, Elsa realized as Nina and Woz emerged from The Beast, much more cautiously than Seth. Everyone on their team of storm chasers wore safety helmets, just in case.

Except for her. She hadn't needed protection from wind storms since she was a child. She'd been trying to convince Nina of that—unsuccessfully—for two years.

Seth reached her and gave her an enthusiastic fist-bump.

"Are you nuts?" Nina yowled. As the eldest and longest-running member of their team, Nina considered it her mission to rein them in whenever one of them decided to do anything particularly insane.

Like jump out of a car and chase after a tornado.

Seth's enthusiasm dropped a few notches, and he stepped back. Nina slung a heavy army blanket around Elsa's shoulders. Shivering and drained, Elsa opened her mouth to thank the woman.

Nina glared. "You're welcome. And certifiable." She pulled Elsa in close under her arm. "Let's get you back to The Beast and get you warm. Doesn't look like this storm's got anything left in it."

Elsa couldn't find the willpower to be bothered by the scolding.

Woz hooked an arm around her shoulders from the other side, warming her with his walking-furnace body heat. "As usual, you're our secret weapon, doll. And"— he pointed at the still-standing house in the field—"we still have a house...probably with people in it."

Elsa gave him a tired grin and walked with them back to the convoy. She paused at the door of The Beast to look back over her shoulder at the torn-up field and damaged tractor bridge, and the still-standing house and barn. Pulling the blanket tighter around her shoulders, she allowed herself a little smile, touched with sadness. One more family, safe and free to go on with their lives together.

Lucky them.

****

"Did you *see* that, Harry?"

Twelve-year-old Rosalie squirmed out of Harrison Litchfield's arms and climbed out of the waterlogged ditch. Big-eyed, she stared after the retreating vehicles picking their way down the debris-laden road.

Harry risked a look upward where he crouched. Through the missing boards of the tractor bridge, he glimpsed moody gray skies. Moody, but tornado-free. Maybe God didn't have it in for him today, after all. At least not in this consecutive five minutes.

A muddy black Lab slogged up out of the ditch after Rose with a whine and an uncertain tail-wag. He shoved his nose under the girl's hand. Rose patted him, but kept staring. "The lady that got into that tank thing.

She *glowed*, Harry. Did you see it? She glowed, like a superhero, and the tornado just stopped!" She looked back at him.

Great. Now the stress is getting to her, too. Harry unfolded himself from where they'd sheltered under the tractor bridge, then climbed out of the ditch. He patted himself down. Soaked, dirty as a losing mud wrestler, and not too happy, but unhurt. He checked his kid sister, and then the dog. Likewise, more muddy than injured.

Then he saw the battered guitar case lying twenty feet away in the field. With a choked-off gasp of dismay, he scrambled for it.

The dog galloped after him, trailing Rose. When the dog wedged himself in front of Harry, he shoved the animal aside to grapple with the clasps of the filthy case. He wrenched it open.

Only when he saw the old Gibson, intact and polished, did he start breathing again.

"Harry? What's wrong?"

"Nothing," he said on a sigh. "We're okay." Now that the danger had passed, fury settled in, and he rounded on her. "What were you thinking, running out of the house like that? We were safe!"

"Sam wasn't," Rose protested. She slung her arms around the dog's neck, and the Labrador wagged its tail again.

Sam, was it? They had discovered the dog just before the storm hit. Rose left the perfectly good house to chase it and, with no alternative, Harry had chased them both into this ditch. There, for the second time in eight months, he'd watched his life flash before him like the proverbial film. Like he needed a reminder of what he'd lost.

Why? Why? He didn't expect an answer, a sign, anything...and he got none, so no disappointment there.

He kicked at the damp, churned earth. "Sam is not coming with us, Rose." At her pouty look, he added, "He's not. We have no business with a homeless dog. We can't afford a roof over our own heads." *Not to mention the hazard of staying in one place,* he added silently, but he'd thought that so often these days that it didn't rate saying aloud.

When Rose gave him a crestfallen frown, months-old bitterness flashed through him. She knew very well that they could have afforded the nicest hotel in the heartland under normal circumstances. Harry had almost forgotten what "normal" felt like...but that line of thinking just plunged him into guilt mode again.

Rose hadn't asked for this. The two of them ought to be enjoying a big house with a sprawling lawn, lush gardens, and garages stocked with expensive, shiny cars. Rose should have been in school, doing giggly stuff with other girls her age. Instead, he sometimes caught a hunted look on her face, in spite of his efforts to make things as steady as possible for her.

Ever since they'd gone on the run, Rose had been fascinated—no, obsessed—with superheroes, as if someone could just emerge from a fallen meteor and save them from their troubles. Harry wished *he* could, but he could barely put food in their mouths. What a joke. If she expected a savior to show up, she'd have a long wait.

Part of him wanted to believe, as she did, that there were superheroes and fairytales where everything ended happily—that a glowing woman could magically wave her arms and stop the world from blowing apart over their heads.

The rest of him remembered why he and his sister were skulking around the Midwest with no money and no identities in the first place.

He sighed, torn between wanting to reassure Rose that they were going to be okay, and needing to hide them both as far from anyone as possible. They were already as close to the edge of danger as he cared to dance, without doing the tornado waltz. "Let's go back inside. We'll talk about this later."

"But Harry—"

"No."

"Can Sam come? For tonight, at least?"

Harry caught the pleading note in Rose's voice, and it tugged at him. A dog was normal.

He ran through a mental resource check: eighty-four dollars and change in his pocket. A bundle of clothes that needed a good wash, once they found a cheap Laundromat. In his army duffel, his sunglasses, a few power bars, a bottle of water, a can opener, a mess kit, and a couple cans of soup.

He pulled the guitar case onto his shoulder by the fraying strap and started back for the foreclosed house at the edge of the field.

The Gibson was worth a few hundred thousand.

The thought alone made him jerk it closer to his body. He'd have to be near death first.

"Yeah, he can come," Harry said at last, checking the sky. It didn't look like they'd get a repeat of the twister, but he couldn't stomach the thought of shutting the dog out into the storm if they did. Even a dog didn't deserve that.

He hadn't seen the woman Rose mentioned. He'd been too busy holding onto his sister and the dog's scruff and the bridge's piling with all his strength. He flexed his hand. The scared Lab had twisted in his grasp, wrenching Harry's fingers painfully, but not bad enough to hamper his ability to play the guitar.

He guessed that having sound hands and avoiding a tornado about tapped his store of luck for the day. Better to get inside, and not push it further. Imaginary glowing people would have to wait.

"We going to sneak back in again?" Rose asked, trotting alongside him toward the farmhouse. The dog rambled ahead, tail waving. Now that the storm had ceased, the mutt seemed content, as long as it kept them within eyesight.

Harry studied his little sister. She giggled whenever the dog loped back to her, and rubbed a hand through his soppy ears. Harry hadn't heard her laugh in months.

A stone or something had hit her during the storm. A little blood welled in a scratch on her cheek. Her tone indicated she knew what they were doing was wrong, but necessary. She'd done way too much growing up, too fast, and done a better job of it than he. *You're too smart for your own good, sweet pea.*

"We shouldn't," he admitted, "but we don't have much choice." He opened the unlocked back window and handed her through first. "We'll clean up after ourselves, I promise. Better this than being out in the open, right? Especially if we get another dose of the weather works."

She nodded. The Lab hopped through the window on his own, clearly unwilling to let Rose out of his sight. Harry went last. "Shoes off," he ordered, "and get that dog to the tub. The water's still on. Rinse him off before he tracks mud all over and gives us away." He handed her a handkerchief to use as a makeshift washcloth. "You, too. You look like—" He almost said *a fright*, but that sounded too much like their mother. Too much like a lifetime ago. "You're a mess, Rosie," he said softly.

His sister didn't seem to notice the near-slip. She nodded and towed the dog toward the bathroom, eager to follow his instructions now that he'd relented.

Harry sank to the floor by the fireplace and began to poke through his duffel. *Stupid,* he berated himself. Rose could do without reminders of home. *He* could have done without reminders of home. He hated that he couldn't just call the police and respond to the dozens of public pleas for news of their whereabouts. He hated that every day he and Rose spent running, he felt farther away from any end to it.

Speculation ran rampant in the beginning that the Litchfield heirs must have been taken for ransom. The family had money, after all, and the news of their parents' murders had been wildly and sickeningly plastered across every possible form of media. Just the mention of their parents was enough to bring Rosalie close to tears. Another knife-twist Harry endured as just one more penance.

After the first month went by with no word and no demand for money, the public suspected that Harry and Rose had also been murdered. A few nasty rumors flew around that they'd had some part in the death of their parents. When Harry heard those, he shook with outrage, but he had no choice except to let them circulate.

He couldn't go home and speak out. They had no home anymore. The culprits were looking for him, and they didn't want money. They wanted the witnesses dead, and everyone knew you couldn't run from the Torellis once they had a sniff of you.

He gave a silent snarl. He'd be ready, when and if they found him. And when they did, they'd wish they never heard of the Litchfield family.

A bitter jab of pain flashed underneath his anger. *You'd be proud of me, Mom. I finally have a goal.*

****

"Ten dollars," said one of the bouncers at a small roadside bar.

"Who charges ten bucks for a no-name blues player?" Seth grumped, indicating the framed poster by the door.

Elsa glanced at the poster in question. The bold, grungy lettering proclaimed the night's entertainment to be Hank Rhodes. Beside it was a picture of what she assumed to be the artist, rendered in heavily shaded silhouette—a man in sunglasses and three days' worth of stubble. He lounged against a crate, looking more like an ad for men's fashion than a blues player. That much, she could see, even though she could barely make out the suggestion of his features...which, she had to admit, promised some pleasant distraction even if the music didn't pan out.

"Ma'am? Ten dollars?"

"Ah, let her in," said the other bouncer. He grinned at her. "Fine-looking girl like you could draw a crowd all by yourself."

She blushed and rummaged in her pocket for a bill.

"I'll pay."

Elsa and her team filed into the darkened bar. The evening crowd had already taken advantage of free-flowing beer. No one had taken the stage yet, but the jukebox pumped out a catchy beat, and the dance floor teemed with patrons enjoying their night.

Elsa watched them. The night might have gone very differently if her team had not caught that tornado.

Nina noticed her faltering smile and gave her an affectionate pat on the shoulder. "I'm going to grab a few beers. Y'all find us a seat."

"Wait, I've got money," Elsa protested.

Nina stopped her with a firm headshake. "I *know* you're good for it. I *know* you can pay your way. Tonight is about celebrating. Even for crazy fools who don't know when not to jump headfirst into disaster."

"I'll take that as a compliment to my persistence," Elsa called to her retreating back.

"C'mon, doll, let's get out there and wear down that wood," Woz said. He tugged her hand, and with a real grin this time, Elsa hurried after him to the dance floor.

An hour of dancing rendered her footsore but happy, and she settled at a table near the stage. The house lights went down, and someone turned on a bluish spotlight.

A tall man with sunglasses and short, unruly dark hair walked onto the stage. Elsa took in his easy saunter and lean, hungry-panther look with a raised eyebrow.

Nina leaned in close with a conspiratorial quirk of her eyebrow. "So far, he's good," she murmured, tipping the neck of her bottle toward the musician.

"He hasn't played a single note yet," said Seth.

11

"Exactly," Nina and Elsa said together.

Polite applause echoed across the room as he stopped mid-stage. He slid the shoulder strap of his guitar forward until the instrument hung across the front of his body, then adjusted the microphone. "Good evening," he said.

He had a voice like spiked chocolate. The amplified sound reverberated through Elsa and settled into all kinds of interesting places. Her toes curled. She closed her eyes on a delicious little thrill and smiled. *Mmmmm. I don't care if you can't carry a tune in a bucket. Just keep talking.*

A jab in her ribs made her open her eyes again. Nina flicked her gaze from Elsa to the stage. Elsa followed it.

The musician was grinning. Even though he wore sunglasses, she had the impression he'd been watching her. Elsa blushed for the second time that night, wondering if he suspected where her thoughts had been leading.

Still grinning—at her, she knew it now—he leaned into the microphone and said, "My name's Hank Rhodes. You've seen the poster outside, so let's get this party going, all right?"

Yes, please, she thought with admiration.

More applause, and a few whistles, one of them distinctly female and very vocal about her appreciation of the night's entertainment. Elsa found herself in total agreement.

Hank launched right into a bluesy cover of a popular song. The promise of his introductory handful of syllables delivered in a sinfully smooth singing voice that went with that guitar like rum and Coke.

Elsa appreciated talent; her foster family exploded at the seams with it. Her sister Morgan was a ridiculously creative chef, and her oldest brother Kincade had elevated horse training to an art form. Even wanderlust-ridden Ethan had a near-magical ability to fix anything without setting eyes on the manual. All that, in addition to their Elemental powers.

This was power with a whole new spin. Hank Rhodes sang with gritty honesty. Even though the words weren't his, she sensed the frustration, determination, fear, and hope in his voice as if he'd lived the song. Elsa leaned forward in her chair, her beer forgotten, and tapped her foot.

If his first selection captivated her, the rest of the set held her transfixed. He sprinkled in a few danceable songs, but while Seth, Rory, and Woz dragged Nina repeatedly onto the floor, Elsa found herself content to sit and admire the view.

Then he started singing about storms, a heartfelt song she'd never heard before about surviving the worst. The rest of Elsa's team had either returned to the floor or lingered up at the bar. Hank's song reached down inside her, grabbed hold, and pulled. She realized her mistake too late. Bereft of the distractions of her team, and with defenses dulled by beer, she struggled with the memories that burst through the dam she'd built in her memory.

Broken glass. Splintered wood. Her father's hand, reaching out from underneath a pile of rubble toward her motionless little sister. Her mother's hair, yellow like hers, but stained red with blood.

She remembered her dog, Grover. The dog warden had taken him away when the ambulance came for her.

She remembered exactly the sound of her own screams, years later, and bit back the echo of them. Her eyes stung, and her breath hitched.

"Doll? You okay?" Woz's voice came from someplace far away behind the memories of ruined buildings and her own sobs. Her teammate stood over the table with a half-empty beer and an expression of concern.

"Yeah," she said, shoving the memories into a dark corner as she always did. Dredging them up wouldn't change history. "I'm fine," she added. "Really."

"All right. If you need me, just holler, you hear?" He patted her shoulder, then returned to the dance floor.

Relieved, Elsa turned her attention back to the stage. Rhodes was still singing—and still, in spite of his sunglasses, appeared to be watching her. This time, his soulful voice washed over her, and the words of his song soothed those aches. Then, instead of soothing, his voice began to feel more like a caress. He had a magic all his own, with a voice like that.

She shuffled her foot and examined her beer bottle. Her ears warmed. How did he make her feel like the only person in the room when she couldn't even see his eyes? He was too raw, too astute, too...everything. Or maybe today's tangle with the tornado had left her vulnerable. Self-conscious, she hunched her shoulders and stared hard at the foil label on her bottle. Hank's voice found her even then, winding through her, unsettling her and comforting her and confusing her.

Toward the end of the night, he wound down his set and then took a last break. She found a moment to escape out the side door of the bar. Sitting on a concrete pylon at the edge of the parking lot, she drew a deep breath and stared up into the star-strewn sky.

Up there, it was clear and wide and endless. She hated being indoors. It reminded her far too much of how her family had looked, trapped and lifeless under thousands of pounds of housing timbers reduced to kindling. She had escaped with a broken arm and spent days in the hospital, but no amount of doctoring could mend that spot in her heart where her family had been.

She rubbed a thumb along the crease in her opposite palm. It was cruel that she should have been given control of the air, years after she'd needed it most. Her oldest foster brother, Kincade, would have felt somehow responsible, as if he could have prevented the incident that had claimed her birth family. He would understand the bitter irony of having her power, and spending the rest of her life wishing she'd received it just a few years earlier.

No matter how much she loved her foster siblings, she'd never told them about her real family. They all assumed she didn't remember.

But she couldn't forget.

"Hi."

She started and turned where she sat.

Rhodes leaned against the side of the building. He'd pushed the sunglasses back onto the top of his head.

She lunged to her feet, then took a few steps back. "S-sorry."

"What for?" Amusement rolled through his voice. "You want to loiter, I'm not the guy to stop you. Got a lighter?"

Elsa chuckled to herself. Her foster brother Ethan, a fire Elemental, never went anywhere without a lighter when they'd all lived at Hope Creek. She wondered if he still carried one in his shirt pocket, wherever he was now. "Sorry, no."

"Never mind," said Rhodes. He stretched something that appeared to be string between his fingers. Then she noticed the T-shirt stuffed under his elbow. He knotted the string on a needle and cut the end with his teeth.

"What are you doing?"

"Sewing," he answered, still with that sardonic ring in his voice. The shirt dropped to the sidewalk, and he made a sound of irritation.

She jogged over to pick up the shirt. She shook it out and studied the flowery pattern. "Not what I'd expect a blues player to wear. Make that squeeze into," she teased, seeing how much smaller it was than the wash-worn shirt currently snugged over his broad chest. She touched the tear in the side of the flowered shirt, then noticed another tear that had been repaired sturdily, but not very neatly.

He gave her a sidelong smirk. "People toss things out when they should fix them," he muttered, holding his hand out.

She smiled. "Here. Give me the needle."

He did, and in a handful of tidy stitches, she mended the shirt. She nipped the end of the string off and went to hand the needle back, but it stabbed her thumb as she did so. "Ouch." She sucked the injured digit.

His eyes were blue, like lightning. Elsa forgot to draw breath. With her cheeks suddenly on fire and the tip of her thumb still against her lips, she found herself unable to tear her gaze away. They stood there what seemed minutes, with only the breeze breaking the silence. The back of her neck tickled as if a charge had passed through the air.

He seemed to sense it too. He slipped the shirt and needle from her grasp. His fingers slid along hers. "What's your name?" he murmured.

His tone brought to mind the way she'd known he was watching her back in the bar, while singing that song that had pulled all her buried memories of her family out of her. She caught a note of sympathy, and a tiny ache settled in her chest.

"Elsa." Lowering her hands, she watched his eyes and how the fluorescent floodlight shifted them from light to dark. Her tongue disobeyed her for several moments, until she finally pushed out the first words she could get her mouth to form. "You don't look like a Hank."

He froze. The charge in the air magnified. Heat. Cold. A curious feeling of shifting, as if the currents were as undecided as he. The fringe of hair on his forehead ruffled in a fitful gust. She hardly noticed the motion when he tipped his sunglasses, and they dropped down over his eyes.

"El. Let's load up."

Woz.

She glanced toward the parking lot to find Woz and Seth piling into her wagon. When she looked back, Hank Rhodes was walking away, and the moment of suspended magic had gone.

Chapter Two

With a hundred extra dollars in his pocket and his duffel and guitar case slung over his shoulder, Harry walked the half-mile to the nearest motel. Given last night's dishonestly appropriated shelter, he'd decided they could splurge on a lawfully rented bed for tonight. He'd left Rose at the motel with strict instructions: *One*, under no circumstances should she answer or open the door; *Two*, hide the dog; and *Three*, get some reading done, or so help him, she wouldn't see a television for the rest of her life.

He arrived, sweaty and in need of a shower, to a face full of dog nose as the door opened before he got to it. He shoved Sam aside and shut the door. "What are you doing awake?" he scolded Rose, who had backed away toward the bed. "And I told you not to open it to anyone."

"Sam knew it was you," she said. "He started wagging his tail as soon as you got close." She must have seen the look of warning on Harry's face, because she added, "And he didn't bark, not once, I swear. Only..."

"Only what?"

"Well, he chewed on the remote control while I was in the bathroom."

Harry sighed, then set his duffel and guitar case in the corner. "I guess that ruled out your trying to watch

TV in spite of Rule Number Three. And for the record, you might be risking Rule Number Two." He plucked the mangled remote from the nearest nightstand with a grimace. One key had gone missing, and the bottom end could have stood in for a cheese grater. They couldn't explain it without making Sam known to the desk clerk, a move which would undoubtedly get them all evicted from their already-paid accommodations.

Rose backed away with her hands outspread. "I swear, I read! They had a newspaper in the lobby—"

Alarm punched him in the gut. "Did you go outside to get it?"

"No! The guy at the desk let me have it when we checked in." She gave Harry a too-perfect expression of frustrated female dignity. "I knew you were going to make me read tonight. You always do when we stay in motels."

"Not going to learn anything if you don't, kiddo. What'd you read about?"

"I dunno, I read the whole thing. Stuff about war, and elections, and a bunch of coupons. Can we get a bag of potato chips at the next store? There's one for half-off."

He found a smile. In spite of the weighty topics in the rest of the paper, his kid sister had zeroed in on the junk food ads. Another little slice of normal. He gave Sam a pat, and the dog settled himself on the floor by the bed. Truth told, he liked the idea that Rose had company and some protection while he was at the bar earning their next meal. He couldn't bring her with him, and things being what they were, the thought of leaving her alone every few nights sat in his belly like an anvil. The extra layout for some dog food would be worth it for the peace of mind. "Sure, potato chips. Tomorrow. *If* you get right to bed."

Rose scooted under the covers so fast, she could have been a superhero herself. He grinned and went to the bathroom to wash up.

By the time he emerged in a T-shirt and jeans, he found the light still on, and Rose fast asleep in one of her clean outfits. They always slept in whatever they'd be wearing the next day. Pajamas had no place in a world where they might have to get up and run in the middle of the night.

Harry stalked to the window to peer out through the curtains. Nothing disturbed the silence, though it looked like yesterday's storm had torn part of the roof off an outlying shed. He thought back to their near escape, and then about Rose's mystery superhero. Rose had been bringing up the incident for the past two days, whenever the opportunity presented itself. Did he believe her, and what did he think they should do about it, and did he think they could find her even if Rose hadn't gotten a good look at her, and could she help them catch their parents' murderers...

At that point, Harry lost patience and snapped at her to keep quiet, then spent the rest of the afternoon regretting it. Who was he to squash her hopes of ending this?

Early on, they'd considered going to the police, only to learn that the Torelli connections had an alarming reach. Where the law couldn't be bought, the organization tapped phones, spied, schemed, threatened, and always escaped unscratched...or so the rumors went, because they never ended up in legal battles. Their influence reached everywhere, except, so far, for dive bars in backwater Midwest towns.

The Torellis were looking for Harrison and Rosalie Litchfield, the golden children of a multi-million dollar dynasty, but those people hadn't existed for months.

Before, he couldn't have asked anything more out of life. He had the nice house, the nice stuff, and the nice car. He had a future. Now all he had was a scared kid sister looking to him to protect them both, and no clue how to do that but to keep moving and stay hidden.

Harry turned away from the window, then settled into a threadbare armchair with Rosie's paper. A quick scan with trained eyes yielded a short article about a seized cache of guns and narcotics in Little Rock, Arkansas. It could have happened in any city, anywhere, but for one detail: a pair of Dobermans had been seized as well.

Marco Torelli.

Harry's heart seized with familiar pain, even as his blood boiled. The man who'd murdered their parents was particularly fond of Doberman pinschers. Harry had profiled him with as much dedication as a veteran FBI agent.

Know thy enemy, the saying went.

Rosalie would have read the article. She'd probably made the same connection. He wondered why she hadn't mentioned it, unless she also saw no end in sight to their wanderings. He had hoped to find someone to whom he could safely provide the evidence to catch their parents' killers and put them away. In the beginning, that had kept him going. As the months wore on, the vengeful fire in his blood reduced to despairing ash. He had money, connections, and influence, but the damned thing of it was, he couldn't use any of it without the Torellis finding them. It would only take one phone call, one ATM withdrawal, one unguarded slip to sign his own death warrant...or Rose's.

Fame had always bought him everything he needed. Except now, when it bought him liability.

He glanced out the window one last time. The sky out here had a peculiar ever-twilight look to it this time of year, even in full dark. It would be dawn in a few hours. He should have been tired, but a dry, restless wind had been blowing through him for a couple of days now. He found it hard to sit still, let alone sleep. Following the low-skimming clouds with his gaze, he let the paper drop to his knee. *It's too bad you're not a superhero,* he said silently to the mysterious woman Rose had seen. *We sure could use one.*

****

"Doll, you are my savior," Woz called. "I'll love you until the end of time."

Or at least until the end of your sandwich, Elsa thought with a smile. Loaded with teetering armfuls of paper sandwich bags, she made her way to the caravan of vehicles parked at the edge of a sub shop's parking lot. The Beast, their steel-on-wheels "weather tank," had, as usual, drawn a few curious onlookers. Woz stood beside them, explaining The Beast's purpose and features with his usual showmanship.

"Leaning tower of pastrami, here," she said with some desperation.

He hurried toward her to rescue a couple of bags sliding off the top. "Courtesy of our much-appreciated benefactor, Kincade Murphy, I presume," he said cheerfully. He waved goodbye to The Beast's knot of admirers, who went back to the sub shop.

"I think we'd starve if it weren't for Cade," said Elsa. "You eat enough for three on a *slow* day. Here. This is your mac salad." She gave him the bag and a grin. If storm chasing ever got old, Woz could start one of those food critic shows, or at least make his living by winning every all-you-can-eat contest in North America. Where he put it, she didn't know, because he was beanpole-thin.

Cade never asked, and neither did she—he just sent money. Hope Creek was more than successful these days, and Elsa often found a generous deposit in her bank account. She never touched more than she needed to feed her crew when the going got tough. They took odd jobs in the off-season to stay afloat, but when summer came around, the storm chasing that required full gas tanks tended to drain their pockets.

Elsa didn't begrudge the expense. She appreciated lots of things that gave her no financial benefit. Helping families who had suffered disaster in the wake of a storm, for example. Or reading a good book. Or admiring a handsome man with striking blue eyes.

Hank Rhodes whooshed into her memory like a gust of updraft, and gave her just as many goose bumps. She couldn't remember ever having been looked at like that, much less feeling her heart pound in such a heady response.

He definitely had the looks to warrant such a reaction, but it was *the* look that had stopped her in her tracks. He'd caught her eye with the snap focus that she gave whenever she sensed a sharp change in the air. She found herself regretting that she didn't know when or where he'd be holding his next performance.

Well, if a look like that was all she'd ever get, she decided she might as well relish it to the fullest. Daydreaming and unashamed of it, she slid into her wagon and handed Nina her share of their lunch.

"Thanks," Nina said. "Rory says the radar's going to be a little quiet for the next couple of days. There's a low-pressure front moving in over Nebraska, but not much more going on than cloud cover and hard rain... Are you even listening to me?"

Sipping at her cup of iced tea, Elsa watched the cloud-studded sky. Her gaze drifted from the puffy white shapes to the swathes of blue in between, and Hank's eyes swirled back to the surface of her thoughts. "Hmmmm?"

Nina remained silent long enough for Elsa to direct her full attention to her teammate. With raised brows, Nina said, "*Someone's* still at the bar. I wondered why you've been so spaced out the past day. Can't be the weather."

"I can look," said Elsa. "Last time I checked, I wasn't dead. Just busy."

"Worried about your power, more likely."

When Elsa scowled, Nina gave her a reproving nudge. "You can't hide forever. Sooner or later, you're going to want to settle down, aren't you?"

"More later than sooner. There's a lot to do," Elsa insisted...though, for the life of her, she couldn't think of a single thing that stood out on her normally extensive list. That remembered intensity on Hank's face crowded out the rest of the itinerary from her brain with dismaying force.

"There will be a lot to do as long as there's a tornado season. El, you told all of us about you,

24

eventually. Don't you think there's someone else out there who will find out what you are, and still love you?"

She hated the gentle reproach in Nina's voice. It wasn't merely her own safety that concerned Elsa. She had an entire family of Elementals to worry about. While Nina might think it a minor technicality when shopping for a romance, and even Elsa wanted to believe the best of people, she knew enough of the world to realize not everyone would view her family's powers with equanimity. People regarded such things with disbelief at best, and at worst, fear. Fear did funny things to people. Made them distrustful. Suspicious. Hostile.

Nothing mattered to Elsa so much as protecting her loved ones. She couldn't afford to waste energy and risk lives getting involved with someone, only to find out later whether she could trust him enough...or worse, couldn't trust him at all. So, single life it must be, regardless of intense looks from wandering musicians. What family she had, she'd fight to keep.

The future flashed before her. Elsa saw herself sitting in her car, decades down the road, still chasing storms, still chasing her life. Her team would all have gotten married and settled down. She looked around in this envisioned future, and wondered who would be sitting beside her.

Loneliness stabbed her right between the ribs.

Elsa recoiled into the present, then stomped on the brake to change gears into drive. With the other hand, she mashed her drink into the cup holder. "Let's go check into the motel."

A soft sigh from the direction of the passenger seat

told her Nina recognized that she was evading talk. They could have kept driving and followed the weather pattern in case anything more might come of it, but that would require sitting in the car with Nina for another few hours. That ranked right up there with a lie detector test. Even now, Elsa sensed her friend and teammate's spotlight eyes on her. Silence reigned for several minutes. Unable to stand it anymore, she flicked the radio on.

"...in the wake of last week's windstorm," the deejay was saying. "There were no deaths, but several area homes and businesses sustained damages, with an estimated total of..."

Elsa smiled at Nina, and found her teammate smiling back. "Better properties than people," they said together. Nina held out her fist.

Camaraderie back in place, Elsa rapped Nina's fist with her own.

The Cozy K wasn't the worst place Elsa and her team had ever stayed, but it appeared to be among the businesses the deejay had mentioned. Part of the siding had been covered with plywood. The clerk in the lobby mentioned there would be no television in the rooms, as the storm had knocked it out, and the cable company couldn't make it over to do repairs for two days. Lack of TV and Wi-Fi for that long might be enough to put the motel out of business, and quite possibly spell the end of the world, at least according to the clerk. She grumped up and down the counter, gathering together triplicate registration forms. "No cable, no Internet. No Internet, no computerized registration. Whole world blows up when these storms come through, I swear. Everything's gotta be done by hand."

"I could take a look at the cable for you," Seth piped up. "I have a degree in A/V engineering."

The clerk gave Seth a raised-brow scrutiny that managed to be hopeful and skeptical at the same time. She wagged her finger at the powered-off television on the wall across the lobby. "Sweetie, if you can get that idiot box working before the cable guy gets here, I'll comp your room. I'm missing *Idol*."

Seth grinned. "Awesome. I'll go get my tools."

Woz and Rory exchanged a long-suffering eye-roll.

Elsa beamed at Rory as the clerk handed her three sets of keys. "Oh, ye of little faith. Seth fixed your radar last week."

"I had plenty of faith in him fixing the radar," Rory said. He shouldered Elsa's second duffel. They turned away from the desk, and left the lobby. With a grimace, Rory added, "Just not sure he's doing us a favor. The world needs no more off-key singers."

Nina elbowed Elsa. "How about on-key ones?"

Woz grinned, but Rory gave them all a blank look as they climbed the stairs to their second-level rooms. After a silent pause, Nina groaned, and this time, jabbed Rory in the ribs. "God, you're going to marry your Doppler, aren't you?"

Rory spread his hands in a perfect gesture of male exasperation. "What?" He looked to Woz, presumably for some solidarity.

Woz, still grinning, just shook his head. No help there.

As they passed an open door on their left, Elsa glimpsed a flash of blue eyes and long brown braids. She looked again. A young girl stared at her from the doorway of her motel room. As soon as their gazes met, the girl's eyes went round as dinner plates, and then she slammed the door. Elsa arched around to Woz with a questioning look.

He arched a brow. "Don't ask me."

****

"She's here!" Rose shouted.

Harry sprang out of a deep sleep with a shout, and was on his feet in an instant. His heartbeat slammed like a sledgehammer as he sought Rose.

She stood at the edge of the bed, flushed and dancing in place like there were hot coals under her feet.

Harry shoved himself between her and the door. "What's wrong?"

"She's here, the lady, the one who made the tornado stop!"

Harry relaxed a little. He drew a huge sigh and sank back onto the bed. "What about her?"

"Well, aren't you going to go talk to her?"

"Why would I do that?"

Rosalie gave him such an effectively guilt-producing look of disappointment that he wondered if she practiced it in private for just such occasions. "Rose, I can't just walk up to total strangers and ask them to help us," he said.

Sam lunged up from his spot on the floor, and then trotted to Rose, wagging his tail. She flexed her fists at her sides. "If you won't, then I will!"

She scooted out the door before Harry even got back to his feet. Wracked with fear, he bulleted out into the hall after her, shouting, "Hey!"

He nearly crashed into a young man with a toolbox and a bunch of electronic wires. The top coil started to plummet off the stack, and Harry caught it. "Sorry," he muttered. He pushed it back at the man and darted after Rose again, following the swing of her braids with anger and worry mixing a frustrated cocktail in his gut.

Then Sam came bounding down the hall. The mutt passed him, still wagging. He heard it draw breath. *Oh, no.*

"Wwwwwuff!" The sound bounced off the drywall in a pinball ricochet that almost split his eardrums.

Another door opened a few steps down the hall, while he was still rushing toward Rose and the dog. Out of the room came a striking blond woman in work-stained jeans and a blue T-shirt.

The same woman he'd seen at the bar outside Denver, Colorado. The one who had fixed Rose's shirt.

Their gazes crashed together, and she looked just as stricken as he. They nearly smashed into each other. Harry lurched to a stop, just shy of putting his hands on her to steady himself.

"Are you following me?" they blurted together.

Rose, farther down the hall, jerked to a stop, then whirled around with—Harry's heart sank—an expression of relief and hope. She hurried back to them.

He realized he still hadn't answered the woman's question...nor she, his. When he turned his attention back to her, she was staring at him with wide blue eyes and a cherry-red flush rising on her cheekbones. His stare cemented on a wisp of golden hair that had loosened from its clip to trail down her slender shoulder. The sun-on-satin lock curled loosely across a delicate collarbone, visible above the low-cut neck of her T-shirt. He skimmed her curvy figure, unable to help himself.

"Are you?" the woman demanded again. "Following me?"

"No," he said. Snapped, actually. He gave himself a mental throttling and pummeled his gaze back to her face.

She turned, just enough to notice Rose. The dog stood so close beside Rose that his tail *thwap-thwap*ped her pant leg. Rose didn't seem to notice. She beamed at the woman. Harry tried to pass his sister a look of warning, but by the expression on her face, Rose had already plunged over the edge of sanity into a dangerous murk of hero worship.

And the woman had hardly even spoken.

He mustered a forceful voice. "Get that dog back to the room."

Rose thrust out a mutinous lip. When she didn't go, he started toward the dog, furious with them both. Any minute, the desk clerk would come charging upstairs—

The dog's ruff stood up. Darting in front of Rose, the Lab growled at him, an uncertain noise that suggested the dog didn't want to bite him, but he damn well didn't like Harry's posture.

Harry didn't much like it, either, being yanked around by his knee-jerk reactions to hide himself and his little sister from suspicious eyes. Liked it less that the woman was watching this little melodrama with obvious interest.

Her laughter startled him, echoing in the hall. Her gaze had gone to his sister's floral top. "I knew the shirt was too small for you."

With the woman's attention now on Rose, a chill slid down the back of Harry's neck. He forced himself to continue toward the dog, with a little more caution this time. "Come on," he urged.

"It's all right," said the woman, kneeling before the dog. She reached a fisted hand toward its muzzle.

Sniffing her, Sam went from growly to goofy in point-three seconds. His tail started *thwapping* Rose's pant leg again.

The woman scratched behind his ears with fearless affection. "You are *such. A sweet. Boy,*" she told the dog. Sam jammed his head against the woman's chest with a little whine of happiness.

Harry had trouble blaming him.

The woman grinned up at him, a sun-flare of cheer bright enough to burn truck-sized holes in his moody rationale. "Bad show last night?" she asked.

"Huh?"

"Dogs can tell when you're out of sorts, you know. Did you play a set, and it didn't go well?"

"No. I just—The dog isn't—" Babbling like a fumbling teenager on his first date. Disgusted with himself, Harry snapped his spine yardstick-straight. "Get back inside," he said to Rose, who just stood there with that worlds-of-disappointment frown on her face.

Too late, he spied the clerk climbing the stairs. "I'm sorry, sir, but we don't allow dogs here."

"Oh, it's my fault," said the blond woman. "Would you accept a deposit for letting him stay?"

The clerk looked unconvinced, but when the blond woman pulled out her wallet and offered a bill, the clerk's brows inched up. "Plus extra if he does any damage, I promise," the woman added.

Keep the remotes out of his way, Harry thought absurdly. He thought of his own wallet, with a few meager bills in it, back on his nightstand in the room.

All at once, the idea of letting this stranger pay for the contraband dog—which wasn't even his, and had already been proven capable of said damage—was too much for his pride. "I can cover him."

"Don't be silly," the woman said, ruffling the Lab's ears again. To the dog, she added, "Is he being silly? Yes, of course he is. Who wouldn't want you with him every single day, you big, sweet baby?"

Sam's tail whipped the air to shreds, and he strained to lick her face while she giggled like a girl and arched out of reach. Rose smiled at them as if the whole world was just perfect.

Not even close.

The clerk went back downstairs. Whatever the woman had given her had clearly been more than enough to compensate for motel policy. Harry wondered which dead president had the honor of smoothing over that snag with such finesse.

Guilt, guilt, guilt.

The woman stood, flushed with laughter, but Harry glimpsed a flash of something sorrowful in her eyes as she said, "I had a Lab when I was little. Great family dogs."

Family. What kind of family was he, dragging Rose across the Midwest in constant, gut-grinding fear of pursuit? "Listen, thanks for that. Let me buy you breakfast in the morning, and we'll call it even."

"I don't need 'even,'" she said. "It's just money." She tipped her head toward the stairs. "Besides, I'm the one who got you caught with the clerk, and I believe in random acts of kindness, Mister Rhodes. It is Rhodes?"

"You never said *your* name," he countered.

She held out her hand. "Elsa Pemberley. Storm

chaser and dog lover."

That grin again. She was full of them, except the night she came to watch him sing. *Something* lingered under that effervescent surface. "And seamstress," he added with a quirked brow. He shook her hand.

"Right," she added. More smiles. Too bad Seamstress Elsa couldn't stitch their lives back together the way Rose believed she could. He wondered who stitched *her* life together, and why it had come unraveled that night at the bar. And how she managed to cover it with all that good cheer.

What if she *could* save them?

No. Nothing useful that way. He ordered himself away from wishful thinking with a mental finger-jab at the grim reality of life as a fugitive.

He still held Elsa's hand, but now, they weren't shaking. Her fingertips skated slowly over the creases of his palm. Even as her eyes widened a tiny, intriguing fraction, a static-sharp tingle of awareness drifted from that touch up his arm, to every corner of his body. A pulse of heat shot straight to his groin.

Her hand jerked in his. Maybe the static wasn't just him. Or maybe it was 'him' enough for both of them, because his body had just started to wonder how much time had gone by since he'd been on the run, and not in a woman's bed. That golden lock of silk on her shoulder sucked all his attention away from everything else. He trailed it with his gaze back down over her close-fitting top, which couldn't possibly hide the shapely curve of her breasts, or the way her torso narrowed at a tiny waist. He could almost have circled it with his hands.

The image of doing that morphed right into one of

pulling those beautifully rounded hips toward him, then devouring that mouth with his own, and seeing if she tasted as good as she looked. Blood pounded through his body in all the wrong directions.

Elsa's cheeks pinkened just enough for him to wonder how much of the same sort of thoughts had flashed through her head.

A door opened, and a tall, lanky man with feral hair ambled down the hall toward them. "Who's your friend, El?" The man took a closer look, then blinked a few times. A grin spread across his suntanned face. "Oh! Hank Rhodes, right? Good music the other night." He thrust out his hand. "Brian Wozinsky, but you can call me Woz."

Harry stamped back a primitive urge to growl, then transferred his handshake with reluctance to the newcomer's. "Thanks. Nice to meet you." To Elsa, he said, "Breakfast in the morning? I like to pay my debts."

She sighed. "It's not a..." She stalled when he gave her a steady stare. A look of cheerful exasperation lit her features. "Breakfast," she agreed. "There's a diner right down the road."

She and Woz went to their respective—and separate, he noted—rooms, and Harry waved Rose and the dog to their own. As she passed him, Rose threw him a brilliant smile he had rarely seen since their parents were alive.

Harry smiled back. It appeared Seamstress Elsa's grins were infectious, as well as plentiful. Almost made it worth the pre-teen rebellion.

Not until he'd closed the door of their motel room did it occur to him he'd gone against his most ironclad rule. He'd be sticking his neck out in broad daylight, with Rose in tow.

Were the lure of the enticing Miss Pemberley and the easing of his pride worth that risk?

Chapter Three

"A date with a singer, huh?" Nina teased Elsa from the bathroom of their motel room the next morning. "Who knew you were such a groupie?"

"I'm not an anything. I didn't even ask him for this breakfast. I was just being nice, and now he's feeling obligated," Elsa retorted from her place on her bed. Lounging on her belly, she shifted her crossword magazine a little closer on the flowered coverlet. She wiggled her bare toes and traced the paper with a fingertip. "The word 'vapid' always makes me smile."

"I like the word 'denial,' myself. Don't change the subject," Nina said, stalking into the bedroom and rubbing her damp hair with a towel. She shot Elsa a wicked grin.

"The word 'interference' has its merits," said Elsa.

Nina swatted at Elsa's rump with the towel, then sat on the bed to give her an affectionate elbow nudge. "It does when your dear, dear friend won't settle down with a nice guy and have six kids, like you know she should. *And* wants to."

Elsa glowered without any real menace. "And what keeps you from settling down?"

"Babysitting you, Goldilocks. What else?" Nina gave Elsa's braid a tug, then frowned at it. "Better brush that out and re-do it, sweetie, it's coming undone."

"What?" Dismayed, Elsa started to pat her hair. And she'd just braided it, too. Darned thing never stayed put the way it should. Breakfast most likely didn't warrant an evening dress, but for some reason, she didn't want to look like a sweaty barn hand in front of Hank Rhodes.

Nina chuckled and stilled Elsa's hands. "I'm kidding, I'm kidding." She gave Elsa's tank top and jeans a once-over, then placed a loud kiss on Elsa's cheek. "You look gorgeous, Gorgeous. As opposed to the rest of us, who need daily applications of cement and spackle to look like something that isn't a moat monster. Better get going. You can use the wagon, if you promise to bring me back a raisin bagel and a coffee."

"Deal," said Elsa, springing up from the bed. She snatched up the keys, then slipped out before the other woman could pester her further.

She had just closed the door on one distraction, when the other came sauntering down the hall from the staircase.

"I was just about to see if you were up," said Hank.

He still wore his sunglasses and a few days' worth of stubble. And maybe that was the comfortably-broken-in shirt from yesterday...or he might have a wardrobe full of them. Elsa struggled not to think about how Hank Rhodes would look with or without the wash-faded shirt. "You're up early," she said, too brightly.

"I usually am," he responded. He held out an arm toward the staircase.

"My car is at the end of the parking lot," she said.

"We shouldn't need it. Nice morning. Diner's not

that far," said Hank.

She studied him, but found it impossible to see behind those shades. "Not a fan of cars?"

"Nothing personal."

"I need to gas it up while we're out," she said, puzzling at his flighty posture. *Skittish horse,* she thought. She tried a smile. "I give you my word of honor that my car and I don't bite, Mister Rhodes."

His attention stayed on her as if nothing else existed. Trying to figure her out, or trying to distract her from figuring *him* out?

Second thoughts bubbled at the back of her mind, stalled only by the sight of Rose, waiting down in the lobby and wearing the shirt Elsa had mended.

He walked single file ahead of her down the narrow steps, presenting her with a distracting view of his rear. He filled out his blue jeans better than any man she'd ever seen. *Great voice, great body, great eyes. What's he got that* isn't *great?* she thought, almost desperately.

When they reached the lobby, she forced her attention away and approached Rose. "Hi, again. Sleep well?"

"The beds are a little bumpy," Rose admitted. "Do you really chase tornadoes? I saw you the other day, you know—"

"Don't start chewing her ear, Rose," Hank said.

Scratch that. Skittish Rottweiler, Elsa thought, watching his shoulders inch up just a fraction as he slid between Elsa and the girl. He reached an arm around Rose's back and urged her toward the door.

Shielding her from a stranger.

Something in his posture suggested trouble for

anyone who looked sideways at the girl. *Is she his daughter?* Elsa wondered. A surprising, and surprisingly disappointing, mental sketch of Mrs. Hank Rhodes floated through Elsa's brain. He wore no ring, but these days, that didn't offer any guarantees. If there were a Mrs. Rhodes, though, where was she?

Elsa watched Hank furtively as they left the motel and crossed the parking lot. She walked. Rose bounced. Hank moved with a smooth, raw power. No threat in his body language...but confidence enough that his look alone would make someone think twice about tangling with him.

One of the farmers back in her hometown of Sagerton, Montana owned a giant of a mastiff, the biggest dog in the county. It scared the life out of any fox, coon, prowling cat, or human who tried molesting old Hughie's flock of prize leghorns. Hank Rhodes could do twice the job at half the size, with just the set of his shoulders.

She did manage to talk him into a car ride to the diner, but before he allowed Rose into the back seat of Elsa's wagon, his eyes went everywhere, on it and in it. The old crossover lacked power everything, and its right rear hubcap had been lost to the ages. The only things in tip-top shape were the suspension, tires, and a rebuilt engine, hidden under a hood rusting at the edges. What did he see with that critical eye? "She's not much, but she can get out of her own way," Elsa said.

He slid into the passenger seat. "Buckle up, Rose."

The girl clicked her seatbelt, then filled the short trip to the diner with running commentary about the heat, Sam's remote control fetish, and envy of Elsa's designer jeans.

"A lucky find," Elsa admitted. "There's not much money in storm chasing, so I get most of my clothes at thrift shops and church sales."

"What does a storm chaser do?" Rose asked.

"Most of the time?" With a chuckle, Elsa patted the seat. "I sit right here on my phone, and report funny-looking cloud patterns to the Weather Service. It's not glamorous, waiting for the big one to show up."

"What do you do when there's a big one?" Rose asked.

She'd been asked this so many times, the answer was as prepared as a presidential speech. "Get photos, graph patterns. Woz does his magic with data and diagrams, and sometimes, we're able to warn people before the real trouble starts."

"But what about when it's already happening? Like the last time we—"

"Rose," Hank snapped, low but authoritative.

Suspicion flickered to life, but before Elsa could ask what Rose meant, they'd reached the diner.

The interior was so similar to every other diner she'd ever seen that she could have predicted the placement of benches, tables, counter, coffee maker, and cash register. The difference now? Definitely the company.

It was more than the way Hank skimmed the entire place in one glance, as if sizing it all up. He *filled* it up, with an air that warned all and sundry to approach him at their peril.

Elsa slid into a booth opposite him and Rose, noticing that Hank chose the seat facing the door. She studied him, doubting whether he even knew he projected such an aura. *What are you running from?*

He pulled a menu from the slot by the condiment dispenser, exuding calm. His lightning-blue eyes never left the list of breakfast specials, but he spoke as if he knew she was watching. "Yes?"

Elsa snatched a menu for herself, then one for Rose. It took all her willpower not to swivel toward the door. "What looks good?" she asked lightly.

"Everything," Rose said. "I'm starved." To Hank, she said, "Can we bring something back for Sam? I bet he's just as hungry as we are."

"Dogs eat dog food. We'll pick some up when we hit the gas station," Hank answered.

"Where did you get him? He's such a sweetheart," said Elsa.

"He's tagging along with us," Hank told her.

"Oh? Where are you headed next?" asked Elsa.

His gaze shot up and pinned her in place. Wary. Hunted.

He *was* running.

A shiver of doubt sputtered down Elsa's back. Maybe it hadn't been such a good idea to invite a stranger to ride with her, even down the street. Her power whispered at her nerve endings, as uneasy as she. Elsa thought about Woz and Nina and Rory and Seth, all of them too far away to get to her if she needed them.

The arrival of the waitress broke their awkward silence. Elsa ordered something small, paying little notice to what it was. Rose asked for a special. Hank followed suit, and even after the waitress left, he didn't bother answering Elsa's question. She was almost grateful.

They stuck to safe topics after that, talking about

weather or animals or the food, without once saying anything personal. Rose stared at Elsa over her plate, looking for all the world like she wanted to say what she hadn't said in the car. Every few seconds, she'd open her mouth to address Elsa, and instead of letting words out, she'd lift her fork and thrust food in.

By the end of their meal, Elsa was only too happy to move on to the gas station. Hank showed no more easiness in the wagon's front seat than he'd been in the diner booth. He swooped out, and then strode into the store while Elsa pumped gas.

She joined him after topping off the tank. Rose bubbled along beside him in the store. Hank had gathered a few items, among them some cans of food, and a probably overpriced bag of dog food that wouldn't last Sam three minutes. She grinned. "Not much of a grocery shopper, are you?"

He didn't answer.

When she looked up from the bag of kibble to his face, he had gone statue-still. His arm was out, pressing Rose back behind him. His gaze had fixed on the man at the front counter.

The customer currently buying a pack of cigarettes had shoulders like a linebacker. He wore neatly pressed slacks and a long-sleeved dress shirt, in spite of the warmth already this morning. Nothing in his demeanor suggested the kind of trouble Hank's posture indicated.

Until he turned around.

An old, deep scar ran from the top of his cheekbone and down the side of his face, to disappear under the starched collar of his shirt. His eyes were dark, and his gaze as hard as the stare of a junkyard dog. He didn't smile, but stepped past her to the door, putting a cigarette between his lips. A spark of fear flared in her chest, and Elsa dodged back. He swept by, taking all the air in the store with him as he went.

After he left, she turned around to ask Hank exactly who that man was, but Hank and Rose were gone.

****

"What do we do now, Harry? We gotta go back for Sam!" Rose whispered.

They stood at the side of the building away from the road. A row of bushes provided them some cover, while allowing Harry a look at the parking lot to see if Vincent, Marco Torelli's right-hand man, had left. He and Rose had delayed their exit from the gas station store by killing a few minutes buying the groceries, but it looked like Vince planned on taking his sweet time getting out of here. The man lazed against the quarter panel of a shiny black Cadillac, puffing on his cigarette in blatant disregard of the *No Smoking* signs. Harry's heartbeat hadn't stopped going Mach Two since seeing him, standing like some terrible apparition at the counter. "I'm more concerned about my Gibson, Rose," Harry said.

"You care more about that guitar than Sam!" Rose accused.

Harry whipped around. "I care about you!" he snapped, in as harsh a voice as he dared. "If I don't get my guitar so we can move out of here, I've got no chance of paying our way, and we're sitting ducks. You and me, and especially Sam, aren't going to matter much if that guy finds us and—"

The stricken look on Rose's face shoved the rest of his words back down his throat.

Awash with remorse, Harry slipped an arm around her and tugged her into the crook of his arm. She went, stiffly. "I'm sorry, Rosie. We'll get him, I promise. We just need to wait a little, okay?"

"What's wrong?" came Elsa's voice.

He and Rose whirled to face Elsa, who had approached from the other corner of the building, behind them.

Harry scrambled for an explanation that wouldn't come.

Rose was faster. "I didn't feel good," she said, pointing at the bushes. "I thought I was going to be sick."

Elsa's features shifted from curious to concerned. "Oh, no, I hope it wasn't breakfast. You okay, Hank?"

"Fine," he barked. "Sorry about the slip." He stole a look around the corner of the building. Vince had gotten into his car, and was exiting the lot. Harry turned to Rose. "You all right now?"

"I think so. Can we go back to the motel?"

"Yeah. We gotta get going to our next stop, though, so get ready to check out as soon as we get back there."

Rose shifted, her gaze darting around. Elsa's brow furrowed. "Can I take you somewhere?" Elsa asked. When Harry looked at her, her cheeks colored a little. She shrugged. "I mean, you never mentioned if you have a car, and I didn't see one outside when my team and I pulled in, and...well..." She trailed off, her cheeks now cherry-blossom pink. "If you need some help..." she added, but that trailed off, too.

At another time, in another life, her self-conscious blush might have charmed him. But Rose perked up beside him as if Elsa were the answer to their prayers, and his hackles went up in reflex. "Thanks, but we'll be fine," he said.

"But—" Rose started to protest.

"We're good," Harry insisted. "A ride back to the motel's about all we'll need."

Elsa didn't look convinced. Given the sudden appearance of Vincent Torelli in the Midwest, Harry was even less convinced...but to her credit, Elsa left that sleeping dog to its own devices.

Rose made not one sound during their return to the motel. With his eyes on the road, looking for Vince's Caddy, Harry didn't add much to the conversation. To his enormous relief, it appeared Vince had decided this no-count townlet wasn't worth a stay. That would be the last of traveling on main roads for a while. It'd be cross-country travel from now on.

The bartender at his last gig had mentioned a rib joint in Oklahoma, owned by his cousin, and told Harry to look him up. Harry rarely got lucky enough to have lined up another show so soon after a previous one. If it weren't for Vince's reappearance, he might have thought good fortune had starting smiling on them, for a change.

Now, he barely had time to say goodbye to Elsa and thank her for breakfast before he and Rose rushed to gather their things and leave.

"Why won't you even talk to her?" Rose asked, sitting on the rumpled bed and scratching Sam behind the ears.

"We can't just blab our problems to the first person you see, Rose," Harry said. He stuffed a few bottles of complimentary shampoo in his duffel.

"She did stop that tornado," Rose insisted. "You don't believe me, do you?"

Harry's blood simmered at the injustice of it all. They couldn't even have breakfast at a diner without it turning into a run for their lives. At this rate, they'd never get back to normal. Frustrated, he threw up his hands. "Even if she did, stopping a tornado is a world away from preventing murder. Do you think I like this, this running and hiding all the time?"

Rose clammed up, but he knew that wounded look. Damn it. If she turned out some screw-up miscreant living on the streets and stealing—or worse—it would be his fault. Sam whined and shoved his nose under Rose's hand. She patted him without much enthusiasm, then got up and gathered her few things.

He stared after her. Doubt crawled through him as he watched her pick up some clothes, all skinny arms and stick-figure legs and messy ponytail that defied brushing. Who was he kidding? He couldn't protect her. He could hardly feed her. *What are you gonna do, Litch? What?*

Disgusted with himself, he grabbed his guitar case, then clipped a new leash to Sam's also-new collar. "Finish up and come down," he muttered, then he headed down to the lobby with the dog to check out.

The quicker they left this place behind, the more distance he could put between themselves and the all-too-near Torellis.

****

Hank Rhodes had whooshed in and out of her life like the dust devil he was. Elsa lingered in the motel lobby, reluctant to leave without one last look at the handsome blues singer...and just as reluctant to admit that to Nina, who'd been hovering since Elsa's return from the diner.

"Nothing to report," she said in response to the incessant questioning. She walked past Seth, who was fielding a thousand thank-yous from the desk clerk for fixing the cable.

"*Idol*'s back," Woz said as he entered the lobby. He waggled his eyebrows and leaned toward Elsa as he passed. "The world is right again."

Elsa smiled and gathered up a worn suitcase, then carried it out to her crossover wagon. *Don't bother looking back,* she ordered herself. *He's probably gone already, anyway.*

Nina slid into the wagon's driver's seat, and Elsa rode shotgun. They were headed next to Oklahoma, following a border between low- and high-pressure fronts that, according to Rory, promised high winds and possibly hail. Just the thing she needed to take her mind off how she'd still be doing this in fifteen years, except alone.

She and Nina sang along to a country station as they usually did, but soon, Elsa had to admit her heart wasn't in it. She couldn't be sure anymore that her heart was truly in anything.

She couldn't blame it on the wistful remembrance of a handsome man, though he was that and more. She couldn't even blame the way Hank had pulled her worst memories out of her, and then soothed them with his song as if he understood her loss.

No. The thing that left her questioning herself, when she'd never done it before, was the simple act of eating breakfast, man and woman and child.

Almost like a family.

"Woof!"

Beside her, Nina flinched. "What the heck was that?"

Elsa whipped around. Sam burst up from the pile of blankets, coats, and equipment in the cargo area. He bounded forward, then hooked his paws over the seat beside Elsa to slurp at her face. Horrified, she grabbed his collar while Nina pulled over to the side of the road. "What are you doing here?"

"I'm sorry, I'm sorry!" came Rose's voice.

Oh, mercy, no.

The girl sprang up from the cargo area, a stack of jackets spilling from her shoulders. She clambered forward, then dropped onto the back seat to tug at Sam until the dog sat beside her. Tearfully, she petted the dog's back. "Please don't send us away. We need your help, Miss Pemberley, I swear, or we'd never have snuck into your car."

Elsa shot Nina a helpless, dismayed look, and the other woman stopped the wagon at the roadside. Nina's hand went toward the cell phone sitting in the console.

"Wait!" Elsa cried, putting a hand on Nina's arm. She studied Rose's tear-streaked face. "Rose, what are you running away from? Is Hank mistreating you?"

"No, no, you can protect us, I know you can. *All* of us," the girl said. Her voice rang with desperation, and real fear shone in her sky-blue eyes.

Elsa reached over the seat to put a steadying hand on Rose's. "Then Hank is probably worried sick about you. We've got to get you back there. God, I'm going to be arrested for kidnapping. You'd better buckle up." She gestured to Nina, who started to put the wagon into gear.

"Miss Pemberley, you don't understand!" Rose cried. "We need you!"

Sam whined, and his tail smacked the worn vinyl seat.

Worried by the terror in Rose's voice, Elsa sought her calmest tone. "Sweetie, if you're in some sort of trouble, I don't think I'm the person who can help you. We'll straighten this out—"

"You're the *only* one who can help," Rose insisted, scooting forward until she sat on the edge of the back seat, practically nose-to-nose with Elsa. "I saw you. I saw you look at a tornado, and stop it with your *bare hands*."

A chill sped through Elsa. She sought Nina's gaze. The other woman stared back at her, the look on her face a mirror of the sudden, violent turmoil in Elsa's belly. Nina's expression said exactly what Elsa was thinking: *Now what?*

Chapter Four

Panic.

Harry tore through the motel. He made the clerk check every single room, but he found no sign of Rose or Sam, inside or out.

And that Pemberley woman was gone.

I never should have trusted her, I never should have trusted her, I never should have—Harry slammed a mental door on the useless rebuke. Standing at the pay phone outside the motel, he clenched his hands on the strap of his guitar case where it hung from his shoulder. A futile effort to strangle something.

Nothing mattered now. Not his neck, or anyone else's. Rose might be dead, a sweet, too-smart kid who hadn't even lived yet. His sister, his only remaining family. Choking on grief, Harry grabbed the phone's receiver and stared at the keypad. Its grid of buttons swam before his unseeing eyes. He refocused on the zero until it was the only thing in the universe. *Press that button, and you die.*

For Rose? Gladly.

He took a breath and reached forward.

The sound of car tires on gravel made him swerve his reach wide. Instead of hitting the Operator button, he swiveled to find Elsa's crossover wagon pulling back into the parking lot. His guts turned to ice when he saw Rose and Sam, their heads poking side-by-side out the window of the back seat. "Harry!" Rose cried. "We're all right!"

He didn't even care that she'd shouted his given name for all to hear. The car had barely pulled to a stop beside the pay phone before Rose and Sam tumbled out. Harry crushed his sister into his arms, hoping that if he hugged her tight enough, it would thaw the fear still freezing his insides. "I thought she took you," he gasped out. "My God, Rosie, I thought she took you."

The Pemberley woman got out of the car. Harry lunged into her face. "Who do you think you are!"

Sam barked and leaped at their feet. Rose yanked on Harry's arm. "Harry, stop!" Her voice came from far away behind the raging of his heartbeat in his ears.

Elsa flinched back a step. "She got into my car! I'm sorry! As soon as I found out, we turned right back around."

Harry herded Rose back from the woman. His sister refused to go, pushing in front of him again. "Stop it! Listen to me!" she cried.

"*You* listen," he snapped at her. "I don't want to see you sneaking off like that again! It's not safe. We have no idea what kind of woman this is"—he jabbed a finger at Elsa—"and she could have—"

Elsa planted her fists on her hips. "I can guarantee I'm not the kind of woman who kidnaps children."

A familiar waking nightmare assaulted Harry, the one where Vince Torelli dragged a kicking and struggling Rose away with one hand clamped over her mouth. With Marco's muscle now prowling around the Midwest, it was all too likely to happen. Shaking, Harry faced off with Elsa, feeling like a blazing neon death's-head must have appeared on his back. Now, it would lead Marco and his droves of killers right to him and his little sister.

Elsa's posture shifted, no longer defensive. "Harry... It's Harry, right? And Rose?"

Harry jerked his guitar strap up on his shoulder in one fist, and with the other, he gripped Rose's hand. He could feel his body shaking, and willed it to stop. It wouldn't. "Let's go, Rosie," he rasped out.

"Please, wait. I want to help," Elsa said. The driver, a dark-haired woman Harry recognized as Elsa's friend, emerged from the vehicle.

"You can't help," he said, a flat, insurmountable brick wall of words that reeked of despair even as he spoke them. Revolted, he began spinning a mental map of their route—a safer route, with no main roads—to Oklahoma.

That would be a damn long walk. Good thing they had no time frame.

Elsa tilted her head. Her blue eyes softened. "I'm putting my safety in your hands, Mister Rhodes."

That brought his attention off the map, and back onto her. *"Yours?"*

"I told you, Harry!" said Rose. "She's a superhero, just like I said. She can stop a tornado just by looking at it!" Rose danced around him, so much like Sam that the dog stopped and gave a hesitant wag, as if he thought only one of them should be acting like he'd lost his mind.

"This is ridiculous," he muttered, still itching to get away.

"Rose is right," said Elsa, with a calm that raised the hairs on the back of his neck.

Again, he stopped. Maybe *she* had lost her mind.

He picked up Sam's leash where it dragged the ground, then thrust the end into Rose's hand. "It's your job to walk him," he told her. "Let's go." He turned, ushering her ahead of him. His sister dragged her feet.

"You don't believe me. You don't believe *her*," said Elsa behind them.

"I don't believe in anything, Miss Pemberley," he called without looking back.

A dust devil burst into being around them, swirling stones and dirt into the air, but none of the debris even came close to touching them. Startled, Harry jerked to a stop. Rose and Sam did the same. The dog whined and looked up at them for reassurance.

A grin bloomed on Rose's face. She squealed and hopped in place. "I told you!"

Harry pivoted on his heel to look at Elsa through the swirling dust. Even as the wind stopped and the stones pattered to the earth, an unmistakable glow faded from her hands.

Elsa's friend stared. "Are you crazy? What if someone in the motel saw you?" she hissed. Elsa ignored her, still watching Harry as if to see whether he would bolt.

The very absurdity of it kept him where he stood. Had the strain of being on the run finally driven him mad? Christ, what if he couldn't trust his own senses anymore? Who would take care of Rose? He clenched his belly against a wave of nausea.

Elsa approached carefully. He didn't even think to back away. "So, now you have something on me," she said. "Please let me help you."

Suspicion was an old friend, and not easily put aside. It was all a trick, a trap. "Help us what?"

"Rose told me you two are in some kind of trouble. She didn't say what. At least let me give you a ride to wherever you need to go."

Main roads. Visibility. This woman. "No."

"El, maybe we should let them go," said Elsa's friend. "He doesn't want our help."

Harry pointed at the woman. "Listen to her. Of all of you, she's the only one making any sense."

Elsa closed the gap between them, then took Harry's hand from where he'd clenched it on the guitar strap. He was too surprised at the touch to pull away. By the time he regained his wits, she'd slipped her palm across his. The smooth softness of her skin reverberated through him like a deep guitar chord. For a second, everything ceased but her guileless blue eyes and the contact of her hand in his.

Where their hands met, his skin fizzed with pins-and-needles. He looked down to find her hand glowing again. Instead of the dust devil, he felt a cool breeze that washed away the heat of the morning. A draft of fresh air wafted into his face, like a welcome escape from a stifling, enclosed room. He breathed it in.

"I'm not a superhero," Elsa admitted, "but I do try to help people who need it."

At a loss, Harry glanced toward Rose, who wore such a jubilant, hopeful look that it almost bulldozed his doubts. He'd have braved ten Marco Torellis if only he could make her happy and safe again.

But he couldn't be sure. He couldn't even trust his own eyes. He glanced at Elsa's hand again. There was no glow now, though he still smelled that fresh-air draft, and he refused to believe it came from her.

Her fingertips brushed the inside of his wrist. A

lightning bolt of instant, thought-obliterating awareness shot through his body. He inhaled sharply, seeking air, some whiff of her perfume, God only knew what. He couldn't recall the last time he'd had the luxury of sex.

Her lashes fluttered once, and she gave a slight shake, as if waking up. She pulled her hand back. "If you'll let me," she said, and her cheeks colored.

He almost said yes, but the absence of her skin against his brought him back to his senses, and instead he said, "We need to go. Goodbye, Miss Pemberley." He turned on his heel, and when he started away down the road, it took him a few seconds to realize Rose wasn't at his side.

When he looked back, his sister was standing where he'd left her, with one hand through the loop of Sam's leash and a crushed look on her face.

"Let's go." He had to force the snarl into his voice, and he hated himself for doing it.

She came forward, much slower than he wanted, and when she reached him, she stopped. For one breath-stealing instant, his twelve-year-old sister looked exactly like their mother, wise and kind and willing to hope that the world wasn't the hell they'd lived in for eight months. "I don't want to run anymore, Harry. We need her. Please?"

Elsa's gaze went to his sister, and the woman's heart was in her eyes. Everything was right there: *I want to help you* and *I feel bad for you* and *Let me save the world*.

Right. She couldn't save *them*.

If the Torellis were using her as a walking parlor trick to reel them in, they must be running out of other, less insane options. Sizing her up, he couldn't help skimming her curves with his eyes.

They'd chosen tempting bait.

Rose must have seen he was about to bolt again, because she grabbed his hand. "*I* need her. *I* don't want to run."

Cornered, he loosened his grip on the guitar strap. Elsa, he could ignore. That longing in Rose's eyes was harder. "I'm sure she has a job to do, Rose, and so do I."

"We can spare a little driving time," Elsa said. "We're always in the car, anyway." She held out a hand, encompassing him, Rose, and Sam. "You can't have been going far on foot."

What a joke. If she only knew.

She might know. He hesitated, pulled in opposite directions.

Elsa's friend broke the silence. "Listen, you guys have some talking to do. I'll call Rory and catch a ride with him." She started away toward the motel, sliding a cell phone from her pocket.

Harry tensed, eyes on that phone. *She's calling Marco.*

Elsa jerked around toward the other woman. "Nina, no. Don't worry about it. Let's just go."

Nina swiveled back. With a shrug, she returned her cell to her pocket.

Elsa came forward. Her attention was all for Rose. She held out a hand, and gave Rose's a squeeze. "I'm sorry I can't help you. It was nice to meet you." Her gaze came back to Harry. It wasn't disappointment he saw, but hurt. The look kicked him in the guts. When she spoke, her tone rang with quiet sincerity. "Goodbye, Harry. And good luck, wherever you're going."

Nowhere, fast, he thought. Elsa turned to go back to her car.

Rose made a hiccupping sound.

When Harry turned his gaze downward, he found Rose crying. Sam whined and shoved his nose at her, but Rose jerked her hand away to scrub angrily at the tears. What was it he always told her? *You can't afford to cry.*

When had he become such a heartless bastard?

Pained, and trying not to let it show, he pulled her closer and slipped a protective arm around her shoulders. "Wait."

Elsa had made it to the door of the car. She looked back over her shoulder.

"Tulsa," Harry said, regretting it. This was wrong, he was wrong, and he and Rose were going to die.

Elsa nodded with that solemn look still in her eyes. "Tulsa, it is."

****

A victory, Elsa thought as she waited for Harry, Rose, and Sam to climb into the car's back seat. Over what, she didn't know, but at least she felt like they were doing something useful. Rose looked ecstatic. As they started down the road, she fired question after question at Elsa, about storm chasing and her power and dogs and everything in between.

Especially about her power.

Elsa had shown them her ability against her own better judgment. It wasn't something to be tossed around lightly. Certainly not to be displayed to someone with whom she hardly had even a passing acquaintance. Only two years ago had she felt confident enough in her own team to show them her power, and they'd become as close to her as her foster siblings.

"Where did you get it?" Rose asked. "Was it a science experiment?"

"An accident," Elsa said, smiling even though the actual event had been nothing to smile about. Elsa sat in the passenger seat, and Harry sat behind her, so she couldn't see his expression. She glanced in the side view mirror, but couldn't see his face there, either. How much did he believe? Could she trust him if he did believe? Her forced smile faded.

"What kind of accident?" asked Rose.

"Rosie, drop it," Harry said.

The blade-sharp distrust in his tone poked at Elsa. She cast a furtive look at Nina, who had decided, wisely, to stay out of the conversation and leave any explanations to Elsa. She twisted around toward Rose. "Maybe we ought to talk about that later, okay?"

Rose settled back in her seat with a cautious look at Harry, who kept his gaze focused out the window. Patting Sam, Rose shrugged. "Sure."

Elsa took advantage of her position to slide a glance at Harry. He stayed motionless, a pillar of stone except for the tapping of his thumb on the back seat armrest. What made him so restless?

Rose and Nina provided most of the conversation after that, an extensive Q-&-A on how they predicted storms, and what they did in between events. Mostly, their days were eaten up by driving time. Having enough team members to take turns behind the wheel helped.

"Do you ever get on the news?" Rose asked. Then, with a glance at Elsa, she added, "Well, probably not,

not with your...what do you call it?"

Elsa turned in the seat enough to face Rose. "I'm an air Elemental," she explained, half amused and half sad. Rose barely paused for breath between questions. How much company had the poor girl had besides Harry? No wonder she clung to the dog like a burr.

"Aren't you worried someone bad will find out?" the girl asked. "Like maybe the government would shut you up in a science lab and run tests on you, or something?"

"I don't make a habit of telling people. My team has known me for a while, and I trust them. And you already knew." Elsa grinned.

Rose grinned back. "Are there more of you? There has to be, if you have a name for it, right? Elementals."

"You're a pretty smart kid," Elsa said. "I don't know about more people like me, but my foster family has other abilities. Earth, water, fire."

"Fire?"

Elsa chuckled. Funny how easy it was to talk about this with Rose. Like other people talked about a family member's talent in art or music. She hadn't expected that. "That's Ethan," she said. "He doesn't use it often. Or he didn't. I don't know where he is, now."

Rose shimmied forward as far as her seat belt would allow. "Why?"

"He travels. Last time he called, it was from Wisconsin."

"So does he just, like, make fire?" The girl's eyes were as big as magnifying glass lenses.

"We can't make an element out of nothing. We can only influence what's there," Elsa explained. "It gets tiring. You know how it feels when you've been running for a long time?"

Elsa meant only the example of hard exercise, but Harry's gaze shot toward her with that hunted look. It flicked away, just as fast. If she hadn't been aware of a problem, she wouldn't even have noticed it.

Rose hadn't. "That's so cool."

Elsa smiled, still watching Harry's expressionless face. His thumb flicked against the vinyl armrest, *tap-tap-tap*. Nice hands—broad palms with long fingers, squared at the ends. "That's a nice guitar," she told him, nodding toward the cargo area where they'd stowed it.

His gaze came back to her, hooded, revealing nothing. "Thanks."

"How'd you learn to play?"

He hesitated, and Elsa stifled a frown. Was even that privileged information? Did he ever really relax? Living like that must be exhausting. And horrible, for himself as well as poor Rose.

Finally, he shrugged. "My father. When I was a kid."

Seeing his discomfort with her focus, Elsa relaxed the set of her shoulders a little more. Nervous creatures the world over hated to be faced head-on and stared at. "I have no musical talent."

"It's true," said Nina. "I love her, but she's fingernails on chalkboard when she sings."

Elsa swatted her with a map that had been sitting on the front seat between them. "Bite your tongue!"

Nina fended her off with a laugh. "Okay, a few steps down from that."

Rose was giggling. When Elsa glanced over, even Harry had cracked a smile. A little one, just an upturn of the corner of his lips, but all her fine ideas about not staring flew out the window. A little humor on the face of such a serious man was a devastating thing.

He caught her looking and froze, looking back. For the barest second, she glimpsed a hunger in his eyes that set her body tingling.

Indecision whooshed through her. She flicked her fingers on her knee, halfheartedly in time with the song on the turned-down radio. The worst storm she and her team had ever faced paled in comparison to the turbulent whirlwind in the eyes of the man in her back seat. Her power tickled at her nerve endings.

Needing to distance herself, she turned to Nina and said, "We really ought to call Rory now, and tell him we'll be late to our stop in Oklahoma, or have them change our route to Tulsa. It's not far out of the way, but they'll worry." When she dared another look at Harry, she found him gazing out his window. Did that expressionless look mean he'd finally relaxed at the idea of the phone call, or was he contemplating escape?

When they finally arrived outside Tulsa, it was midday. Rory and the rest of the crew had promised to meet them. The van and The Beast had parked at the edge of the motel lot where they'd agreed to meet.

"I'm hungry," Rose chirped. "Aren't you, Harry?"

"No," he murmured, studying the building.

"Are we staying here?" asked the girl.

At that, Harry's gaze went to Elsa. He said nothing, guaranteed nothing, just opened that car door with a lithe, silent motion, like a puma about to slink out of sight.

Rose was the exact opposite. She bounded out of the wagon with Sam in tow, and practically danced around to Harry's side as he emerged. "Please, Harry?

Let's stay! Let's see what Elsa's team does. And I'm starving. Can I have the rest of the chips?"

Elsa's heart went out to the girl. "We have plenty of sandwich fixings in the weather van's fridge. Want to join?" she asked Harry.

He shifted on his feet, just a little, ready to run again. Somehow, she doubted her power had caused his restlessness. She doubted he believed in it, even having seen the evidence. If he did believe, he took it far too much in stride...which meant that she presented the lesser of the evils troubling him.

Which meant, in turn, that he was running from something really, really bad. Rose was an open book; she said Harry tried hard to take care of her, and Elsa believed the girl. But a man with Harry's—Hank's—charisma and talent could be cutting records in Los Angeles, and here he was, blowing through little town after little town, gone almost as soon as he arrived.

Elsa had made the choice not to put down roots, too. She couldn't, not when other families needed her.

Not when putting down real roots of her own meant having something to lose.

Her heart spasmed with pain, and she turned away from that thought almost by reflex. "I'd better help with the weather gear," she blurted, going to the wagon's tailgate, then flinging it up. She grabbed an armload of whatever came first: laundry and cables and a bag of what looked like Woz's books. The bag slipped.

Rose caught it. "Did you go to school for storm chasing?"

Elsa smiled. "Not exactly. A little architecture. Storm chasing kind of came on the side."

"Because of your...you..." Rose trailed off. "Your

thing you do," she said in a stage whisper. She set the bag in Elsa's arms.

Elsa laughed. "Yeah."

Sam sniffed at a candy wrapper someone had left on the ground. Rose scooped it up before he could mouth it, then hurried to drop it in a trash can at the edge of the lot. All this time, Harry had not moved an inch, even though his gaze went everywhere.

Pretending not to notice his tension, Elsa walked toward him and smiled. "I'm sure the boys have already checked in. Come and eat something. Otherwise, I'll worry."

The corner of his mouth twitched as if he thought not eating should be the least of anyone's worries. And maybe it should have been, but then he glanced toward Rose, who jogged back to them with Sam gamboling after. The dog reached them first, straining at the end of his leash to snuffle at Harry's hand. He rubbed the dog's head absently. She could almost see him thinking: *Feed Rose. Then run.*

Who took care of him?

She moved closer, as close as she dared. "Harry?"

"All right," he said, watching his sister lead Sam toward the motel. When he looked at Elsa, his expression was cautious, but she glimpsed a heart-wrenching weariness. Elsa glanced from him to Rose and back.

Right. She had made it her mission in life to help people who needed it. In all her years of storm chasing, the signs of someone needing her had never been plainer. It was easy enough to see that people needed help during an oncoming storm. She and her team weren't the only ones who pulled together and offered assistance when that happened, or picked up the pieces afterward. What made Harry and Rose different—what set them apart—was that they needed her help, but for whatever reason, they were afraid to ask for it. She stole another look at Harry, knowing that if he caught her scrutinizing him, he'd bolt.

Just what sort of help he and Rose needed, she didn't know. Not yet, but she swore she'd find out.

Chapter Five

NOAA, National Severe Storms Laboratory, Norman, Oklahoma

Malory Sternberg flipped from one computer-printed page to the next. And then the next. And then back to the first. "Unreal," she murmured.

"What's the matter?" asked Dan Poulsen. Her colleague's attention was still glued to his monitor, and his tone suggested he didn't really want to know. The map on the screen reflected off his glasses.

"Look at these," she said, laying the packet on the desk beside him. He didn't move his gaze from the screen, so she added, "How does an EF1 tornado, moving 104 miles an hour, just fizzle out to nothing the instant before it hits the Topeka city boundary?"

Dan ignored her.

"And then an EF3, almost three weeks later, in Missouri? No casualties. Not one."

Dan ignored her.

"Then an EF4, Dan, in Piedmont, just last week. Blew itself out before touching anything but fields. Really?"

At last, he dragged his gaze away from the computer. "Dumb luck?" he asked in that same blasé tone.

"Your golf scores are dumb luck. This is a pattern."

He sighed. "Do you *want* a job in the mailroom?"

"Just look at it!" she snapped.

He grabbed the packet, then paged through it. She doubted his gaze even landed on words. "Ever since the director bumped you down to my area, I've been thinking of moving my stuff," he muttered. "I don't want to get demoted by association."

"Dan!"

He eyed her. "Aren't you supposed to be on vacation?" When she didn't respond, he sighed again and flipped back through the pages, a little slower. "What pattern? There's no pattern. They're not even in the same weather system."

"The pattern isn't how they start, it's how they stop. Every single one just poofs out of existence right before doing any real damage to people or property."

"Which is what we'd like to happen," Dan said, in that I'm-talking-to-a-toddler voice that rubbed her nerves raw.

"There isn't even a discernible stutter in the mesocyclone, not on any of our radar," she added. "Steady on, right up until *Smack*, it hits a wall and stops completely. The whole storm system forming the thing just falls apart at once. What does that?"

For a second, it looked as if Dan might be interested. His gaze twitched to the papers again, and he started to turn a page. Then he clapped her packet shut and put it down. "Get out of here, Malory. Take a break from chasing ghosts."

She gave an inarticulate huff and turned back to her workstation. She couldn't take the report home with her—it became government property, once she'd filed it—but she grabbed a stack of sticky notes, then scribbled the major data points down. They were her own data, damn it, just numbers.

Just numbers to NSSL. To her, maybe something bigger. Maybe the break in luck she'd been waiting for.

With a last glare at Dan, who had returned to mooning over his computer screen, she stuffed the little notes in her briefcase, then snapped it shut.

Her trip to Paris could wait. Tornado Alley couldn't.

****

At a picnic table behind the motel, Harry watched Rose wolf down a ham and cheese on rye as if she thought she'd never eat again. Sam had his nose buried in a bowl of dog food. Harry was so used to sacrificing meals to his little sister he hardly even noticed his own stomach when it growled.

Elsa's teammate, Seth, pushed a wrapped sandwich toward him. "Dude, there's still plenty. Grab one before Woz eats it."

The rest of Elsa's team erupted in a round of friendly jeers at Woz, who fielded them all with good-natured snarking of his own.

Harry laid a hand on the sandwich wrapper. *Eat half. Save the rest.* He might not get dinner.

God, he hated this. Resented having to worry about food, about where to sleep, about how much cash he had in his wallet. Unwilling to look at Elsa or her team, unwilling to let them see his frustration, he kept his stare on Rose, making sure she had her fill. Already, he'd begun thinking ahead to his next gig at the rib joint. It shouldn't be too far away. The bartender at his last set had given him the address, and Harry thought he'd seen the turnoff to that road at the last intersection.

Not too far a walk now, as long as the weather held.

"If you ever want to come back and play another set, you're pre-invited," the bartender had said. "We ain't seen business that good in three months."

Harry tried not to play the same venue twice. It wouldn't be wise to get too familiar to anyone, even if he did look light years away from the clean-shaven, tuxedo-clad playboy he'd left behind in Los Angeles. Hank Rhodes was Salvation Army, not John Varvatos. He doubted anyone would pick him out of a crowd even if he did go somewhere without his dime-store sunglasses.

"Wakey, wakey," Elsa said from across the table.

He came back to the present with a little head-shake, and pulled the wrapper off the sandwich. "Sorry. Cobwebs. What did you say?"

"I said, if you want, there's going to be an extra bed in Seth's room. We usually take doubles at motels, and there's always an odd one out." She shrugged. "Nina and I can get a cot for Rose, and Sam could stay with her."

A look at Seth revealed him nodding. "Long as you don't mind bunking in a room full of cables and computers," he said around his mouthful of German bologna.

Rose sat bolt upright. "Stay with you? Can I really?"

"Sure, if it's okay with Hank," Nina added. "We were going to rent a movie." She grinned at Rose. "Something girly, so the boys don't want to join in."

Looking from Rose's elated expression, to Nina, and then to Elsa, Harry gave a soft outward breath, hardly enough to be called a sigh. "Talk to you a minute?" he muttered. "Alone?" He pushed onto his feet and then started away, out of earshot of the rest of the group.

He didn't realize how close Elsa had followed until he turned to find her right behind him. Rather than looking irritated at the way he'd ordered her around—which would have been easier—she looked troubled and curious.

Out of earshot, he realized, but not eyesight. Rose was still watching them, clearly eager to know what they were discussing, and trying not to appear so.

He pushed aside his own discomfort, not wanting a public confrontation, but unable to let Rose out of his sight. Harry turned his glare on Elsa. "I don't know what your game is, whether you think you're Robin Hood, or what—"

"I'm who?"

"—and I appreciate the food and the ride, but I'm not some charity case."

"No one said 'charity case,'" she protested.

"You said you wanna help," he snapped. "The best way you can help me is to stop helping me. Stop getting her hopes up."

Elsa's lashes flickered over those blue, blue eyes. "Why?"

The hurt on her face pulled at him. He struggled for a gentler tone, and failed. "You can't help us. No one can help us."

Her hand slipped into his. When she spoke, her voice went as soft as that look in her eyes, threatening to disarm him. "Harry, what are you running from?"

He barked a bitter laugh and tried to remove his hand from hers.

Instead of allowing it, she reached for his other hand. "You can trust me. I'm trusting *you*."

He laughed again, quietly, still skeptical, still searching for that chink in her story that would lead the Torellis to him and his sister. "Parlor tricks."

Her brow knotted. "Parlor...?" She let go of him to thrust a hand in front of his face, and before his eyes, her fingertips started glowing. The rest of her didn't move, but a cool breeze rushed off her palm and ruffled his hair. Her eyes sharpened with irritation, and something more that hurt to see. "Check it out, Harry. No wires, no magic flimflams. Just me, trusting you. You've already seen it, and so has your sister. What would I gain by proving it, besides trouble of my own?"

He hesitated. Took half a step back. With a cautious glance at her face—just a glance, because he didn't trust himself to look longer—he reached up to take her hand again in both of his. He held her as if she were made of glass, and stared at her skin. The illumination flickered, swirled like currents along the creases in her palm, faded, and then flushed bright again. The breeze tickled the little hairs on the backs of his hands. Where his thumbs skated over the lines in her palm, he felt the buzzing he'd experienced before. Disbelief eroded away, leaving a tiny shoot of wonder. "How do you do it?" he murmured, almost without realizing he'd said anything. He brought his gaze up to hers.

A huge mistake. The empathy in her eyes plowed through him like one of her tornadoes. "I don't know," she said. "I don't know how, I don't know why. I don't know why *me*. All I know is, if I have it, I should use it." Elsa stepped closer, gripping his hands tighter.

"Please let me help you, Harry," she whispered.

Pain twisted in his chest. "Why?"

She surprised him when an echo of his pain flashed across her own features. The downturn of her mouth punched a reflex button inside him, made him want to kiss her, to erase it, to see her smile again. "Because there are people I couldn't help, and they're gone now."

They stood there, frozen, with his hands in hers and that wind fluttering their hair. Harry sucked it into his chest, wishing it could blow away the ashes in his past and still leave him something to hold onto. Something permanent. Something that stayed. Somewhere *he* could stay.

He kept watching her mouth. Even in the lowering evening light, he saw her lips trembling. Her lashes fluttered again, and her eyes had dimmed a little.

He wanted to trust her. He wanted to trust *anyone*. If there was someone to watch Rose while he played his next set—someone besides Sam—it would be so much easier.

And he had something on her, he realized, still holding her hand.

Still holding her hand.

He dropped it at once. "We'll stay tonight," he said. "Just for tonight. Truth is, Rose could use some company, other than me."

Elsa looked just as flustered as he. When she glanced up at him, she smiled a little, and somehow even that shaky upward curve of her lips eased the weight in his chest. "Don't you have another show to do?"

"Yeah, a couple days out. I gotta find the place, talk to the guy."

She opened her mouth to say something else, then closed it again. Harry could see her deciding not to push her luck. His mistrust wavered. She didn't seem the type that could carry a lie. Could it be she had nothing to do with the Torellis?

He stomped on that nascent hope. *Rose. Think of Rose.*

Ha. He'd thought of nothing but Rose for months.

He tucked his hands into his back pockets to keep them away from Elsa, but it was no good. He could still feel her skin against his fingertips. His groin pulsed.

Christ, he was sick of being alone.

He stalked back to the group without another word. Better she thought him rude than the truth: that all he wanted right now was to take that look in her eyes and turn it into a week in bed with her, erasing both their demons. Even if it couldn't last.

****

Waiting for Nina to get back from the store with popcorn and snacks, Elsa flipped through the movie channels on their room's television. Sam lay on her bed. Whenever she scratched his ears, his tail thumped the bedspread.

She smiled at the dog as he slurped her hand. Rose had told her they'd found Sam wandering loose before the tornado. She gave the dog's broad head a rub. "Maybe there's a reason we were all put in each other's way, huh, boy?"

"Elsa," came Rose's uncertain voice from the bathroom.

Concerned at the girl's tone, Elsa got up to move to the closed door. "What's wrong, honey?"

A few seconds passed, then the door opened a

crack. Rose's face appeared, flushed and frowning. "I'm bleeding," she whispered.

Startled, Elsa thought immediately of the first-aid kit in the weather van. "Did you hurt yourself?"

"No," Rose said. "My period. I think I just got my period."

"Oh. Don't you have any—"

"I've never had one," Rose interrupted, clearly as hesitant to discuss the subject as Elsa was to intrude on it.

Elsa's first thought was of Harry, towing this poor girl around the Midwest for who knew how long. Rose was growing up under his nose. Had she even had a woman to talk to her about any of this? Did he know how alone the girl must feel?

"Right," she said. "Don't worry. I have a bunch of stuff in my bag. Stay right there."

By the time Nina returned from the store, Rose and Elsa were giggling on the bed over a story of Elsa's disastrous first school dance. "What's with all the merriment?" Nina asked, setting bags of groceries on her own bed.

"I was telling her about Ricky and the chocolate fountain." Elsa fizzed with laughter.

Nina grinned. "Don't ever do that," she told Rose.

Rose's expression sobered. She turned her attention to Sam, patting his back. "I've never been to a school dance."

As Nina removed more groceries from the bags than they could have eaten in a week, Elsa said, "Nina, can you pick the movie? We've narrowed it down, but we wanted your input. I'll be right back."

"Sure." Nina withdrew a package of peanut butter

cups from the grocery bags and dangled them in front of Rose. "A little birdie told me you like these."

Rose lit like a fluorescent bulb. "Thanks!"

With a last smile, Elsa left the room. Rose's enthusiasm rubbed off in the best of ways, all the more surprising because she remained buoyant in spite of her unexplained but still obvious troubles. She was a bright girl, and shockingly knowledgeable about current events, for a kid her age. At twelve, already used to hiding her power, all Elsa had worried about was riding horses and learning to swing down from her foster parents' hayloft when they weren't looking. Rose knew about crime trends, foreign officials, and the stock market. Elsa had a day-old newspaper on her nightstand, and when Rose noticed it, she tore through it as if it were the latest teen magazine.

Outside, Elsa marched toward Seth and Harry's room. She rapped on the door.

It opened on Harry, damp-haired and in a fresh set of clothes. The shirt, worn thin, hugged his broad chest. Elsa's attention stuttered on that enthralling sight for several seconds before she remembered herself. "Um...yeah. Got a minute?"

He stepped back to open the door wider. In the room, Seth was gathering a small bag of shaving supplies. "Me?"

"No, just Hank. Outside, if that's okay," she added.

"'Kay," Seth said, trotting toward the bathroom.

Harry gave a shrug and stepped outside, closing the door behind him. "What's wrong?"

"Nothing's wrong," she said, walking to the end of the building and around to the back where they'd eaten earlier. A few sparrows picked at crumbs that had spilled onto the cracked pavement. When she approached the table to sit on its edge, they fluttered away into the trees.

She faced Harry, who came to a stop in front of her. "Look, Harry, it's obvious you care about your little sister," she began, then hesitated. "I'm not trying to pry."

His brows drew together. "Say what you gotta say."

"She needs a woman around."

The expression on his face was just as she'd expected. Guarded. Offended. Suspicious of her motives. Before he could unleash the hostile words she knew would follow, she added, "Rose is what, twelve?"

"So?"

"Harry, she's just gotten her first period, and she's afraid to even tell you because she thinks that's one more thing you've got to worry about in taking care of her. She's smart enough to know she should be seeing a doctor about her healthcare, but she won't. She doesn't want you two to be found. She was embarrassed to talk to me, but she did, because there's no one else."

His outburst stopped in its tracks. The misery that flashed through his eyes tugged at her heartstrings.

"She loves you," Elsa added gently. "Whatever trouble you're in, she loves you enough to protect you, the way you protect her."

Harry's shoulders slackened. His weariness was palpable. "I'm failing her."

His admission and choice of words were so at odds with the T-shirt-and-jeans man before her that she blinked in confusion. "You're not," she urged. "She's smart, she's healthy, and she's fed and clothed. She has family." Her voice shook.

His attention snapped to her face, alert to that little catch. The startling blue of his irises sent a tiny thrill through her belly. "Where's your family?" he asked.

She jerked her gaze away and forced a laugh. "All over the country. My two foster brothers and a foster sister. And my team, of course."

His stare never left her face. She could feel it, could feel the intensity of it, in the air around them. "What about before all of them?" he prompted.

Her throat tightened. She'd talked about trusting him. For some strange reason, part of her even believed she could, regarding her power. He might not believe what he saw—not completely, not yet—but she sensed he understood she wanted to help him and Rose.

But that wasn't the same as tearing open that old wound he'd touched with his song, the first night she'd met him. Some wounds never really healed.

She sensed he understood that, too.

"They died," she said finally. It was all she could get out.

A stray breeze fluttered his damp hair. She caught the spicy, clean scent of shampoo and breathed it in, willing the pleasant smell to soothe the ache in her heart.

He seemed to find no such solace. When he angled his head, compelling her to meet his gaze again, his eyes had clouded. She doubted it had anything to do with her confession alone. "I'm sorry," he said. "I know people always say that."

"It was a long time ago."

"They say that, too." He sighed and pivoted on his heel to lean against the edge of the table beside her, then crossed his arms loosely over his midriff. "It never seems like as long a time ago as people say. Not to them."

She almost asked him where his parents were, but that prickling sense of a sensitive subject detoured her away from the question. For a few silent moments, it was enough just to be there beside him, not saying anything. Somehow, it felt better.

It almost felt right. And she hardly knew him.

The sun sank ever lower. A few streaks of red and orange remained on the western horizon. The air had taken on that golden wash of twilight peculiar to summer evenings in the Midwest. The sparrows chittered themselves to sleep in the trees.

Their chatter gave her an excuse to peer sidelong at Harry on the pretense of searching the trees. He watched the birds, too, but his mind was clearly on something else. She waited. At last, he uncrossed his arms, then reached behind him to prop his hands on the edge of the table. "Thanks. For talking to her."

Warmth flowed through her. "You're welcome," she said.

He brought his gaze back to her. Pushing off from the table, he turned to her. "She knows not to...when a boy...?"

"I think she understands about boys and sex," Elsa said, then grinned. "She's smart, that girl."

Harry grinned, too. Dimples creased his stubbled cheeks. His eyes lit with humor, all the more riveting because of that shocking blue. Elsa's breath stalled, and her heart, starved of oxygen, drummed in her chest.

His smile was more than just devastating. It obliterated all semblance of logic.

When his gaze met hers, her skin prickled with a charge in the air. They stilled, their eyes locked on each other.

In a rush, Elsa's senses were bombarded with awareness of him. His eyes. His big, lean, muscular frame. The rakish waves in his short, dark hair. The way that shirt molded to his body. A body that could stop a train. She opened her mouth to say something—God only knew what. She'd forgotten how to speak. Nothing could possibly be important enough to say, anyway.

He stared at her, his gaze suddenly sharp, so intense she shuddered. She went hyper-alert to every shift of current in the air. Heat wafted from him as his gaze coursed over her body, and suddenly, even her skimpy tank top stifled against her skin.

An instant. Only an instant. And then his mouth slammed over hers.

Her senses fired all over her body where they touched. She hesitated only a second before sliding her hands over his magnificent chest, molding to the curve of his pecs.

His arms circled her body. He slid his hands up her back, pulling her to him, claiming, possessing. His mouth was hot and hungry. His body was hard and hotter, a living wildfire in her arms. Elsa gave a tiny moan that he devoured with his kiss. *More,* she thought.

He pressed her back against the table with a groan, and his hands clenched in the back of her tank top, dragging her still closer. His erection ground against her belly. Elsa slid her hands around his waist to curl over his taut buttocks, to pull him against her.

In answer, he brought one of his hands to her

breast, cupping it, sliding hard over the sensitive nipple through her thin shirt. Her nerves pinged wildly, overloading her. She gasped and clutched him tighter.

Harry's mouth swept across her cheek to her neck. His snarl vibrated her tender skin, sending scorching pulses straight to her core. "Oh, God, Harry," she breathed.

He stopped. Froze, really. His forehead dropped against the hollow of her neck. "Holy shit," he whispered harshly. His breath burned against her exposed skin.

She hated to speak. Hated to come back down to earth. "What's wrong?"

He raised his head, then shook it. "No. This can't. I can't. *We* can't." He jerked his hands away and pulled backward as if he were dodging a snapping dog.

Still trembling, still on fire, Elsa struggled with his rejection. All she could do for several seconds was stare. "Harry?"

"No!" he snapped, then checked himself. His forehead creased, and he closed his eyes. "No." He held himself rigid, a rope pulled taut and about to snap. Several more seconds went by before he opened his eyes again, but he met hers only briefly before his gaze fell away. "I'm sorry. Good night."

He retreated, leaving her there, shaking, bewildered by the way the air went cold and empty. *No,* she thought. *Horrible night. Horrible, horrible night. What did I do wrong?*

Tormented by a sense of something huge and unfixable, she barely slept all night.

Chapter Six

Harry knew it was a nightmare, the minute it resolved itself into the too-familiar shape of a hallway with an emergency door at the end. He had the same dream almost every night. Even knowing it was a nightmare, he couldn't shake himself out of it.

Rosalie huddled in his arms, clinging to him, terrified. No matter how hard he ran, the door stretched farther and farther away. "Harry?" she sobbed. "Harry! Harry!"

The voice calling his name changed. Softer. "Harry?"

Elsa's voice. A mental flash of her eyes demolished everything else and Harry started awake. He found himself staring at the gray ceiling of the motel room. Still seeing Elsa's face and that expression when he'd left her last night, it took him a minute to remember where he was.

Seth still slept in the bed on the other side of the room. Not chatty, that kid. When Harry returned to the room, he must've looked angry—and he was. Furious with himself. After a preliminary question, Seth didn't press him about the issue. Harry found himself grateful the kid knew a boundary when he saw it.

Weather gear still littered the room. Seth hadn't been kidding. He brought an A/V studio worth of equipment with him wherever he went.

Elsa. Her face. God damn it. Harry rubbed his eyes, trying to grind the image out of his memory.

Time to go.

He rolled out of bed, then snagged his guitar case and duffel in a motion so smooth, it was practically military. He left the room, then stalked down to Elsa's door. All of her team's vehicles remained in the lot. No others had come since last night. He glanced up and down the road. In these Midwest flatlands, you could see for miles. Not one car traveled the road yet. Powder-gray clouds covered the sky. The birds had hardly even begun to wake.

He stopped at Elsa's door and stared at the fading white paint and the crooked *Three. Knock, damn it. Knock, and get your sister, and blow this pop stand.*

He barely rapped it once, and the door opened. Nina appeared with her finger to her lips. With a grin, she pushed the door open wider.

The cot was empty. One bed was likewise unoccupied, probably Nina's.

In the last bed, Elsa teetered on the edge where she slept. Rosalie slumbered on the edge of the other side. In the middle lay Sam, stretched out to his fullest. Elsa's hand lay on the dog's back, and Rose's on his head.

"I wish I had a camera," Nina whispered. "Elsa's such a sucker for dogs and kids."

The sight of the three on the bed wormed its way under Harry's skin. In a flash, he saw a sunlit bedroom on a Saturday morning, with Rose and Elsa giggling while the wriggling, wagging dog slurped their faces to wake them up. The mental image was so clear, he could make out a white bedspread, and the woodgrain in the

Mission oak bedframe.

His parents' home. Their room. His, now, if he could ever lay claim to it.

Harry crushed the vision. Eventually, the lawyers would give up and declare him and Rose dead. Their assets would be frittered away to wherever such things went when they were unspoken for. Harry would be just as poor as he was right now, so none of it mattered, anyway. Certainly not his wishes for things that wouldn't be. "Rose," he growled, startling Nina with his gruff tone.

His sister sprang upright. The fright in her eyes pierced him, but he forced himself past it. Sam bounded up and launched himself toward Harry.

As Harry caught the dog's collar, Elsa shot up, rubbing her eyes, her hair in such disarray it almost made him smile. He forced himself past that, too.

Without words, Rose gathered her things. She found Sam's leash, then clipped it to his collar. "Are we going to stay here until your next show?"

"Dunno yet. I have to go see the guy. Should've done it yesterday." He hated staying in one place, more so now that he'd spotted Vincent Torelli. Granted, they'd put some miles between them since that sighting, but anything less than a few states away was still far too close.

Christ, he had the proof that could put the Torellis away, and he couldn't even use it. The minute he plugged himself into the grid, it would be over.

Sam strained in his grasp, whining to go out. Harry looked down at Rose. Made himself smile. "Happy Birthday, sweet pea."

"Birthday?" Elsa echoed, her voice husky with

sleep. She swiped at her hair, which did little to smooth it. "It's your birthday, Rose? Why didn't you say so?"

Rosalie blushed. "It's okay. The movie was perfect." She pulled Sam from Harry's grasp, then led him outside.

Harry swallowed hard. Rose's thirteenth birthday. What the hell could he give her? He had nothing. *They* had nothing.

More guilt. Would it ever stop hammering at him? "Listen, thanks for watching her last night," he muttered to Elsa and Nina.

"Our pleasure," Nina said. "We had a ball."

Harry tried to keep his attention on Nina, but it snapped to Elsa, rising from the bed. She wore the tank top from last night, and a pair of high-cut shorts that exposed long, slim legs.

The mental picture of the sunlit bedroom returned. This time, it was just Elsa and him, and those endless legs wrapped around his naked body.

He backed out the door as Rose and Sam passed.

"Wait, are you leaving?" Elsa called.

Still backpedaling into the lot, Harry checked over his shoulder to see Rose leading Sam to a patch of weeds. The sun had risen. A couple of cars passed by. *Need to get off these main roads.* "Look, Elsa. Thank you. For everything, really. But we can't keep taking advantage of your help."

Everything happened at once. Sam barked. Rose yelled the dog's name. A look of horror filled Elsa's face. "No! Rose, no!"

Harry dropped his bag and guitar case in the dirt. He whirled around to find Rose chasing the loose dog into the road—and another car was coming.

Adrenaline exploded through him. Harry sprinted toward his sister, and Elsa followed.

He caught up to Rose and Sam as they reached the middle of the road. The car's horn blared, and Harry gave Rose and the dog a violent shove. Girl and dog tumbled to the roadside.

The car slammed on its brakes and fishtailed toward him. He scrambled, stumbled, too slow. His booted foot slipped in gravel.

From the corner of his eye, he glimpsed Elsa, still standing at the roadside. Light burst from her hands, and a fierce wind blasted his body, thrusting him toward Rose. The car hurtled past him, and the corner clipped his fingers. Pain streaked up his arm. He shouted in agony, and toppled end over end into the weeds on the far side of the road.

"Harry! Harry!" Rose screamed.

For a few seconds, he could only lie there on his back, staring up into the overcast sky and making sure he could force air back into his lungs.

Rose's teary-eyed face appeared over him. Sam shoved his nose at Harry, slobbering and whining.

"Get off me!" Harry snarled. He shoved at the dog, and when his left hand brushed the Lab's head, needles of pain shot through his fingers. Harry swore loudly and curled himself into a sitting position over his throbbing hand.

"Hey! *Hey!*" came Elsa's angry shout. A squeal of tires made him look up.

The car that had hit him slammed on the gas, and then screeched away down the road.

Elsa rushed across the road, then knelt before him. "Harry, are you hurt? Say something!"

Pain. Fuck. His hand. The joint of his ring finger pounded in time with his speeding heartbeat. The knuckle was rapidly swelling and turning red. He considered swearing again, but even that took too much energy.

"Oh, God, Harry," Elsa said, crouching beside him. "Can you move? Did it hit you?"

"My hand," he said. "It's fine, it's fine, it barely winged me." He glanced over his shoulder. The car was long gone. Nondescript, he recalled. Thankfully, not a black Cadillac.

Elsa followed his gaze, but only for a moment. She turned her attention back to Harry's hand. "Is it broken?"

Oh, Christ, please don't be broken. Ignoring the pain, he tested the joints with his opposite hand. Everything moved as it should, without undue pain, but the joint smarted like a sonofabitch. A sprain, if he was lucky. "I gotta get ice on this. *Now.*" He lunged to his feet.

Elsa rose beside him, holding out her arm as if she wanted to help him, but couldn't tell if he welcomed the support. She glared down the road. "I can't believe that bastard just hit-and-run like that!"

"Good for him," Harry muttered. "I don't need the publicity."

The uncertainty in Elsa's posture moved to her face. "What can I do?"

He checked his body. Not much more than scrapes and bruises, except for that sprain. He'd be sore as hell. Already, his left arm protested movement. Alive—he and Rose, and even the dog. Shaking a little with shock, he stared at Elsa. "I think you just saved my life."

She gave him a watery smile, and an instant later, Rose launched herself at Elsa in a bear hug. "I told you she was a hero, Harry!"

He started to open his mouth on a tirade, berating Rose for chasing the dog across the road, but the fact that she was alive and unhurt shut his mouth for him. He should have kissed his lucky stars he'd escaped with only a finger sprain.

He wouldn't be playing the guitar for the next few weeks.

Everything crashed down on him. He did swear now, repeatedly. Rose paled at the outburst. Harry stalked back across the road to his now-useless guitar, lying in the motel lot.

"Shouldn't we get you to a hospital?" Elsa called.

He whirled on her. "I go to the hospital, I'm on the grid, and me and Rose are dead. Right now, I can't even feed her, but at least I'm *alive*." He thrust his injured hand in the air.

Elsa's face drained of color, too. "Just what kind of trouble are you in, Harry?"

He froze, realizing he'd just blown any remaining chance of safety out of the water. He sighed, then picked up his bag and guitar case. "Look, it's better if you forget you saw us. We've already hung around too long."

"No!" Elsa cried, her voice sharp with outrage. "Not a chance, especially not now! Harry, tell me what's going on."

He turned on her, about to yell, scream, something to drive her away. Elsa stood with her hands fisted at her sides, trembling. Tears glinted in the corners of her eyes.

His hand throbbed. He glanced to Rose, who clutched Sam's leash as though it were a lifeline. His little sister shook, too. For a few tense seconds, he debated what to do. What was best for Rose. "Ice," he repeated, then stalked back toward Elsa's motel room.

Nina stood in the doorway, wide-eyed, clearly concerned. He acknowledged it with a nod.

She unfroze. "We've got some emergency stuff in the van. I'll get it." She dodged back into the room for a set of keys, then bolted toward the team's vehicles.

Rose, Sam, and Elsa followed him into the room. He sat on Elsa's still-rumpled bed. That sunlit room flashed into his thoughts again, but now, he gave the image a brutal kick.

His temperament must have shown on his face. Elsa sat beside him, looking worried—and worse, sympathetic. "How can I help?"

He laughed, completely without humor. "I thought we covered that. We are beyond help, Miss Pemberley."

Elsa glanced to Rose. "Why don't you go wake Rory and Woz if they aren't already up, honey?"

His kid sister glanced at him, a silent request for permission. Harry sighed and gave another nod. Rose and the dog left. The door clicked softly shut behind them.

He expected questions. Lots of them. He would have been full of them. But Elsa just sat there, watching him stare at his useless hand. Her gaze was palpable, like a soft stroke of her hand across his cheek. His shoulders tensed in response. "You could have exposed us at any time," he muttered. "The gas station. The diner. You didn't have to stop that car from hitting us."

"Of course I did," she murmured.

"If you wanted us dead," he added.

Her brows twitched upward. "Harry, why in the world would I want you dead?"

He shrugged his shoulders, trying to ease the tightness. A few seconds of silence passed. The room's air conditioner kicked on, trying to compete with the already-warm air outside. "We're on a hit list," he said in a rush.

The door opened again, and Nina ducked in with a box of first-aid supplies. Harry took a glance at Elsa's stunned expression, and clammed up. Nina seemed to sense the tension in the air, because she didn't move a muscle.

Finally, Elsa rose from the bed and took the box from her. Her voice trembled a bit. "Nina, can you check on Seth?"

"Sure," she said, and disappeared again. Harry couldn't blame her for not wanting to be part of the shit-storm about to happen. *He* didn't want to be part of it.

Oh, hell on a trampoline. What was he supposed to do now?

Elsa busied herself pulling an ice bag and finger splint from the box. She was shaking, but gamely trying to ignore the fact.

He watched her, admiring her nerve even through his own pain. "Girl Scout?" he guessed.

"Just prepared," she said. "In our line of work, we've had near about everything."

He shifted, then winced when the motion jarred his hand. "Even with your...?"

"It's not perfect," she replied when he trailed off.

She set the box on his other side, then poked through it for tape. With her eyes on her work, and not him, she asked, "D-Do you want to tell me why?"

A gentle question, not a demand. He would have demanded, after a bomb-drop like that. Did he want to tell her? *Not really,* he thought, but the words wouldn't come out, and he couldn't, for the life of himself, figure out why. *No* should have been the first word out of his mouth from the moment he met her, and he should have kept saying it until she went away. Elsa Pemberley was a force not unlike her tornadoes.

His gaze fused to her lips, to the way the lower one was just a bit fuller, and how it gave her a pensive expression. The faint line between her slender brows amplified the look. "Why do you need to know so much?" he murmured. Completely not what he'd meant to say.

Her gaze met his at last. Her voice cracked with a touch of what he'd have sworn was desperation. "Tell me what I can do that will help you and Rose."

He gave another humorless laugh. "Unless you have an inescapable arrest warrant in your superpower bag of tricks, Miss Pemberley, we're screwed."

She went to a cooler in the room's corner. For a few seconds, he watched her crouching over the box. Even sleep-rumpled, she was hard to resist—all long legs and slim curves, and an ass that almost made him forget the spearing pain in his hand.

He suspected her pauses between questions were to let him think what to say, to keep it from feeling like she was pushing him for information. To decide whether to tell her at all. The suspicion that had kept him going all this time poked at him, a residual warning that he shouldn't reveal anything. But his suspicion had never prepared him for a woman who claimed she could control the very air.

And he'd thought his life couldn't get any more surreal.

She brought him the ice pack. "This is going to hurt. I'm sorry." She cleaned the abraded skin of his fingers with swabs and alcohol. Focusing on her face, on those lips and long, lowered lashes, he ignored the discomfort.

Then she straightened his finger to set it on the splint. Agony flashed up his arm, and he grunted.

Elsa flinched. "I'm sorry, I'm sorry."

"Stop apologizing."

Her gaze came up to his. Neither of them moved. There was a spark of pain in her eyes that he recognized only too well. Something in his gut twisted on that look, echoing it, defying his need to put her at a distance. "None of this is your fault," he murmured.

She went back to setting his finger on the splint. "I know."

She wouldn't acknowledge it, he realized. Didn't believe he and Rose were marked to die. Still thought, somehow, that she could help them, and he meant to deny her that chance.

He opened his mouth to say something, then shut it when it became clear no words would smooth this over. He put his good hand over hers, trying to thank her for what she'd done for them, even though it was no use.

It wasn't enough, not with the way a frown lingered on her lips and the tension lingered in her shoulders. "Elsa, if you hadn't pushed me out of the way of that car, things would be a damned sight worse for us right now. I'll find a way to take care of her."

Without meeting his eyes, she said, too casually, "You could come with us."

"Storm chasing?" He snorted. "What the hell do I know about storm chasing? And you, you don't even know what kind of trouble you're buying."

Now she looked at him. The sudden, naked intensity and worry in her eyes washed over him, and stabbed him as neatly as a switchblade knife. There was no faking a look like that. "Then tell me," she urged.

He stared at her, waiting for what, he didn't know. For Marco Torelli to come bursting through the door with his hitmen and shoot Harry dead. For the moon to fall. For Elsa to tell him to forget it, that she didn't really want to know. For all of this to get easier, just for a second.

It wasn't going to get any easier, though—not until something changed. Not until he sucked it up and took a leap of faith in something. Or someone.

Maybe her.

He swallowed hard, but didn't move his gaze from hers. When he spoke, his voice was hoarse, as if it were worn out from all the screaming he'd wanted to do in the past eight months, but couldn't. "My name is Harrison Litchfield, Junior."

****

The evening had been beautiful—way too beautiful to be indoors—and yet there they were. Harry's parents had taken him and his sister along to a pricey hotel, where they were attending a dinner benefiting the local hospital. Enough money in this place today to run the country for a solid year, truth be told...and a crying shame they had to waste a perfectly good Friday night in a stuffy banquet room. Harry glanced out the hotel room window with a wistful look at the cloudless sky.

Los Angeles in the autumn. Perfect. The blistering heat of summer was over, and the rains of winter hadn't started yet.

Rosalie hopped on the edge of the bed, staring at the coverage of an upcoming Halloween festival on the suite's enormous television, but not paying much attention. "Mummy, can I go swim in the hotel pool?" she called, wheedling just a little.

Their mother entered the room from the walk-in closet. She fastened a pair of diamond earrings in her ears, then examined Harrison's untucked button-down shirt and slacks. "Why aren't you ready? The benefit starts in half an hour. Your father's going to spit nails."

Harry slouched farther into the chair. "I would pay to see that. Rosie doesn't want to go, either. Who's going to watch her if we're all cavorting at this supremely dull dinner?" He gave his mother a look of mock censure. "You aren't becoming one of those parents who lets the television do the babysitting, are you?"

"All right, all right." She kissed the top of his head. "I find them as boring as you do, but don't tell your father that. He likes to think I'm having the time of my life while we dance to terrible music." She gave Harry a wink, then held up a diamond choker. "Help me?"

Harry stood and took the necklace to fasten it around his mother's neck. He knew his parents well enough to understand that they could have been at a tax audit and still had fun, as long as they were together. He admired that. Some families were torn apart by the disappointments of years of childlessness. Harry had been a lucky break early in their marriage. Nineteen years later, Rosalie became lucky break number two. And from what he'd seen, his parents had spent the years in between just as in love with each other as they'd been on day one.

"There," he said, clasping the necklace. "Knock them dead." He kissed his mother's cheek.

"I'd rather knock them generous," she said. "With just a little more funding, we'll be able to open a new children's wing at the hospital."

Harry smiled. His mother's experience with fertility problems had led her into a crusade for would-be mothers and the health of their children. Privately, he wished he had such a worthwhile pursuit in his life. Something more worthwhile than upholding the family traditions with public appearances and toothy smiles, anyway. Life as the son of wealthy philanthropists might seem exciting, but in reality, it was a lot like watching paint dry.

"Off to it, then," he said brightly. He passed the bed, taking Rose's hand and towing her toward the door. "Rose and I will go to the pool and pray to the water gods to wash buckets of money out of the pockets of the teeming masses."

"Bye, Mummy!" Rose hopped after him. They paused in the adjacent room to let her get her swimsuit on under her clothes, and then grab a plush towel. Harry grabbed his guitar case from its spot by the dresser, then slung it over his shoulder. The guitar was a birthday gift from his father the week before, and he had barely let the expensive instrument out of his sight or hands since. Even he had a hobby, and an hour of the pool room's humidity was worth the risk for the pleasure of playing the antique Gibson.

"Aren't you going to swim?" Rose asked.

"You swim. I'll serenade you." He tweaked her nose, and they made their way down to the pool.

They boarded the elevator behind a pair of burly men in suits. The smaller one shushed the other with a slicing hand motion as soon as Harry met their gazes. He thought nothing of it while the elevator doors slid shut. He and Rosie stepped back into the corner of the elevator behind the men. The pool was on the bottom level, and it looked like these two might be heading for the benefit in the ballroom.

He adjusted the guitar case over his shoulder. His wandering gaze landed on a tiny, spiky tattoo peeking out from the collar of the second, bigger man. *Odd*, Harry thought, contrasting the gritty ink design with what was clearly a four-digit business suit.

Not one sound disturbed the whirr of the elevator for three floors. Then there was a buzzing sound, and the whirring stopped.

Emergency lights flicked on. Dimly, Harry heard surprised voices in one of the hotel hallways. There was no indication of a floor number on the screen overhead.

"What happened?" Rose asked.

"Power's out, or something," Harry said. "Don't worry, they'll come fix it." He looked to the smaller man. "Can you press the Call button for help?"

He didn't. The men shared another look. No one moved.

Harry tried again. "Hey, mister, I don't want to be stuck in here. Do you?" He made a move for the button.

"Just cool it," the man said, blocking him.

Rose took a big step toward Harry. She bumped

him, and Harry stumbled. He thrust out a hand automatically, brushing the tattooed man's waist as he righted himself.

And under the man's jacket, tucked into the waistband—even though he hardly believed it—Harry felt the unmistakable outline of a gun. "Sorry," he muttered, stone-faced, and stepped smoothly back. But under his falsified cool, he started sweating. Whoever these men were, they weren't cops, and he'd have bet his family's fortune they weren't security.

The smaller man gave him a lingering look. Harry wanted to step closer to Rose, but he feared it would only endanger them both. Every second that crawled past, his heartbeat hammered louder.

"Shouldn't have taken the elevator," the tattooed man muttered.

"Whatever," the other man snapped.

At this, both men craned their necks behind them. Harry was suddenly, sharply aware that they were trapped in a small metal box with these men. The hair on the back of his neck prickled at the flint-sharp stares in their eyes.

Rose crouched and scooped something small off the floor, then turned it over in her hands with a curious look.

"Whatcha got, sweetheart?" asked the smaller man.

She moved closer to Harry. "Nothing."

He took half a step toward her as if to grab the object, but Harry pulled her behind him with a stern look. In the silence that followed, every breath was like the roar of a freight train. Most especially, his own.

Something mechanical kicked to life in the elevator shaft. The elevator bell rang, and the doors slid open.

Rose whimpered.

Harry squeezed Rose's hand in what must have been a punishing grip, and lunged forward. With only a cursory "Excuse me," he banged the men's shoulders and burst into the hall with her jogging at his side, trying to keep up.

"Hey!" one of the men shouted. Footsteps came fast behind them. Then, an unmistakable sound he'd never have thought to hear in real life: the *pop* of a silenced gunshot. Rose shrieked. Even then, Harry didn't believe it until he heard a *smack*, and saw a bullet hole in the drywall beside them. The men started swearing at each other.

Harry scooped Rose into his arms, and bolted down the hall with his heart pounding and his head screaming *What-the-hell, what-the-hell, what-the-hell* all the way to an emergency door. The two men were still snarling. Another gunshot, and one man's voice stopped in a strangled grunt, followed by a thud. Rose started crying, her eyes huge as she stared over Harry's shoulder. "Harry? Harry!" Her voice ascended with panic.

He hid her face in his chest and ran through the emergency door. He ran down the steps, ran through another hall, ran through an Employees Only door. Ran, ran, ran, and kept running.

They made it to the parking lot, and then snuck onto a bus leaving for the fairgrounds. The entire time, Rose hugged his neck, shivering even though she'd worn her shirt and pants over her bathing suit. Big-eyed, she stared at him, staring at her, all the way to the fairgrounds.

Only when they pelted across the unused midway

and into a barn did he even try to unscramble his thoughts. "Rose, what did you see? What did you take off that floor?" he demanded between gasps for air.

Sobbing, she shoved the little object into his hand: a flash drive. "I don't know. Harry, I just grabbed it, and he scared me, what do we do, I don't know, I don't know!" Tears poured down her cheeks. She begged him with her eyes. "He had a gun. Harry, he k-k-killed that man—"

Harry thought of their parents. Were they safe? God, he hoped they were safe. Could they go back? Should they? What the hell had just happened?

He brought his attention back to his sister's face. She was still crying, hiccupping, hugging herself like she thought no one else would.

He scooped her up again, squeezing her shivering body against his. "It's going to be okay, Rose. Whatever that was, it'll be okay."

But it wasn't. Whatever else it was, it was definitely never going to be okay again.

Chapter Seven

Elsa couldn't think of anything to do but sit on the bed across from Harry and stare.

Hit list, he'd said. *Hit list.* The words still wouldn't sink in. Nothing had prepared her for the unlikelihood of such a confession, and she and her foster family were masters of the unlikely.

The flash drive Rose had picked up contained deposit records for a Swiss bank account. The figures were obscene—enough money to buy a major corporation, and run it for six years.

Instead, the Torellis had been using the money to buy law enforcement, district attorneys, media moguls, and anyone else who might smooth their way. Gun-running, narcotics, gambling, prostitution, and even terrorism, if it suited them. Elsa had heard some of the hype about the Torellis on the news. Once in a while, a story would air, and then, mysteriously, get hushed up. Busy with storm chasing, she never gave it much thought.

Harry must have thought about it every single day.

"We tried giving the flash drive to the police," he said at last. "I made a copy. Don't know why. I guess, after what happened, I just figured I couldn't trust anyone to get it right. That's when I realized we couldn't trust the Feds, either. Least, not the ones we gave the flash drive to. After that, we just ran."

"Not everybody is crooked. There's got to be someone who will protect you," Elsa said.

He scoffed, and she felt foolish for her idealism. "Problem is, you can't tell the good guys by looking at them," he rumbled. Even his tone chastised her.

Hit list. The craziness of his confession settled in her brain. No crazier than her Elemental power. So why did it have to be any less true?

Oh, poor Rose. Poor, poor Harry.

She slid off the bed to kneel in front of him. Resting her hands on his knees, she gave them a light squeeze. "Harry, you've done the best you can. You've kept her safe. Kept both of you safe. It's hard to trust. Believe me, I know."

That electric-blue gaze settled on her at last, bottomless, hopeless. That same, drifting look she must have worn after her birth family died. The crush pressed in on her own heart, and she had to draw a deep breath to stem it.

"An electrical fire. That's what the fire marshal called it," Harry said. "Three hundred and sixteen people died in that hotel." His voice hitched. "But I heard about the cover-ups afterward. The banquet room doors had been barred, and the hotel safe was empty, and a lot of people whose families were at that benefit declared bankruptcy. So don't talk to me about safe."

Good God. Three hundred and sixteen people. His parents. Kids. He and Rose must have been the only ones who escaped.

The determination to do something drove the words out of her mouth. "Come with us," she repeated. "You've tried everything else, and we can help you until your hand heals." When he said nothing, she added, "No one has to know, not if you don't want them to. I won't say a word."

"Your friend already knows enough," he said, gesturing with his good hand to Nina's bed.

"And she'll keep her mouth shut. I've trusted her with my power, and she hasn't ratted me out. She won't rat on you, either. As far as the rest of my team knows, you're Hank Rhodes."

He narrowed his eyes at her, searching her face. "How do you do it?"

"Do what?"

"Live like this. Believe people are...good."

The disillusionment in his voice drove needles of echoed pain into her heart. Elsa bore down on the hurt, denying it, dismissing it. "Because some of them are."

His eyes darkened, shuttered. She had seen that look before, on people who'd given up hope after devastating storms wiped their homes off the face of the earth. She clenched her hand on his thigh as if she could keep him there with a touch. "Let's make a deal to trust each other. Just for a little while, Harry."

He glanced up at her, and then away, as if looking at her cost him too much. His gaze went to her hands, still resting on his thighs, and a flash of heat crossed his face as if he were recalling their kiss. He stifled that, too, and his expression was as passive as before. "I don't have much choice."

She lifted her hands away from him, casually, carefully, but that brief look had unsettled her like a swirl of storm winds. Resting her forearms on her own knees, she said, "There's always a choice. Every day you wake up, you make the choice to keep going or give up. You've kept going, and you've kept Rose going. That's a crazy amount of courage."

He gave a soft snort. "Is that what you call it?"

She smiled a little, even though she ached for him. "That's what I call it."

****

"Really? You're coming with?" Woz sounded like Harry had just offered to send him on a Caribbean vacation. Was he always this enthusiastic?

Harry shrugged—wincing when it aggravated his sore shoulder—and held up his splinted fingers. "Can't play my guitar like this, can I?"

Beside him, Rose gave a little squeak and jumped in place. She ran at Elsa, and then hugged her around the middle, while Sam barked and wagged at the pair.

"Stellar!" Woz proclaimed. "You want to ride in The Beast with me and Seth, or do you want something tamer?"

"I want to try it!" cried Rose. "Can you show me how everything works?"

"Sure, my wee weather girl," said Woz. He held out an arm, and after Rose handed Sam's leash off to Elsa, she jogged toward Woz. He shepherded her toward the steel monstrosity on wheels. It bristled with camera equipment and antennae where it sat at the edge of the lot like an audiovisual porcupine-slash-beetle.

Harry noticed Rose's blushing, sidelong look at Seth, who circled the vehicle, checking the exterior equipment and making adjustments. Good-looking kid. For a kid. With a brotherly grumble sticking in his throat, Harry realized that young Seth was just the sort of kid girls Rose's age swooned over. He had that boy-band look to him, and Rose stared at him as if he were the cutest puppy in the pet store window. Seth couldn't have been older than sixteen or so, himself. What was he doing flitting around the country, poking at radar equipment? Where were his parents? At least he didn't seem to be aware of Rose's gooey stares.

Yet.

Harry suddenly and vividly recalled his father's stern advice to him when he'd begun to notice the opposite sex. Harrison Senior had never outright told him "hands off." It had been more of a "proceed with caution" rule of thumb. The Litchfields were wealthy and often in the public eye, two very good reasons not to get embroiled in anything that might result in a public scandal.

Now, it wasn't the threat of scandal that worried Harry, so much as whether he really ought to have the birds-and-bees talk with his kid sister. He fought an inward cringe.

The instinct to stick with Rose had never stopped kicking at him since he'd agreed to tag along with Elsa and her storm chasers. If anything, it had intensified. Next to the Torellis, talking to Rose about boys should be cake. He took half a step toward The Beast.

"You can go with them, if you want," Elsa broke into his thoughts. "Or you can ride with me. Nina's going with Rory in the van. She thought you might want to—I don't know—talk to me some more. Given...everything." Elsa shrugged as if his answer mattered nothing to her, but her gaze remained conspicuously on her wagon.

He hated his own indecision. All he had to go on was what little he knew of her and her team, and that still-impossible revelation of her command of the air. Even if it were true, what did that get him? Just a cold war of his secret versus hers, and the uncertainty of who would break first. The whole thing couldn't have been more insane if it tried.

Christ, he'd give his right arm for a decision that didn't feel like a deathtrap. Just one damned sign he was doing the right thing by Rose, by his parents...but if God knew how this would end, He wasn't talking.

Elsa waited, clearly content to stand there until Harry made up his mind. Disgusted with himself, he shook off his thoughts and started toward her wagon. Whatever happened, he couldn't stand here in the open like a shooting-range target. Not with Vincent Torelli on the loose.

The farther they were from him, the better. At least that much was clear. "Where are we heading?"

"Texas Panhandle, roughly," Elsa said, walking toward her wagon with Sam, as naturally as if Harry's decision to come with them were no big deal. She opened the back door to let the dog up onto the seat. "Tulsa fizzled out, so we're following a storm system Rory's been tracking."

She slid into the driver's seat. Harry got into the passenger side, all too conscious of his nearness to her. The Panhandle was at least five hours' drive from here. Five hours of sitting beside Elsa and wondering whether his luck were improving at last, or everything had just taken a nosedive into hell.

For the first ten minutes or so of the ride, she remained silent. Harry couldn't stop himself from glancing in the side view mirror every other second, but The Beast stayed right behind the wagon.

As their drive lengthened, he also found himself looking sidelong at Elsa. She'd rolled her window down, and the breeze fluttered at her hair, teasing wisps of it into escaping from her ponytail. Fingers of sunlight found their way into the car's interior and burnished the pale blond into still paler colors—a silvery yellow here, almost white there. He only realized he was staring when the musical chirp of a cell phone interrupted him.

"Oh, shoot," Elsa said. "Grab that, and hit the speaker button."

Harry reached toward the console under the dashboard and found the cell, a new-ish one with a plain black case. Not much for frills, was Elsa Pemberley. The screen flashed with the name *Ethan*. He recognized the name as Elsa's foster brother, and tapped the button.

"What's up, half-pint?" came the voice over the phone before Elsa even got the chance to say hello.

She beamed. "Ethan! Where are you?"

"Currently, some Podunk town in Illinois, on my way to some Podunk town in Ohio."

"I miss you," Elsa said, and the longing in her voice jabbed Harry in the gut. "Come see me."

"Yeah, I would, if you ever stopped moving around and putting yourself in front of Mach-five wind storms."

Elsa glared at the road ahead as if she could see her foster brother's face. "You've been talking to Morgan again."

"Saw her and Trent a couple of weeks ago," Ethan confirmed. "She gave me the third degree, too, if it makes you feel better. She wants to see everybody for the holidays. Big announcement of some sort."

Elsa gave a little squeal, not unlike Rosalie. "Is she pregnant?"

"Didn't say, and I didn't ask. Not really my kind of conversation. Call her when you stop your summer weather dance."

"Yeah, about that," Elsa said.

"What, Elsa?" Ethan prompted, drawing out the question. Harry cracked a smile at the brotherly warning in the man's tone. If only he knew what his foster sister was up to.

"Tell you what," she said, sunny-voiced. "I'm on my way to Texas. I promise I will call you, and Morgan, and Kincade, all when I get there."

"Elsa." Ethan's voice was stern. "I don't care what you do, but you know Cade's gonna blow a gasket if he hears you're still jumping in front of twisters."

"Now I'm getting secondhand scoldings?" she complained. "I thought at least you were on my side."

Harry couldn't help chuckling.

"Just be careful," Ethan said, in the same tone Harry used on Rosalie. He grinned in complete empathy.

When Elsa asked him to disconnect the call, she groaned. "Brothers!"

"My kind of guy," Harry said, setting her phone down. He shot her a crooked smile.

"You all live in a time warp where your little sisters don't grow up," she grumbled.

His good humor took a hit, but he forced it back in place, not wanting the lightness of the moment dampened. "I beg to differ, Miss Pemberley, and I submit yesterday as my evidence."

As soon as he said it, his thoughts shifted from their previous discussion of Rose to their kiss right afterward. Judging by the blush on her face, Elsa's thoughts had followed suit. Harry's fingers itched to run through her white-blond, sunlit hair. Rose wasn't the only one paying special attention to a member of Elsa's crew.

He made a fist to blot out the urge to touch her, then used the fist to rap against the passenger door's armrest. "Do you chase storms every summer?"

"Every summer since leaving home," she said at once, as if she were just as eager as he to change the subject.

"Why'd you leave?" The moment he asked it, Harry realized how curious he was about this irrepressibly optimistic, walking challenger of nature's fury. What would cause her to leave a family she clearly held so dear? What made her the kind of person who'd pick up a guy and his kid sister and their dog— and their problems—as if she ran some kind of rescue?

What made her that compassionate?

Envy pinched him. Before his parents died—were murdered, he reminded himself—he'd never looked past the end of his own nose. There had never been a need. He'd had everything he could have wanted, so the future had never been a problem. Now, the future was a problem that stared him in the face each morning, big as life and insurmountable as the Great Wall of China.

"I liked working the farm with Cade," she admitted, bringing him back to their conversation. "It was tough, but at the end of the day, I really felt I'd put in an honest effort. But..."

"But?"

"Well, part of me always felt we were sort of holding him back. He puts his family before himself...to a fault." She offered Harry a sympathetic smile. "He worries a lot. He's a little like you, actually."

He shifted uneasily at that look. "Must be charming and handsome, then."

She chuckled, and he thought they were safely away from serious topics until she added, "What were your parents like?"

He shot her a wary look. "What about yours?"

For a second, it appeared she might insist he answer first. That stubborn expression crossed her face, the one he was beginning to recognize as sugar-coated steel. Finally, the set of her shoulders relaxed. "They were killed in a storm that wiped out our neighborhood. I was about four years old at the time."

A strange ache settled in his chest. No, not at all strange. Elsa knew how it felt to have one's family smashed apart in a single, horrible moment. Somehow, the fact that she understood that grief lessened his, if only a little. He thought about reaching for her hand, but didn't. Still, he added, "I bet they'd be proud of what you're doing."

When she looked at him again, there were tears in her eyes. She gave a little laugh and looked back to the road, as if embarrassed to have been caught in such a state. "Thanks."

Something shifted then, something almost imperceptible. Elsa was suddenly unsafe, but in a way he hadn't expected, hadn't looked for. Harry rubbed his still-itching fingers against the rough denim of his jeans, as if it could erase the haunting sensation of her skin against his. No good. In this small space, he was alert to everything about her, and not just in the physical sense. He tried like hell to stop it, but as he looked sidelong at her flustered expression, something in him began searching for maybes.

He knew this woman could pin him down, if he let her.

He checked the side view mirror again. The Beast trundled along behind them, just as it had for a few hours, barring a stop for their convoy to change drivers. "How'd you meet these guys?"

Her voice brightened a little. "The first year I left Hope Creek, I went straight to Oklahoma. I knew I wanted to do this, so I started searching online for other storm chasers. That's when I met Nina. She grew up in Oklahoma, watching storms. The rest of us fell in line, and Seth joined us about a year ago when she took him on."

"*She* took him on? I thought you ran this circus."

"Technically, yes, but Nina's been doing it longest. And she's Seth's...well, mentor, I guess you'd say, not guardian. He's emancipated."

Harry raised his brows.

Elsa noticed. "His parents were abusive. They abandoned him, eventually. But he's crazy smart, like a junior genius. He's already done with his A/V degree, all learned during his downtime. Nina still makes him take his high school classes in the off-season." Elsa beamed. "Says she won't give him a permanent spot on the team if he doesn't keep up his education."

With a residual twinge of envy, Harry stared out the windshield. "You seem pretty tight-knit."

"Yeah. A different kind of family, but still family," Elsa said, her voice filled with an obvious affection that tugged at Harry.

He cleared his throat. "And how did you break the news about your way with tornadoes?"

She laughed. "Totally accidental. I literally rescued a cat out of a tree."

The confession startled an answering laugh out of him, his first real feeling of good humor in...well, he couldn't say when. The sensation shocked him in how welcome it was, in how much he wanted more of it. He chuckled again, pleased to find he didn't have to force it in the least. "You really are one of those types who needs to save everybody," he teased.

She picked up on his mood, and reflected it back at him. Her eyes gleamed with mischief. "Which brings me to my next point. I may not know much, Mister Hank Rhodes, Traveling Blues Player, but I was a girl once, and I have just the idea to make Rose's thirteenth birthday her best one ever...if you're brave."

He hesitated, but this time, it wasn't borne of distrust in her motives. The look in her eyes could only be called devilish, and his body reacted with electric sparks. "Brave enough to withstand an evening of...?"

"Makeovers," she said, shooting him a haughty glance. "Nina and I want to take her to a salon. Nothing too big, I promise. A haircut, maybe a little blush and eye shadow."

He groaned, totally fabricated. When was the last time he'd had this much fun sparring with a woman? Good to know he wasn't too far out of practice. Just for good measure, he added, "God save me from makeup and mud masks."

"You stop that," Elsa ordered, still lofty-voiced. "That young lady needs a night of girliness." She checked her nails, unpainted but neatly trimmed. "As a matter of fact, so do I."

The electric sparks intensified, shooting down his

spine and leaving searing trails. Harry's body reminded him in no uncertain terms that Elsa was all-woman without even trying. Instead of squashing the reaction this time, he wallowed in it, unsure when he'd have another chance to feel such a raw surge. Even this was a long-denied extravagance.

Damn, it felt good.

With her attention on the road, he was free to watch her. Big, blue eyes. Lightly tanned skin, plenty of which was visible over her low-cut tank top. *Thank God for low-cut tank tops.*

Her lashes were fine and golden-tipped, only a shade darker than her hair. Slim, arched brows. One curl of her hair spiraled down loosely along the side of her neck where it had escaped from her ponytail. And sweet Jesus, she had the sexiest ear. He imagined nuzzling that lock of hair aside to nip at her earlobe. Funny, he'd never thought ears sexy before.

What could a few days with Team Pemberley hurt? With his left hand useless at best, he couldn't feed himself or Rose, at least until he healed. And as far as he knew, they were driving *away* from Vincent Torelli.

Harry called the rib joint from the motel's pay phone and explained his injury. The guy was cool about it and even invited him back, though the odds were slim that Harry would take him up on it. But once Harry's cash ran out, he'd have no way at all to earn their keep. He had a couple days' worth of scratch at most, if he stayed conservative.

But the temptation of tagging along with Elsa's team was more than financial. He sat close enough to touch her if he just reached out his arm. He glanced down at his splinted finger. She'd doctored him as well as any ER might have done. Better, even. All things considered, he much preferred the experience of seamstress-slash-nurse-slash-storm chaser-slash-superhero Elsa to anything he could have gotten at a hospital.

No ER doctor could possibly drug him with anything more potent than Elsa's body. As long as he was absorbed in studying her, pain receded into virtual nonexistence. Why, again, had he stopped kissing her?

"Harry?" she asked, drawing out the word.

"Yeah?"

"You haven't said anything for, like, twenty minutes. What's on your mind?"

You and me, naked in my pool at home, in the middle of the night, he almost said. *And then in the bedroom. And then on the kitchen counter. And a few other places after that.*

Elsa was still waiting for him to talk, but eight months of pent-up sexual tension jackhammered at his every nerve ending. "I'm not tagging along with you just to mooch off your sandwich fixings for the next two weeks," he warned her.

"Of course you aren't," she said with a scowl and a glint in her eye. "You're going to work like a dog, just like the rest of us. I've got plans for you, mister."

He went straight back to that countertop scenario without any elaboration from her. He didn't even care what she had in mind. He'd pull the damn Beast to Texas with his teeth, if she wanted. His groin pulsed insistently in time with his now-rampaging heartbeat.

Silence reverberated around the car's interior for several seconds. He bit back whatever he'd been about to say, because he couldn't guarantee it wasn't going to be X-rated.

She must have noticed him not talking, because she glanced over. He was still staring helplessly, and for once, he didn't give a crap.

Her large, pale blue eyes went wide. The tips of her ears went bright pink. The car swerved on the shoulder. With a yank, she righted the wheel and, now pink-cheeked as well, jerked her attention back to road.

And *Smack!* Just like that, Harry knew resisting her was a lost cause. He'd been living like a monk, a martyr, a damned saint. For one day, even for one goddamned hour, he wanted to take something for himself.

And he wanted her.

Chapter Eight

Elsa sensed a shift in the environment of the wagon's interior, a subtle heating of the atmosphere that outstripped the efforts of her sluggish air conditioner. The warmth wasn't her—or not *just* her— even though her cheeks were on fire. She'd always hated the way any self-consciousness showed up on her face like movie listings on a neon marquee.

Harry didn't seem to mind it. Elsa would never have touted herself as a first-rate judge of men's signals, but the look on his face left no room for doubt. He was thinking sex.

Her power coursed through her body, lighting up every nerve ending. Her skin prickled all over, a billion little jabs from her gift, demanding to be let free. She reined it in, but only out of habit. Harry knew about her power. She didn't need to hide it from him, the same way she didn't need to hide it from her team.

She trusted him.

The realization made her as giddy as if she'd made a headlong rush toward a tornado. She trusted this man, whom she barely knew, who was a mob target on the run, who was looking at her right now with dangerous heat in his eyes.

A heat her body answered, with neither her help nor her interference. She squirmed on the seat, then bit down on a whimper when the motion sent zips of friction to her most hypersensitive places.

Harry picked up on the stifled noise. She saw it in the way his eyes went positively feral. Her skin tingled, reminding her of the intense dreams she'd had last night—dreams that had begun with him kissing her, and had not ended with him walking away. Her skin burned with her blush, all the way down her neck.

The corner of his mouth tilted upward. "What's on your mind, Miss Pemberley?" he murmured. His voice wound through her lazily, musically, touching off sparks like well-placed blasting caps.

Her heartbeat sped up. She clenched her now-trembling hands on the wheel. They'd been talking about makeovers a moment ago—harmless, innocuous. How had he turned her around so suddenly? With just a look?

She felt the heat of his hand before it even reached her. His callused fingertips slid along her neck, rough against the tender skin. If the contact against his splinted finger bothered him, he gave no indication. He trailed a loose lock of her hair over his hand, then tucked the strands back behind her ear. Slowly. Indolently. Without the slightest indication that it was anything other than the intent to touch her.

She gasped, forcing her attention onto the road, where it most certainly did not want to be. Her skin tingled where he'd brushed it.

"Does your team ever change places in this convoy?" he drawled, stroking little circles on the bare skin where her neck sloped into her shoulder.

The pins-and-needles sensation of her power rushed to that point of contact, as if she were one of those plasma balls sold in gift shops. "Sure they do. S-sometimes."

"Fall back, then," he said. His fingertips criss-crossed a ticklish spot.

She had no other option but to obey. Conscious thought had shut down to all but the familiar route, and the restless heat that gathered where Harry stroked her skin. She switched lanes, then let off the accelerator. The Beast took point, and the van moved ahead as well. With her ears burning, Elsa refused to look toward them, to see if they'd noticed the reason for her swerve and slowdown.

Harry chuckled, low and quiet. When she dared another glance at him, he was eyeing her, his lids at half-mast like a drowsing tiger. The sight, coupled with his touch, made her want to purr like a cat, herself. "No one's looking, darlin'," he told her. "Except for me. Is this bothering you?"

"No." The word came out a whisper.

"Is it welcome?"

She paused, trying to control her trembling and keep her attention on their route. "Yes."

Immediately, his fingertips slipped from her neck to her collarbone. The rough edge of his splint bandage rasped her skin, and she gasped. "You'll hurt your hand," she protested.

"My hand is feeling *no* pain."

"I thought...I thought you didn't want to..."

"Shouldn't." His fingers stroked their way toward the slope of her breast, and she squirmed again. "There's a difference between 'shouldn't' and 'want to.' And believe me, I want to." His hand paused, and for a moment, he sounded like his warier self. "Trouble follows me. I don't want to get you caught up in it."

She quirked a smile at him. "I look for trouble all by myself."

"So I've noticed."

The amusement in his voice revved her power. She clenched the wheel, trying to shut off the sensations before her skin began to glow. His fingertips inched lower, then trailed along the neckline of her tank top. "Harry..." Her breath rushed out, and she couldn't catch it again.

"Yes?"

She gave an incoherent groan and the briefest of glances, pleading with her eyes, before looking back to the road.

"Stop, or don't stop?"

"Don't," she whispered. "Don't stop."

He gave a low rumble, almost a growl, and slid as close to her as his seat belt would allow. His unsplinted index finger slipped under the neckline of her shirt and the satiny edge of her bra to curve over her breast. The callused tip of his finger brushed her nipple.

Elsa gasped and stomped on the accelerator. The wagon leaped forward, too fast. She came too close to the back of the van and, with a muffled yelp, let off the gas.

Harry chuckled. "Thought you storm chasing types were supposed to be cool under pressure." The rest of his fingers nudged under her shirt collar. He traced her nipple again.

She bit her lip for a full five seconds. "I don't think this kind of pressure is typical to the job," she said, glad suddenly that she was now following her team, instead of leading them. The route receded to a fuzzy, unimportant background noise in her brain.

"Hmm," said Harry. His fingertip continued its maddening circles, hotwiring her body. "How good's your driving?"

She tried to force some indignation into her voice. "Very good, thank you." Her squeak at the end made it clear her attempt at self-control was an epic fail.

Harry's fingers cupped her breast, then gave it a gentle squeeze—barely any pressure, but enough to make her sigh. He gave a soft grunt, but she couldn't tell if it was discomfort in his shoulder or hand, or a response to touching her. If she looked, would she find that electric stare turned on her heated face? On what he was doing to her? Would he be coming apart like this?

He slid his middle and index fingers along either side of her nipple, pinching ever so lightly. His breath caught.

"Your hand," she protested again, her fists convulsing on the wheel.

"To hell with my hand. You think any red-blooded man in his right mind would turn down a chance to touch this gorgeous body when invited?" All the same, his left hand slipped away. She mourned its absence at once.

He leaned a little nearer. As big as he was, filling the space beside her, it didn't take much effort to get close enough to brush her ear with his lips. "I really shouldn't have stopped kissing you that night."

"No, you shouldn't have," she said. Her nerves knotted and unknotted, and knotted again.

"My bad," he muttered into her neck. His lips pressed against the skin behind her ear, then he suckled gently.

Elsa nearly forgot where she was. A heady

euphoria fuzzed her brain, and only the habit of following her team's convoy kept her in line on the road. She focused on staying far enough behind the van to prevent an accident. Maybe she ought to be a little farther back, actually. She raised her foot off the accelerator a little more.

Harry's tongue flicked at her skin, and her breath rushed out. Good God, what had he done to her? She was on fire from head to foot. "Harry...oh, my God...Harry...you need to...I can't..." She lifted a hand from the wheel long enough to clutch at his knee, reaching, needing to touch him back. Had he turned her into a sex-starved madwoman?

His right hand clapped over hers, stopping it. "Uh-uh. Hands on the wheel, Miss Very Good Driver. This is all about you, as much as I'd like you to be participating." He lifted her hand back to the wheel, then stroked her fingers briefly before lowering his own hand to her knee.

"If this is...mmmph...about me...why aren't we stopping, for God's sake? You're turning me inside out!"

His breath tickled her ear. "Glad to know the attraction isn't one-sided." His thumb circled her kneecap.

"God, no." She sucked in a breath as his fingers trailed higher above her knee. "Harry, please," she begged, barely able to sit still. His rumbling chuckle sent a rush of heat from her ear down her spine, to settle between her legs until she throbbed with need.

Her cell chimed. Elsa, who wasn't prone to bad language, swore colorfully.

He drew back and lifted his brows. The gleam in

his eye was unmistakably smug. "I'm impressed."

She shot him a glare, then tossed her cell phone at him.

Still chuckling, he pressed a button on the keypad. "Pemberley residence," he said with amusement in his voice. He listened a moment, then pressed another button.

Rory's voice blared over the speaker. "Looks like we've got a live one, El. I'm getting some sketchy conditions over the Panhandle. Could be setting up for a blowout."

"What kind of time do we have?" she asked.

"Based on my models, about thirty minutes until it starts picking up wind speed. Maybe forty-five until it's noticeable on the ground. Not sure yet if we'll get anything out of it. Are we going after it?"

"Let's do it." She stepped on the gas.

****

Harry never regretted the existence of phones so much in his life. His entire body was in a state of snarling, trembling, rigid arousal. From her very first sigh, his sex drive had been pinballing back and forth from his brain to his groin, faster and faster, until he was sure he had TILT written in big-ass neon letters on his forehead.

Crap. Crap, crap, crap. Had it been so long that he was about to lose it before anything even started? Any cool he'd possessed in the past thirty minutes went straight out the window, along with his good sense. He gave a groan, unable to smother it, and just as unable to will away the excruciating tightness of his hard-on against his zipper.

"Harry?"

Elsa's breathy query made his shoulders tense in a wholly unnecessary, alpha-male response. They were damn lucky there were no other men present. He might club them and drag Elsa off like some stupid caveman.

Her voice came louder now. "Harry."

He clenched his good hand on the armrest under the passenger window. "Trying really hard to think about tornadoes right now," he bit out. "Pretty sure Team Pemberley needs you, wherever we're going."

From the corner of his eye, he saw her open her mouth. A doubtful look crossed her face. "I could—"

"Don't give me a reason to tell you to pull this car over," he snapped. He risked a look at her to find her still blushing, and he was suddenly dying to get her clothes off and find out how far that blush went.

He'd had scratch-an-itch sex before. Back home, there had been no shortage of women wanting a piece of him when he went looking. Money did that for you.

This was entirely different. This was a woman who loved dogs. Who loved people. Who cared enough about a drifter and his kid sister to scoop them up and drag them along with her traveling circus, in spite of the price on his head. Who—

His attention snagged on a blue sedan in the side view mirror. "How long has that car been behind us?"

Elsa checked her rearview mirror. Still red-faced, she gave Harry the briefest of glances. "I've been a little too distracted to notice."

Harry punched the redial button on Elsa's phone. "Rory—Hank. Have the team take the next exit. We're pit-stopping at a gas station," he fabricated.

Elsa raised her brows, but after another look in the rearview, she gave no protest. She followed the line of vehicles off the highway at the next exit.

And the blue sedan followed them.

Harry swore and squinted into the side view mirror, trying to see the car's occupant. The sun glare off the windshield prevented it. "Move ahead of your team again."

With another glance in the rearview, Elsa switched lanes, and did as he instructed. Now four vehicles back, the blue sedan kept tailing their convoy.

"Hang a left here," Harry barked.

She did, without question, and her team followed. They passed a gas station, and Elsa's teammates must have wondered why she didn't stop, but they continued along behind. Watching for their pursuer, Harry fisted his good hand convulsively. "Go right."

She did. And the sedan did, too. He gave a faint, hostile snarl.

Another gas station loomed ahead down the road. After a moment, Elsa's gaze flicked to the rearview, and then to him. "I won't let anything happen to her, Harry. You know that."

"I know," he said.

Elsa's voice firmed. "Or you."

He shot her a startled look before he could catch himself. No one had felt the need to be protective of him in so long he'd forgotten what it felt like. They held each other's stares. He couldn't find anything to say. Her eyes were drowning him.

An instant later, she veered off into the gas station parking lot.

"What are you doing?" Harry demanded, but she was already pulling into a parking space.

Elsa unbuckled her seat belt, then flung open the

door and swooped out of the car. Her team was just turning into the lot behind her.

The sedan pulled into the parking lot behind the convoy. Elsa stalked purposefully toward it.

Forgetting his need to be inconspicuous, forgetting that Rose was safe inside a bulletproof tank of a vehicle, Harry ripped his seat belt off, and then leaped out of the wagon. "Elsa!"

The sedan parked in a space close to the building. Out climbed an auburn-haired woman with tortoiseshell glasses and a huge leather tote bag.

Harry hesitated mid-stride. Not exactly mob material. He stalked faster toward Elsa, just in case.

But Elsa seemed to be holding her own. She walked right up to the woman. "Can I help you?"

The woman frowned at Elsa. "Excuse me?"

Elsa propped a fist on her hip. "You seem to be following my team. Can I help you?" she repeated firmly.

"Oh, you're part of them," said the strange woman, with a look suddenly full of flattery. She stuck out a hand. "I'm Malory Sternberg. I work at NSSL, the—"

"National Severe Storms Laboratory. I'm familiar." Elsa shook the offered hand, and flashed such a sweet smile that no one could have picked up on the warning in her tone unless they were attuned to it like Harry was. "Elsa Pemberley."

"I wondered if you have some time to talk, Miss Pemberley," said Malory. "I've been noticing some strange weather patterns, and I need opinions from professionals in the field. Not for official business, of course, just a private project..." Malory poked through her tote bag.

So, she's gone from one of 'them' to 'professional in the field,' Harry thought darkly, watching the newcomer. *What are you* really *after, lady?* He reached Elsa's side, with no qualms about using his height and shoulder width to intimidate the woman now drawing a fistful of pages from her enormous tote.

Malory noticed his presence, then blinked rapidly as if she were in shock. Harry allowed himself a satisfied smile and held out his hand. "Elsa's colleague, Hank Rhodes," he murmured, putting a little extra emphasis on *colleague*.

Malory shook his hand. "How do you do? Um...here...could you hold these?" She pushed the papers into Harry's hands, then dove into her bag again.

Elsa shot Harry a brief, wary look before turning to Malory. "We're on kind of a tight schedule, Miss Sternberg. Storm front moving in, and all. Maybe I could take your number?"

Harry glanced to the pages in his hands. On top was a hand-scrawled sheet titled *Defused, No Casualties*. It listed a dozen storms and tornadoes, their locations, and dates, the last of which was the one Elsa had "defused" the day he and Rosalie and Sam had taken shelter under that farm's tractor bridge.

A warning tickle traveled from the base of Harry's neck, all the way down his spine to the small of his back. He gave the woman a steady glare.

"Can I follow you?" Malory asked quickly. "I'm on a deadline to get this information."

"I thought you said it was a private project," Harry said.

Malory seemed to catch herself, and then said, "It is, it is. But I want to bring it to my boss. I want my old job back, see, and—" She fumbled for a smile, and Harry sensed the desperation behind it. "You know how it is, when you're trying to butter up your boss."

Actually, he didn't. He'd never had a boss. He'd never had to work until now. If he had a boss, it was his perpetually hungry, thirteen-year-old kid sister. And even now, he couldn't work. He flexed his left hand at the unsplinted joints.

"Of course you can follow us," Elsa said before he could form a comment.

Harry glanced at Elsa, unable to hide his alarm fast enough. Quickly, he brought his attention back to Malory. "It's dangerous," he snapped.

"I've been through a little bit of 'dangerous' in my line of work, Mister Rhodes. You don't work at a place called 'National Severe Storms Laboratory' without seeing one or two of them, up close and personal."

"You must really want this information," he muttered, allowing the full measure of his suspicion into his tone as he handed the sheets of paper to Elsa.

When Elsa read the title on the top sheet, her brows shot up. She frowned, skimming the page, then glanced to Harry, a brief flash of sky-blue eyes full of shock. But as soon as that look punched him in the belly, Elsa was turning back to Malory with supreme calm back on her features. "You understand there are inherent risks to what we do. You're assuming all liability for your own safety and property."

Malory nodded, all eagerness. "Of course."

Elsa appeared to consider a moment. Harry expected nervousness—some sign of agitation, at least. This woman had her, point-blank, even if the nosy Miss Sternberg didn't yet realize it. What would happen if

Malory discovered that the mysterious force defusing the storms was Elsa? His skin crawled with the need to step between the women.

But Elsa merely nodded back at Malory. "Okay."

Wait. What? Harry passed Elsa another wary look, but Elsa was handing the sheaf of papers back to Miss Sternberg with one of her should-be-patented sunny smiles. "We're stopping off for about fifteen minutes. Meet you back on the road after that."

"Sure thing," Malory responded.

Harry fell into step with Elsa as she strode toward the station's convenience store. "This doesn't bother you?"

"Of course it bothers me," she answered. Her gaze remained on the glass doors of the store, and her tone was steady, but Harry saw a little frown tugging at her lips. "She's been trying to connect the dots. But if I've learned anything about keeping my ability under wraps, it's that only people with something to hide act like they have something to hide."

"Which means...?"

"Which means we let her tag along and see what we do."

"That'll be interesting, when it comes time for you to show her how to stop a tornado."

Elsa smirked. "I'll jump off that particular bridge when I get there."

Getting gas was a blur. Elsa picked up a few snacks, which they brought to the rest of the team. "How are we doing on time?" she asked Rory.

"Not bad, if we hurry," he answered. "Who's the tag-along?"

"Weather watcher from NSSL," Elsa said.

"Aw, hell."

"No problem," Elsa told him. "We just do what we do. Let me worry about her, okay?"

"Sure," Rory said, with about as much conviction as Harry. They exchanged a guarded look.

After that, there wasn't much talk on the way to the Panhandle. Harry kept checking the side view mirror, half hoping that Miss Sternberg would decide to give up her search for answers. Tense minutes ticked by, broken only by the muted thump of imperfections in the road.

Elsa made an indecipherable noise, and pulled off to the road's shoulder. Harry redirected his gaze to find her staring out the windshield at the sky.

It was greenish-black, and as ugly as an old bruise. The scrubby grasses bent low, as if bowing to the storm in greeting. A lonely windmill spun furiously. Harry watched the blades spin with wild mental images of it flinging off its tower and into their convoy.

"This has got to be it," Elsa said, barely a murmur as she studied the sky. "Look at that cloud formation. Almost perfect, if we get a decent wind shear. Nice work, Rory."

"Glad you're calm about this," Harry said.

"It's nothing yet," she said. "When they get really bad, I can feel it in my skin."

Her casual comment brought his attention from the storm-bruised sky to her slender arm, stretched toward the steering wheel. For a second, he just fixated on her skin, flawless and clear and made to be touched.

Which he'd been doing earlier, and might still have been doing, if that NSSL woman hadn't barged into their lives.

Out the windshield, he saw The Beast pulling to the roadside. As they passed the wagon, Woz and Rose gave him a dual thumbs-up from their windows. Harry decided about then that the entire team had gone completely out of their tree, and were doing their best to drag him and Rose with them. "What. The hell. Am I doing?" he muttered.

Elsa giggled. "Come on, get out." She was already doing so, herself.

"Uhhhh, no."

She leaned down into her open doorway, providing him a too-tempting view of the skin peeking over the top of her scoop-necked shirt.

Hell of a motivation.

She gave him a full-on grin, with far too much mirth for someone about to face a possibly windmill-flinging storm. "Bawk, bawk, Rhodes. Everybody else is getting out. Even the NSSL lady."

Rueful, he opened his door. "Heard the one about your friends jumping off a bridge?"

"Yep," she chirped. More seriously, she added, "We'll be safe, I promise. I have...kind of a plan."

"Kind of?" He pivoted to stare at her, but she was already walking toward the other vehicles with purpose in her step.

Harry watched the clouds boiling in giant, finger paint swishes overhead, and wondered how much safer it was to chase storms than to flee murderers.

Chapter Nine

Elsa reached the weather van as Nina and Rory were climbing out. Rory checked the various weather sensors against the readout on his handheld device. "You sure about this?" Nina asked, just loud enough to be heard over the gusting wind.

"What, about the NSSL bloodhound?" Elsa asked with more unconcern than she felt. "Sure."

"El." Nina's tone rang with a familiar warning.

"I got it," she said, more firmly. "If the storm gets out of hand, you can distract her while I fizzle it."

"We've got wind shear formation and a horizontal roller," Rory reported. "Moving a slow southeast, no populated areas. Could just be a case of watch and learn."

Nina glared at him. "Don't help."

Elsa gave him a smile. "You guys keep our bloodhound busy. I'll wave to you if it's time for the dirty work."

Rory glanced toward Harry, who stood beside her wagon with an uncertain eye on the sky. "Is he going to be okay with this?"

"He'll be fine. Do your thing," she said cheerfully.

Woz, Seth, and Rose climbed out of The Beast. Woz joined them at the side of the road, while Rose and Seth walked around the monstrous steel vehicle. Seth made adjustments to the sensors, while Rose chattered at him near-nonstop. With a private smile, Elsa checked Harry's reaction to his sister's obvious interest in Seth. She found him eyeing the pair with a look that said he'd rather see her try to bull ride an angry rhinoceros.

Elsa couldn't help a chuckle. Had Cade ever been like that about her when she was younger?

Woz photographed the cloud pattern as Elsa stalked into the field. She crouched down, letting the breezes closer to the earth talk to her.

It began as the routine investigation of a promising storm, but the longer she remained there, the more strongly she felt Harry's gaze on her. Was he thinking about what they'd been doing in the car earlier today? She didn't seem to be able to get the images—and the sensations—out of her head.

Think. NSSL woman. Team's watching. Pay attention, she scolded herself. Looking from the flattened scrub grass to the heavens, she studied the sky. Rory was right—textbook. Based on the cloud movements and past experience, Elsa figured they were looking at a baby supercell. They didn't always develop into severe storms, and certainly didn't spawn as many tornadoes as the movies would have one think, but it was best to stay watchful.

A fact which Harry's presence was not helping.

She glanced over her shoulder to find him standing beside Woz, but a little closer to the field, as if he wanted her to come back toward the convoy.

Sparse rain spat down. Her skin prickled, seconds before Rory shouted to her. "Radar's starting to turn Technicolor, El. We're getting our updraft," he called.

She could have predicted that. The tingling in her skin told her the ground-hugging drafts had begun to shoot skyward, turning the horizontal spiral on its head.

That could mean tornadoes. And it often meant—

Pellets of ice slammed down in the dust around her. One smacked her shoulder, and she hurried back toward the cars.

Hail.

Darn it. She hadn't wanted to "bubble" herself from the assault with that NSSL woman watching, if she could help it. Marble-sized chunks of ice thunked off the vehicles. Lightning erupted below the massive shelf cloud forming in the sky. The very air went utterly black in an instant.

Her team had already begun pulling out helmets and jackets. Seth scooped Rose under his arm and ran for The Beast. As Elsa passed Woz, shooing Harry toward her wagon, Woz called, "Might want to give this one the hiccups, doll."

"No, it's fine," she insisted. This was nothing. Sternberg was watching. She wanted storm chasing, and this was it. Elsa snagged a spare helmet and pushed it at Harry. "Put that on, or get in the car," she said over the rising wind.

He arched away to look toward The Beast, even tried wrestling his way around her.

"No. She's all right. Seth and Woz will take care of her, I promise. Get to the wagon!"

"What about your own head?" he shouted.

Elsa glanced toward Malory, who was talking to Rory what looked like a mile a minute. The woman had dressed all wrong—no coat, no boots, no protection for her head. Rory snagged a blanket and extra hardhat for her from the weather van.

Harry tried holding her spare helmet out to her.

Hail battered against his shoulders. A few pieces pelted his injured hand and he winced, but didn't budge.

She grinned and turned her power on, just enough that she knew it would only show as an illumination in the creases of her hands. Invisible even then, if she fisted them. The air formed its bubble around her, deflecting the hail and the worst of the rain. "Thanks, but I come with my own weather protection," she said. "Into the wagon, Rhodes."

They climbed back into her vehicle. Sam, who'd been curled up all this time in the back, leaped up and tried to clamber over the front seat to lick their faces.

"We're fine, mutt, we're fine," Harry grumbled, pushing him back, but Elsa caught the smile he tried to hide. The Lab was clearly nervous from the *rat-tat-tat* of the hail against the car, but Harry chuckled and rubbed the dog's head. "You're all right, you big chicken."

Elsa's heartbeat stumbled, then picked up speed. What a smile he had. What a shame he didn't do it more.

"You sure this is nothing?" he asked, peering out the windshield as the hailstones rattled against it.

The storm blurred everything beyond the glass into dim, watercolor grays, but her power fed her the story without having to look outside. "For your first storm, this is practically gift-wrapped," she said. "You heard Rory. It's moving away from us, and where it's going, there's miles of nothing."

He glanced at her shimmering palm as she reached for the steering wheel. "So you don't defuse all of them?"

"No," she said. "It's kind of a triage system. When

they're going to get bad, I can almost always tell. Like static buildup on my skin—that tingle just before you get a shock." She turned on the heater to dry out the dampness in the air. "This is cranky, but not full-out ticked-off. I want Miss Sternberg to get a complete dose of undiluted storm chasing."

"So you can scare her off?"

"With any luck," she admitted. "Or, who knows? Maybe she'll learn something useful for her project."

Harry raised his eyebrows at her.

"Seriously," she added. "Just because I have to hide who I am from people doesn't mean I don't *like* people."

Harry's look didn't falter.

She giggled. "Okay, I like them in general," she said. "She is pretty nosy."

"She should've been a reporter," Harry agreed. His gaze lingered on Elsa a second too long. "So, what do we do now?"

Elsa's cheeks warmed. Without thinking, she breathed in deep. Harry's clean, shampoo scent had been amplified by the rain, and the heater in the car did a bang-up job of spreading the scent around until there was nowhere to hide from its lure.

His gaze sharpened. Clearly, he'd already gone where her thoughts were heading. She trembled a little.

Harry's arm slid around her, pulling her closer. His good hand slid up to her cheek, rough and warm and a little rain-damp against her skin. His lips came down on hers, not hard, but exactly right, like he and Elsa were made to kiss each other. She gave a little sigh and leaned into him, forgetting about her team, the storm, and Malory Sternberg.

Harry lifted his head just enough to turn his kisses from her lips to the line of her jaw. "I really...*really* want to do more than this," he murmured.

"You're not the only one," she whispered.

He gave a low chuckle, but then his eyes took on that familiar serious expression. He cupped her face. "I don't know how to thank you for what you've done for us."

She raised an eyebrow. "A little more of this is a good start," she teased.

For a few glorious moments, all they did was sit there in each other's space, and Elsa stared at him like a moonstruck teenager. She breathed his scent in, relishing it, letting it flood her senses. It was so delirious just to be with him. How much more incredible would it be if they were free to follow where these kisses led?

Did she have the nerve to find out?

A gust of wind rocked the car just as her cell rang. Elsa jerked away from Harry to fumble for her mobile, which clattered to the floor of the passenger side.

She and Harry both went for it at the same time, and their heads thumped together.

She yelped and drew back. With a rueful-sounding moan, Harry rubbed his forehead and picked up the phone for her. He handed it over with a crooked smile that charmed her to her toes.

She clicked a button. "Hello?"

"El?" Rory blared over the line. "Our bitty supercell is having kids. Think we should get out of here."

Elsa turned her wipers higher. "Oh, boy."

"What's 'Oh, boy?'" Harry demanded.

"Get your seatbelt on, Rhodes. We need to get out of here." She scrambled to buckle herself in, then slammed her vehicle into reverse and peeled out of her parking spot.

Harry stared out the window at the storm. "What is it? *What?*"

"Damn it," she muttered. She'd been too wrapped up in Harry—or wanting to be—to notice the static charges now rumbling along her nerve endings. Aloud, she said, "Hang on, Harry. We're about to go on a roller coaster ride without the benefit of a track."

****

As they spun out of their space, Harry whipped around to see if The Beast had followed. It had, of course, as well as all the other vehicles in their convoy.

Elsa pushed a button on her cell, then dropped it in the console. "Find us a hole, Rory."

"Nina's on it," he shouted from the speaker of the cell.

Nina's voice blared over the phone a second later. "Up ahead, about half a mile on the left. There's a road, kind of."

"Kind of?" Elsa echoed.

"Only one for miles. Just take it!" Nina said.

Harry risked a look out the passenger window, then wished he hadn't. Elsa's 'gift-wrapped' storm had spawned a funnel cloud—no, *two* of them. One had whirled off in the predicted direction. The other had broken off the main storm, and was spinning toward them.

An icy wave skimmed down his back. "This is your 'nothing?'"

"Relax," she said. "I'm a professional." She veered

onto the road Nina had mentioned—dirt and ruts and not much else, as far as he could see through the pounding rain and hail.

The wagon barely bounced as they drove along. Harry opened his mouth.

"She may not look like much, but she's built for this," Elsa said, answering the question he hadn't asked.

Still itching with distrust, Harry glanced behind them. "I doubt we can say the same for Malory Sternberg's car."

The wagon tipped into a rut, then back out. "I did say any damage to it was on her head."

She jerked the wheel to avoid another rut. As they sped along, Harry marveled at her coolheadedness. He'd been running for his life for eight months. Elsa had made a career out of it.

Maybe they really were safer with her than they could be with anyone else.

In the middle of a dangerous storm, racing down a road that should have been a goat track, he laughed out loud, uncertain whether it was humor or hysteria. "You are some kind of woman, Elsa Pemberley."

She beamed. "Thanks."

"Looking good, guys," Nina reported over the phone. "Radar has the first funnel already snuffing out. Second one should follow suit."

Elsa's eyes went wide. "Before or after it hits the power station?"

Harry's attention shot forward to the skeletons of four transformer towers, grouped around an enormous fenced compound at the end of their access road. "Oh, shit."

"Hang on," Elsa shouted. She cranked the wheel,

and suddenly, they were careening over the scrubby plain.

"Somebody's got to get that Sternberg woman," Nina said over the crackling cell. "Her car will never be able to off-road this. Elsa?"

"Damn. Punching it, Nina." Elsa leaned toward her door, then put one hand on the window crank. "Take the wheel. I've got the gas pedal."

Harry slid toward her seat to grip the wheel with his sound hand. "What are you gonna do?"

"Fix this."

"Defuse it?"

"Not much choice." She rolled the window down. The storm rushed inside, spitting hail, rain, and debris.

"Elsa?" Harry shouted over the roar. Sam whined and barked from the back seat.

"I've got to be in it to stop it," she called, leaning out the window as far as her seat belt would go. She reached her arm out. Her skin began to glow, and Harry stared in shock. As they lurched across the uneven ground at insane speeds, a burst of light blinded him. He clenched his eyes shut in reflex before remembering that he was driving. He snapped his eyes back open.

But the storm had died out.

The wagon slowed, then stopped. The wind and rain still gusted through the open window, but the hail had ceased. Harry looked southward. The funnel clouds had receded, and light fingered its way through the storm-blackened sky.

Elsa shifted the gear into park. Harry lifted his hand from the wheel and, with an amazed sort of detachment, realized it was shaking. He lifted his gaze to Elsa, who slid back into the cab with a whooshing

AIR

sigh.

Harry pulled his hand back, vaguely embarrassed at how it trembled. "*Almost* always sense it?"

She ducked her head. "Almost."

"El?" crackled Nina's voice.

"We're fine. You?"

"We're good, and The Beast is all right. I think Malory's stuck in a rut back there. Nice save, loony girl. That one was about to cross the road after us." The condemnation in Nina's voice carried an undertone of affection.

Elsa grinned. "I'm starving. Let's find a restaurant."

"Woz's favorite words," Nina said, then the line clicked off.

Harry said nothing. He doubted there were appropriate words for the occasion...unless they were four-letter ones.

Elsa turned the wagon around, then headed back for the access road. Malory was indeed stuck in a rut where they'd turned off into the field, spinning her rear tires. "Hmm," Elsa murmured. "The boys'll push her out." She must have noticed, as they regained the road, that he wasn't talking. "Are you okay, Harry?"

"Oh, sure," he drawled, loading on the sarcasm. "After this, armed hitmen? No problem."

She angled a censorious look at him, but after a few seconds, her eyes gleamed, and a grin spread across her rain-soaked face.

Harry couldn't help it. Lightheaded with adrenaline, he burst out laughing. "Holy shit, Elsa. That was closer to the Weather Channel than I've ever been in my life."

She laughed, too, then reached back to give Sam a reassuring pat. "Welcome to the team."

He stayed quiet most of the way to what was now a late lunch. After Woz and Rory helped Malory get her car out of the ditch, Harry rode along with Elsa in a surprisingly comfortable silence. After the madness of a double tornado and an off-road run for cover, the quiet was almost serene.

Harry couldn't stop smiling.

When they reached the restaurant, he even had enough goodwill to exchange a few polite words with the distressed but dogged NSSL woman.

"I knew I should've bought a four-wheel drive," Malory said, shaking her head.

He held the door for her. "Elsa's got one, and I still feel like I've been through a pinball machine."

As they sat at their tables, Malory turned to Elsa. "Do you mind me asking a few questions for my research?"

"Not at all," said Elsa. "That's why you're here, right?"

Malory started off with the usual "how long have you been doing this" sort of thing, along with a few particulars about storm chasing. Elsa answered thoroughly, shirking nothing, even when Malory asked about the storm that had killed Elsa's birth family. He learned that not even Elsa's foster siblings knew she remembered it. She hadn't wanted to burden them with that event.

Team Pemberley knew. Each of them wore kind, empathetic looks while Elsa spoke of the tragedy.

Sitting on Elsa's far side, Woz gave her back a rub. "You've got us, doll," he murmured.

Elsa smiled and bumped his shoulder with hers.

Sitting across the table from him, Rose gave him a brilliant smile of her own. She'd been bursting with facts after her ride in The Beast, as safe as if she were in an underground bunker. The weather tank was equipped with off-road harnesses, all-terrain wheels and suspension, and bulletproof glass. All things considered, Harry figured she was safer in that, outrunning storms, than he could have made her in some motel room with a flimsy lock on the door. "The Beast is the coolest thing ever. You gotta try it, Harry!" she bubbled.

"Elsa, I saw something odd back in that storm," Malory said. "While I was stuck on the road, I saw a flash of light in the field where you were driving."

The group's cheerful atmosphere slipped a notch, but Elsa recovered fast. "An electrical surge? We were near the power station."

Malory gave a shrug. "Maybe. Are you sure you didn't see it? You were right there."

"No, but I don't put anything past a storm anymore. I've seen a lot of unusual behavior in the past couple of years," Elsa said.

She made a good show of innocence.

The food arrived, saving them from a hazardous turn of conversation. For several minutes, everyone busied themselves passing ketchup.

Harry studied the NSSL woman from the corner of his eye. She started on her salad, and he thought they were in the clear.

Then she looked right at him. "Woz tells me you're actually a blues singer."

Harry paused in the middle of a mouthful of

cheeseburger. "I guess so," he said as casually as possible.

"How did you take up with a team of storm chasers?" Malory smiled. "Is this what traveling singers do in their down time?" Her gaze fell on his bandaged hand.

He acknowledged the prodding look with a tilt of his head. "For a while."

Malory seemed to pick up on his lack of wordiness. She directed her next questions at the rest of the team. Harry listened until it became clear she was no longer poking too closely into his business, or the truth behind that mysterious flash she'd seen.

"I want to thank you for letting me tag along with you," she said at last. "If nothing else, it's given me something to take back to NSSL on the storm chasing experience."

The team told her they were glad to do it but, when Malory paid her portion of the bill and took her leave, Harry suspected they were even gladder to see the back of her.

"Well, that was a rip-roaring good time," Woz said.

"It's all right," Elsa said. "Hopefully, she got what she wanted, and she'd done with us."

Seth reached across the table for the salt shaker, then shook out an alarming amount onto his onion rings. He chuckled. "More likely, she scared herself off when she drove her car into that ditch in the middle of the storm. Dude, her face was totally white."

"Whatever the case, that's the end of it, and goodbye," said Nina, angling a cautious look at Elsa.

"She didn't see a thing," Elsa griped.

Nina frowned. "She did, too, and you're getting

careless."

"Would you rather I have let the storm blow her car into that power station?"

With a sigh, Nina dipped one of her french fries into a puddle of ketchup on her plate. "No," she answered in a tone of irritation. "But you do need to watch it, El."

Harry passed his sister a look of amusement. The discussion had all the earmarks of his reminders to Rose to keep her head down and her nose clean.

Rose grinned back. She'd been smiling and laughing a lot more lately. How much of that was the companionship of Elsa and her team? He soured a little with brotherly grumpiness. How much of that was Seth? Well, he seemed like a nice kid, and he treated Rose with respect.

He hadn't felt so isolated, either, this past couple of days. And he had to admit, he liked it. *I guess storm chasing is the new normal.*

The day was pretty quiet after the morning's excitement. Most of the team buried themselves in the data Rory had gathered. Some of it, he had willingly imparted to Miss Sternberg for her "report." The rest, he'd forwarded on to NSSL, himself.

In fact, everything stayed so low-key that Harry, for once in eight months, allowed himself to take a full breath and forget that he was on the run. He helped Rory give the weather van a minor tune-up. He hauled cables for Seth, who was making some upgrades to The Beast's dash-mounted video camera. And every once in a while, as he worked, he found himself humming.

All in all, he thought, watching a spectacular sunset outside their chosen motel that evening, a damn good day. Rose and Sam had cozied up in Elsa and Nina's room with a stack of magazines and a video. For once, he had no immediate worries on his mind.

"There you are," came Elsa's voice. "I thought Rory had commandeered you again."

Harry looked up to find her picking her way toward him across the scrubby field beside the motel, with her hands in her jeans pockets and a smile on her face. "Nope," he said.

"Whatcha doing?"

"Nothing. And it's nice."

She joined him to gaze at the sky, patched with enormous, billowing, rust-colored clouds edged in firelight. "It's crazy how we get the most brilliant sunsets after the worst storms."

He intended to pass her a smile, but when he looked, she was still staring at the clouds with what seemed like wonder.

He stared at her with the same reaction. A lick of heat whisked down his back to spread through his lower belly, and suddenly he felt like that sky, blazing all over for anyone to see. He thought about the pathetic few bills in his wallet, and the clean-but-impersonal motel rooms, and how he used to be able to afford the Ritz-Carlton. He wanted her. Good God, how he wanted her. But not like this. A woman like her, with guts and grit and a heart as big as that damn sky deserved roses and crystal and silk.

All he had was himself.

"Elsa," he said hoarsely.

She turned to him, and in her eyes he saw the echo of the same sensation running through his body.

It had been inevitable, really, since the moment

they met. Everything about her had driven him to her, from her incredible power down to a smile that had him hoping there might be something beyond this endless running.

And he knew, even as his lips met hers, that tonight—just for tonight—if all he had to give was himself, he would make damned sure it was enough.

Chapter Ten

Elsa shook, knowing, as Harry's lips came down on hers, where this kiss would lead. Not because she feared it. It was impossible to be afraid of something that had been waiting to happen since she first met him. Her entire body thrilled at his nearness, from the slightest whisper of his mouth against hers, to the heat radiating through the air around him and into her. A tornado whirled through her body without leaving a ripple. She grabbed onto him as if he could keep her from blowing away under its force.

His arms circled her and dragged her against him, like being mashed against a wall of feverishly hot rock. She reached up to bury her fingers in the wild waves of his hair, pulling him closer, closer, and still not close enough. He gave a groan that sounded like agony and snatched her hand in his sound one, then he was off, towing her swiftly behind the motel. "Where are we going?" she asked, panting as she hurried along with him.

"I dunno. Anywhere. Away from everybody."

He stalked around the corner of a tool shed butted up to the back of the motel. They slammed up against the clapboard wall of the alcove it made with an inside corner of the building, barely still again before they were kissing in the dimming shadows. Elsa's heart battered against her ribcage, and she wondered if someone would come looking for them, wondered if the shed was enough to hide them.

Too many people around. They could be discovered any second. She wanted to jump in her car with Harry and drive away—somewhere they could be alone. She wanted him all to herself for hours, but she couldn't wait.

Harry's mouth burned a path down her throat to the bare skin above the neck of her tank top. Fiery shivers raced through her body. She pulled up on his shirt, crushed it in her fists, whimpered when her searching hands found the hot skin of his belly. Eagerly, she spread her fingers through the dusting of wiry hairs leading down to the waistband of his jeans, kneading the hard muscle under his skin.

With a soft snarl, he pulled the fabric of her shirt and bra downward. Cooling air flushed across her breasts, but a split second later, his scorching mouth replaced it. He devoured her like a starving man. Elsa moaned and pressed against him, offering herself unreservedly.

His mouth skimmed her breast, almost but not quite reaching the nipple. She gave another whimper and reached around him to draw him closer.

He stilled, then straightened with an explosive sigh. "No. Not here. Not like this." With a tug, he straightened her clothing.

Hurt flashed through her. She opened her mouth to reproach him, but he was already taking her hand and stalking out of the shadows of the alcove. "Harry...wait. Harry," she protested.

"Don't tell me not to stop," he said, his voice hard-edged. "We aren't going to do this behind some seedy motel."

"But..."

"No buts." He tugged her around to the front of the motel, then paused to stroke her cheek with the tips of his fingers. "I'm broke. I'm being hunted. I'm busted-up," he said, holding up the splint, "but God damn it, I've still got a few principles left. Stay there." He pointed to the spot where she was standing, as if daring her to object, then strode toward Nina's door.

What he told her teammate, she couldn't have said, but a few seconds later, he stalked toward Elsa's wagon with her keys in hand. He tilted his head, indicating she should follow. She jogged toward her vehicle, curious.

He got into the driver's seat. Elsa slipped into the passenger seat, intrigued by the dark look on his features. "Where are we going now?"

He waited until she'd buckled her belt, started the car, then slammed it into gear. "Somewhere better."

He said nothing more for the rest of the drive. Elsa longed to touch him, longed to ask about their destination, but a part of her thrilled at not knowing, at putting off the fireworks she knew were waiting.

But Harry didn't bring her to a hotel. They pulled into the parking lot of a nice restaurant. Classy, she saw, but not so posh she'd feel underdressed in a tank top and jeans.

Except the steamy look in Harry's eyes made her feel like she wore nothing at all.

His gaze traveled over her, unhurried and very, very deliberate. "This is what normal people do, isn't it?" he asked. "Go on dates? I've got enough left in my wallet to take an amazing woman out for a late dinner. Or just drinks. Or—" He leaned toward her to kiss her again, and murmured against her lips, "a very hurried dessert, which might be considered an appetizer."

That thrill pelted through her again, and her breath came short. "Are you sure you want to wait that long?" she asked, trying to pull him closer.

He slipped away with a chuckle, then got out of the car. To her delight, he rounded the front to open her door for her. "Elsa," he assured her, his eyes gleaming as he helped her out, "you are worth waiting for."

****

He felt like an untried kid on a first date with the prettiest girl in class. Through the waiter's greeting, and picking out a sampler plate, and deciding on dinner, he could hardly sit still. He insisted she order whatever she liked best off the menu. For once, damn it, he was going to do something right. Something to thank the incredible woman sitting across from him for coming into his life. What she'd given him—a taste of the world outside his forced rootlessness—was nothing short of the work of a superhero. She might as well have fallen to earth from some distant star, after all.

He watched her study the menu, enjoying the way the light from the dim art glass chandelier picked out the paler tones in her hair and eyelashes.

He had taken stuff like this for granted so often. Dinner with a woman had always been a formality, a perk of his position in society. Almost overlooked in its pleasures.

She shifted in her seat and, with an elbow on the table, put a finger to her cheek in a pensive attitude. Shadows fell across her face and down her slender neck. He'd never given much thought to how beautiful women were. They just were, and as a Litchfield, he'd

147

had his pick. Models and movie stars, jet setters and socialites.

Elsa was none of those, but somehow, just sitting there, existing, she eclipsed all of them.

"Are you sure you don't mind leaving Rose?"

"She's fine," he said. "Nina bought some nail polish, and they're doing the girl thing. Precursor to your makeup day, no doubt." He gave her a wry grin, then fell silent, just looking at her.

Her posture shifted again, and a smile curved on her lips. "You're staring," she said at last, and her gaze came up from the menu. "What's the matter?"

He sat back in his chair and stretched his legs out under the table. "Don't mind me."

She looked back to the menu, but her smile didn't fade. "I'm beginning to feel like a goldfish."

"What?"

Quirking a full grin at him, she said, "Swimming around, getting stared at?"

"Can I help it? You're stare-worthy."

Her cheeks pinkened, and her laugh revved that part of him which wished they hadn't stopped for dinner. He forced it into check, unwilling to rush this.

She ordered a chicken dish, even though he suspected her eyes were on the grilled salmon ordered by the woman at the neighboring table. Disappointment nipped at him. She was probably trying to spare him some expense. Suddenly, he wanted to order one of everything on the menu, and let her pick at whatever tickled her fancy. If he'd had access to his money, it would be a five-star meal, the best bottle of wine in Texas, and a night of dancing in a dress he'd bought her just for the occasion. And after that...

Well, here he was, back at trying to rush things.

When the food arrived, he pushed his fries around the plate, more interested in watching her than in his bacon cheeseburger.

She mistook his lack of attention to the food. Halfway through her own meal, she asked, "Not hungry?"

"Trying to make the night last," he said without thinking.

Her gaze shot up, and the smile on her face hit him like a TKO. He realized what he'd said, and returned her look with an embarrassed grin. About as slick as a first-date teenager, too.

"You're amazing, Harry," she said, propping her chin in her hand.

"Me?"

"Yeah. Not too many guys out there who would drop everything, risk everything, for their little sister the way you do."

"We do what we gotta do," he said. "Look at you, storm chasing your way around the country. That's a whole class of guts by itself."

"It helps to have a bit of an edge," she said. Her conspiratorial smile faded a little. "Is there anyone—anyone at all—who you can go to?"

"I think you're it. And really, I keep telling myself I shouldn't have dragged *you* into my mess." He tapped at the leg of the table with his foot.

"I *want* to be dragged into it," she insisted. "I want to help you and Rose get your lives back."

The sincerity on her face made him smile. She leaned forward with an imploring expression in those big blue eyes. He could easily see how she got her way, more often than not.

Suddenly, he wanted to know everything about her. He wanted her to know all about him. He'd spent so long hiding from the rest of the world that the idea of telling her was a drug to his system. He wanted to show her his favorite haunts in L.A. He wanted her to see the hospital wing his parents had opened to help kids with birth defects and childhood illnesses. He wanted to laugh with her over cocktails at a club, or take her out on the yacht, which was probably still sitting there at Marina del Rey right now.

How incredible would she look on that boat, with the wind in her hair and the skirt of her dress hugging those long, tanned legs?

His body hummed with eagerness. "Please tell me you don't give a damn about dessert."

Her lips curled into a sly smile of her own. "I don't know. That brownie à la mode is looking pretty spectacular."

The teasing note in her voice revved him up further. "You can get one to go," he suggested.

Her eyes shone in the low light. She traced a finger along the edge of her plate, and he followed the motion like a man glued to the television during the playoffs. "I thought I was worth waiting for."

"I could find a few alternative uses for that ice cream."

Her eyes widened a little, and he allowed himself a satisfied smile. A relief to know he hadn't completely lost his touch. He reached across the table for her hand.

She gave it, and he allowed himself a slow, thorough exploration of her fingers with his own. Over the narrow tips, the neatly trimmed nails, her knuckles, the back of her hand. Soft, smooth skin that could put silk to shame. He traced the skin of her wrist, sensing the fine bones underneath the skin, then turned his touch to the inside of her wrist, where the pulse sped madly. Drawing little circles on her skin, he raised his gaze from her hand to her eyes.

Her lips were parted and her cheeks flushed. The pulse in her wrist echoed the one he saw racing in the hollow of her throat. Her gaze was fixed on his hand like one hypnotized.

He grinned. Exactly what he wanted. "What do you say I pay the check and we get out of here, Elsa Pemberley?"

****

She barely made it through the door of their hotel room before she was reaching for Harry again. All the way there, she'd wished she hadn't chosen to do the driving. With his attention unfettered by the road, Harry was free to torment her with feather-light touches that traced from her ear down the side of her neck. The result left her shivering, even though she was far from cold.

Now, she closed the hotel room door, then pounced on him with an urgency that startled her. She wasn't *that girl*. She'd never been *that girl*...at least, not before right now.

She'd dated. She'd even had a few abbreviated relationships, none of them truly serious. None that made her shake with the need to touch, the way she needed to touch Harry.

And he responded. The moment she slid her arms around him, his hands were in her hair, his mouth on hers, his body pressing against her. She tried to take it easy on his injured hand, tried to pull it away.

"Hell with my hand," he muttered, then kissed her again. His stubble scraped her chin, rough and masculine. Little zaps of sensation sparked along her nerve endings, and she dug her fingers into the back of his shirt.

His hands warmed her skin as they slid along her arms, around her back, into her hair. "You smell like fresh air," he murmured against her cheek. His breath washed across her skin, deliciously hot. "Like getting outside after you've been in a suffocating room all day."

"I smell like air?" She smiled.

He grinned, looking somehow rueful even so. "I tell a woman she smells nice, and I get crap for it?"

Elsa tried smothering her smile without success. "Sorry. Go ahead."

He nuzzled under her hair to kiss her neck. "You smell nice." Kiss. "You smell nice." Kiss. "You smell nice." Kiss, kiss, kiss.

Her toes curled inside their shoes, and she forgot all about teasing him for his unusual compliment. Instead, she towed him toward the large bed that dominated the room. "It might interest you to know I've been thinking a lot about this," she said.

"Oh?" He followed her with one eyebrow arched upward, so adorably she found herself grinning again.

"Oh, yes," she assured him. "From the moment you walked onstage at that bar, in fact. Probably much more often, and more extensively, than is good for me."

"Is that so?" He slipped his arms around her waist, then guided her backward until she bumped up against the side of the bed. "Well, it might interest *you* to know that I haven't had one damned second without you in my head, Elsa Pemberley. And now that I've got you to myself"—he tipped her backward onto the bed with a decadent gleam in his eye—"I plan on taking *extensive* advantage of the occasion." With a wolfish grin, he settled on one knee over her. "Now, where was I?"

"Something about how I smell?" she suggested helpfully.

"Ah. Yes. Nice, that was it." He leaned downward to press a lingering kiss at her jawline, then paused to inhale, just as lingering. His breath puffed across her throat. When she squirmed with thwarted pleasure, he chuckled. Little thrills of electricity raced back and forth through her body.

Harry ran his hands up her sides, unhurried as he traced the curves of her hips, the narrow sweep of her waist, and then the flare of her breasts.

She gasped as his thumbs whisked across her nipples through the thin tank top, and nearly came up off the bed.

His big hand pressed her gently down. "Now, don't go rushing this," he said with a teasing note in his velvet voice.

"Wouldn't dream of it," she managed, even though she wanted to tear that shirt off him.

"If this is my opportunity..." Kiss. Kiss. Kiss. "I'm making the most of it." He inched her tank top upward, and his mouth drifted along with the hem. Kiss. He paused to nose at her navel, and she shivered. Kiss. Kiss. He dragged his mouth up her midriff.

The pulsing in her ears raced far beyond the most heady sensation she got when facing a tornado. She squirmed, trying to rush him, unable to stem the excitement throbbing in her body.

"Oh, no you don't," he said. His voice rang with a note of playful reprimand. He bent over her again, staying just at the bottom of her breastbone, and not one inch higher. Kiss. Kiss. Kiss.

"Harry, *please*," she whispered.

The tip of his tongue flicked against her skin. "In an awful rush, aren't you?"

She tugged at his shirtsleeves, trying to bring his mouth upward to her breasts, her mouth, her throat, anywhere but that spot where he teased and tickled. "You're unfair."

"Unfair?" Amusement rolled through his tone. "Unfair to let you lie here and be completely..." Kiss. "...and thoroughly..." Kiss. "...kissed, by a man who thinks you are just as incredible here..." Another kiss at her breastbone, and she arched to meet it. He moved up to her forehead, then pressed another kiss there. "...as here?"

She melted utterly, putty in his hands and not caring. She beamed up at him, heedless of how silly she must look.

He grinned, full of male smugness. "Where was I again? You keep distracting me. It's really rude, actually."

She tapped her breastbone. "Right here."

"Mmm. Yes. You know, you taste just as good as you smell." He flicked his tongue against her breastbone one last time, then slid his hands up underneath her tank top to spread his sizzling palms against her breasts.

Elsa bit off a moan and lifted off the bed to press herself against his hands. Arching her back, she sighed,

AIR

loving the way the heat from his skin spread through her body like an expanding ripple.

He gave a long, low rumble, part purr and part growl. "And as for how you feel..." He curled his fingers back to slide them up underneath the lower edge of her bra.

She cried out as his fingertips reached her nipples.

He stared into her eyes. The hungry look in his gaze made her shivery and hot and needy, all at once.

A little smile tipped the corner of his lips upward as he stroked her in tiny circles. "I'm not sure there are words good enough to describe that," he finished.

Unable to help herself, she curled her legs around him to pull him closer. "More," she begged shamelessly.

His eyes flashed. "Oh, there's more." He reached around her back and unhooked the bra, lightning-fast, then swept her shirt and bra off over her head before she knew he'd meant to do so.

His mouth came down on hers, so hard and hot she blazed all over. His tongue swept her mouth, stroked her from the inside the way his hands stroked her now-bare skin. The cloth of his shirt chafed lightly against her bared nipples. She moaned and tightened her legs around him. His erection ground against her.

A hoarse groan ripped from his throat. He jerked his mouth away from hers to press his forehead against her chest. "Oh, God, Elsa, don't," he pleaded. "I don't want to rush this."

She splayed her fingers along his back, tracing his spine through the T-shirt. With a flash of wonder, she realized he was as rigid and trembling as a big cat about to leap. "Harry?"

He lifted his head again. His electric-blue eyes were half-wild with heat, but under that, she glimpsed a need so raw, her heartbeat stumbled.

Words failed her for an endless stretch. She stroked upward until her hands reached his face, then brushed the soft stubble there. Finally, she found her voice. "I'm not going anywhere," she whispered.

Harry traced the curve of her cheek with his good hand. His gaze followed where his fingers went: along her jaw, her chin, her lips, until at last he fixed on her eyes again. He smiled, just a little. "How the hell did you get so damned beautiful?"

The sincerity in his voice made her heart stutter in an unsettling sort of way, like maybe there might be a time beyond this wandering life she'd chosen. The very thought that it might be possible scared her, a breathless pause at the top of an impossible high-dive, with no certainty of a pool at the bottom. She forced a smile. "Lots of practice?"

He seemed to sense her nerves. His smile went from pensive to provocative. "No, I think you were just there the day they were handing out extra helpings of incredible," he said. "For instance..." He traced a lazy outline around her breast.

She forgot her reservations entirely.

"I think I've done an awful lot of talking, here, and not enough other things," he drawled.

"You are the one who didn't want to rush—" she began. An instant later, she stifled her own words with a long moan. Harry had closed his mouth over her nipple, and was drawing gently on it while flicking at the underside with the tip of his tongue.

Elsa fisted her hands in the back of his shirt. "Oh!"

she gasped out as his teeth pinched lightly on the sensitive tip. Her head whirled, and the pleasant heat building within her slid downward in a slow, relentless molten wave. "Harry, please." She tugged on his shirt, trying to get underneath it.

But Harry was a man completely intent on his work. He turned his attentions to her other breast, circling the nipple with his tongue, flicking it, then blowing cool air on it.

She cut off a very un-Elsa-like whimper. He made a low noise that might have been dry amusement, but his hands were oh, so serious as they seared their way down her body to the button of her jeans.

She lifted her hips at once, eager to rid herself of the clothing restricting her from his touch. His fingers, even one-handed, were as nimble with her garments as they were with his guitar. He slid her pants and underwear off with only the slightest of hitches, then hovered over her on one knee as if drinking in the sight of her. His gaze went everywhere, slow and thorough.

She tugged at the front of his shirt. "Come back down."

The corners of his eyes crinkled as he smiled again. "Just appreciating the artwork. I don't intend to miss a thing, Beautiful." He bent back down to kiss her again. His tongue teased at hers, pouring fresh waves of heat into her body. Shaking now, she reached for his shirt, and this time, he helped her slide it over his head.

He was breathtaking. Awestruck as she'd never been at any storm, she ran a hand over his chest, exploring the contours of hard muscle over skin like hot satin. Stopping at the waistband of his jeans, she dragged her stare back up to his eyes. "Seems a little one-sided, still. I'm naked, here."

His eyes gleamed with mischief. He kissed her again, then guided her hand to the button of his jeans. "I'm nothing if not fair."

Spurred by his response, she unbuttoned and unzipped his pants, then slid her hand inside. She'd never done this with a man she hardly knew...but she'd never spent an hours-long drive being teased and tormented into a sensual frenzy by one, either.

Harry gave a guttural groan as she grasped his rigid, pulsing erection. He pressed hard into her hand, and already, his breath churned. "Easy with that, honey," he said on an exhaling breath. "I'm already too tempted to hurry this."

"You and me, both." She stroked him, just a little. He bit off another groan, then dropped his head to her breast to suckle it with desperate ferocity.

Her body burst into flame. She twisted, trying to get still closer, turning inside out with the sudden force of her desire. Half-conscious of doing it, she clenched her hand on him.

He swore and slammed his hips forward. "Elsa!"

Her name washed across her ears and sent heady, hot shivers straight down to her core. She sensed the clenching of his fists in the bedspread. His arms shuddered with restrained force.

She inhaled in wonder, somehow shy, even as she reveled in a completely different sort of power. The slightest of touches, and he responded like a wild thing, pinioned to the earth only by the touch of her hands. "Kiss me again," she whispered.

He swooped down, and the moment his tongue invaded her mouth, her awareness of anything else blew apart.

His hand slipped between her legs, and those agile fingers she'd so often admired began to play her like she was an instrument, herself. With a sharp whimper, she arched upward. He stroked and circled and teased and strummed, and always kept her on the peak without letting her tumble over. Her nerve endings fired and recoiled, and fired again. Moisture rushed to meet his hand. Every time his fingers retreated, the emptiness was torture. "Please, please, oh, Harry, please..."

"You keep begging me like that, honey, and this is gonna finish a lot faster than I want it to," he said. "Oh, God, you're hot."

Unable to take it anymore, she dug her fingernails into his back. "I want you. Take them off. I want you, and I can't wait," she gasped out.

He gave a fierce, warning growl. "As the lady says," he grated. With one backward lunge, he was up, just long enough to shove his jeans off. His penis sprang free, as hard and gorgeous and mesmerizing as the rest of him. For only one second, was she able to admire him before he plunged back down.

He crushed his hips against her in a long, slow thrust. The ridge of his erection dragged along the moist, sensitive folds between her legs. Again. Again. She sucked in, starving for breath that refused to come, and just as she was ready to beg, he drove inside her.

Her hovering climax pounded into her and went endlessly on. Stars burst in front of her eyes. She heard herself call his name, felt herself wrap her legs around him with reckless abandon, heard him saying her name, too, again and again.

Buried to the hilt, Harry thrust his hand into her

hair to guide her back to his mouth for another drugging kiss. From there, he dragged his lips to her throat, her shoulders, her breasts, kissing everywhere. All the while, his hips rocked against hers in deep, thorough strokes that kept her whirling. Each slide touched her throbbing center, stoking the fire within her until she was ablaze. She clenched her eyes shut, hardly able to take the intensity. Her skin tingled at each point of contact. The pounding of her heartbeat echoed the sensation of his against her sweat-slick skin. Her power climbed higher, ever higher.

"You're amazing," he whispered.

She opened her eyes to find him watching her with something like awe. His hand was on her cheek now, stroking it with such tenderness that she thought her heart would break. And when she climaxed a last time, he tumbled with her over the brink, still gazing at her.

Joyful tears sprang to her eyes. She forgot about her work. Forgot about nosy scientists. Forgot about the shadowy murderers hunting the man in her arms. She even forgot that lonely, storm-orphaned child, so far away in her past.

Because the future was going to be so much better.

Chapter Eleven

Marco Torelli sat back in his dining chair to watch the morning sunlight lancing through the tall, mullioned windows. The heavy brocade curtains and sheers layered underneath blocked some of the golden gleam, but one sliver of light fell exactly on the opposite wall's oil painting of Lady Kettering. "Edmonton!" he shouted.

His rabbity servant skittered into the doorway. "Sir?"

Marco picked a sausage off his plate, then popped it into his mouth and chewed slowly, savoring the flavor of the imported and expertly seasoned meat. His chef was imported, too, from Sicily, and eating his food felt like a slice of the home he hadn't seen in three decades. Cooking was only one of the chef's many talents. A double win, that. Marco would have to hurry up the man's green card.

He took an unhurried sip of his coffee. Edmonton watched him, nervous, awaiting orders, but Marco merely dipped his fingers into his water goblet, then wiped them carefully on his linen napkin. When Edmonton was good and fidgety, he said, "Move the painting of my bitch. It's in the sun."

Blinking, Edmonton turned his gaze on the large painting. The sleek Doberman bitch who had begun Marco's passion for the breed stared imperiously out of the gilded frame. "N-Now, sir?"

Allowing a little of his warning tone into his voice, Marco said, "Is there a better time than now to do what I tell you to?"

The dog lying at Marco's feet raised his head and perked his ears at the tone. Marco plucked the last sausage from his plate and fed it to the animal. The dog was a fine example, a descendant of Lady Kettering, but not fit for show or breeding. Too volatile a temper, but he made a perfect bodyguard. A well-trained dog couldn't be persuaded or bribed off his watch like a man.

Some things, the animal kingdom still did better than humans. Loyalty was one of them.

With a pat to the dog's head, Marco returned his stare to Edmonton.

The servant shifted toward the painting, then hesitated. "It's rather large, sir. I'll need to get help to move it."

"Do it, then!" Marco snapped. "And bring me the papers!"

Edmonton bulleted out of the room. Not five minutes later, he returned with another pair of servants. One of them laid a stack of newspapers in front of Marco. Then, the three of them fumbled about with a stepladder like circus players.

"Damage that piece, and I will be very disappointed," Marco said quietly from behind his *Los Angeles Herald*. He sensed the servants freezing where they stood, and shared a private smile with Lucas. The dog wagged his cropped tail, then shifted to a more relaxed pose on the parquet floor.

The circus shuffled a little less awkwardly after

that and, peaceful mood restored, Marco took his time looking through the newspapers. Most days, he searched for business opportunities. He owned a quarter of the city as it was, but a business that refused to grow would soon find itself failing. After the Internet, he fanned through a selection of papers his servants brought him every morning. He usually went across the time zones in his searches, but a little blip in *The Oklahoman* caught his eye.

From Strummer to Storm Chaser, it said.

The oddity of the two things together made him take a second look. Reporters loved to start out with that catchy bullshit, and usually anything was fair game, if it got readers to pay attention, but guitars were something else altogether.

Harrison Litchfield Senior had had a stunning guitar collection.

> *You wouldn't think a traveling musician could hold forth on storm chasing, but guitarist Hank Rhodes knows his stuff. This is a man who totes an antique Gibson Les Paul around the countryside. But after a matter of days with a team of storm chasers headed by Montana-born weather enthusiast Elsa Pemberley, Hank fits right in with this motley assortment. When he's not watching his weather-minded younger sister, he can be found repairing a faulty...*

Marco paused in reading long enough to look at the tag line of the article. A filler column, just bullshit and fluff, but it had been submitted by some broad from the Severe Storms Laboratory out of Oklahoma. The whole thing was barely a couple of paragraphs. Big fucking deal.

Except.

Traveling. Gibson Les Paul. Younger sister.

The missing guitar from Litchfield Senior's collection.

The thrill that went through Marco's body was ten times more satisfying than sex. The prospect of picking off a threat did that. "Edmonton," he called.

The man left off the crap with the painting to hurry to Marco's side. "Yes, sir?"

Marco was already getting out of his seat. "Get me my cell phone. I'll be outside. Lucas, heel."

The dog sprang to his feet, then ticked across the polished floor after him as Marco stalked toward the French doors leading to the garden.

He walked slowly among the trimmed boxwood and stone statues sprinkled throughout the manicured garden, barely seeing any of it. The dog followed him, attention fixed on his face as if awaiting orders. Marco spared him another pat, but remained restless until the skittish servant came rushing down the path with his phone.

He took it, then shooed the man away with an irritable swipe. Edmonton rushed off the way he'd come.

Marco hit the first number on his speed dial. The line hardly rang before it was picked up. "Yeah?" came Vincent's voice.

"You got some better respect for me in your tone than that?"

"What's wrong?" came the answer, less snappish.

"I'll tell you what's wrong, you stupid *cafone*. Litchfield slipped right out from under your fat foot."

Silence, and then a muttered curse. "Where?"

"Oklahoma, last I saw. You're looking for a bunch of storm chasers led by some bitch named Pemberley. I'll send you the article."

"On it."

"You find him, you hold him until I get there. I want to see that son of a bitch with my own eyes. You got me?"

"I got you. I got you."

"If he slips you again, little brother, your head's gonna slip."

"Yeah, I got it." The line went dead.

Marco clicked his phone off, and muttered the same curse. Working with family was the biggest advantage, and the worst pain in the ass, about going into business.

****

Harry didn't want to open his eyes. He'd been dreaming, a gorgeous, slow-motion, on-repeat dream of his night with Elsa. Opening his eyes would only mean the end of it. Eager to return to that blissful experience, he reached out to Elsa's side of the bed.

But she wasn't there.

He snapped his eyes open and flipped onto his belly. The sheets tangled up around his waist. Cursing, he wrestled out of bed and onto his feet.

The bathroom door opened. Elsa stood in the doorway, already dressed, with her cell to her ear and her skin paler than Harry had ever seen it. "He's up. Hold on." She held out the cell to Harry. "I'm so sorry."

Rose. Plunging him into ice water couldn't have frozen his heart faster. He vaguely recalled reaching out, but Elsa had to put the phone into his numb hand.

165

A few seconds passed, so suddenly crammed with memories of last night and the guilt of leaving Rose, that Harry didn't react at all.

"Answer it," said Elsa. Beyond the paleness of her skin, she gave no clue to who, or what, waited on the other end of the line.

Harry raised the phone. "Hello?"

"Harry," said Rose, and his body started to function again until her next words. "You gotta get back here, quick. We're in the paper."

From absolute stillness, Harry shot into motion. He went everywhere at once, without words, grabbing pants and socks and shirt, checking for his wallet, looking automatically for his guitar. Only after he remembered it wasn't there did he stop tearing apart sheets and furniture.

The entire time, Elsa hadn't moved. She stood in the middle of the room, hugging herself and looking miserable.

"We gotta go," he barked. "Grab your stuff, we gotta go."

"Harry?"

"Not now," he snapped. He gave an inward flinch at his tone, but didn't check himself. Darting around the room, he scrabbled, one-handed, to get his clothes on. Stupid! Why had he thought for even one second it was safe to have something for himself?

"Harry." Elsa's voice came again, gentler. She crouched beside him and eased the cell from his injured hand.

Harry realized Rose was still on the other end, and paused in the act of jerking his pants on.

"Rose?" Elsa said into the cell, calm-voiced.

166

"We'll be there in twenty minutes, okay? Don't worry." After a pause, she disconnected the call.

And after that, she wouldn't look at Harry. He dressed in silence while she gathered her few things. He fumed at himself the entire time. He had known—*known*—it was dangerous to tie himself down to anyone or anything. Like a fool, he'd ignored his better judgment and selfishly gone off with Elsa. He should never have joined her team in the first place. They were far too visible, motoring around in that monster vehicle, chasing storms, getting attention.

His heart froze all over again. "That woman. That NSSL woman."

"I know," Elsa murmured. She scooped her keys from the nightstand, then fidgeted with them, turning them over and over in her palm. "Harry, I know my apology can't even touch this."

"We're not gonna do this now," he snarled. "I left my kid sister with a stranger to come away and f—"

The sudden hurt in Elsa's eyes made him bite back the rest of his words, but he knew she heard them clearly in the ringing silence. *Fuck you like a dog in heat.*

She swallowed, and the pain in her expression gouged at him. Fresh guilt piled on top of him, made him glad he'd stopped what he'd been about to say, even though his bitterness was aimed entirely at himself.

What they'd done last night was nothing short of incredible, and with a few words—even unsaid—he'd fucked it up.

Elsa met his gaze squarely. "Let's get back to Rose, then."

Their return drive was silent. There was no traffic. The road stretched away, as deserted as if it were the end of the world.

Which it might be. Harry flicked his fingertips against his leg, restless and impatient. The first thing he would have to do would be to change his name. Rose's, too. And no more guitar. He'd have to sell it. He regretted that prospect at once...but every shred of Hank Rhodes would have to disappear, even if it meant losing his last link to his father.

He closed his eyes. *Give me something, God. What do I do?* Only the road noise answered him. He leaned back against the headrest, too weary to sit upright.

"This is my fault," Elsa said finally. Her voice rang with resignation.

He knew he should deny it, that he'd had an equal share and more in what happened, but talking took too much energy. He remained how he sat.

"You can't leave us," she added.

He opened his eyes to stare at her.

Her attention was on the route, but she sat stiffly. When he didn't respond, she glanced at him. "Do you hear me, Harry? You can't. You can't take care of either of you right now. And I can't let you leave, knowing that."

"You're not my bodyguard," he said.

"I'm what you have to work with," she shot back. "Last night aside"—her breath hitched, but then she forged on—"we'll have to work together until your hand is better or we find a way to stop these people from coming after you." She paused and, seeming to sense his impending objection, she snapped, "I will not take no for an answer."

168

Moodily, he stared out the passenger window. A hundred possible replies sprang to his lips, but none of them made it out. She was right. He had no other options. "Let's just get back there."

****

Elsa had made compartmentalizing an art form. She had survived the loss of her birth family, the rejection of childhood crushes, the teasing of her foster brother Ethan, and the pain of watching Hope Creek slide downhill before Kincade was able to rescue it.

Harry wasn't going to go into a neat little box like the rest of it. Not after last night.

As they pulled into the motel, she sighed. Worry prickled at her until she saw Nina's door open. Rosalie came running outside as they pulled into a parking space. Relieved that the girl was all right, Elsa let herself relax a little.

Not Harry. The moment the wagon pulled to a stop, he was out, and jogging toward his sister. His arms went around her with a speed that squeezed Elsa's heart.

As she got out of the vehicle, Elsa heard him telling Rose to get her things. "You can put them in my car, Rose," she called.

Harry shot her a glare full of loosely restrained fury.

She returned the look with the same vehemence, then stomped toward him so she could speak without her teammate overhearing. "You two are my responsibility until your hand is better," she said, "and don't think you're just going to slink off into nowhere the minute my back is turned. I *will* find you."

Rose's gaze ping-ponged back and forth between

169

them. "Harry, we've got to go with her."

His lip curled, and it appeared he would argue, but Nina came toward them with Sam on his leash.

Harry's expression still seethed, but he edited whatever he was about to say. "Fine," he muttered, then thrust his left hand up. "The *second* this splint is off, I'm gone."

Gone. Was it that easy to go, even when she promised him her help? After everything they had done last night? Elsa swallowed her pride and tried to remember this was his life on the line. Rose's, too. There were more important things at stake.

The hurt would just have to wait.

Nina came to a stop in front of her. Sam wagged and tried to jump up to lick Elsa, but she warded him off with an upraised hand. Nina tugged the dog back, and Sam went to Rose to lick her instead. Nina's brow furrowed with tiny lines. "What's the story, El?"

"Not mine to tell," she said. Her voice came out hollow.

Scowling, Nina rounded on Harry. "Then *you* tell. Did you hurt her? I'll kick your—" Nina shot an apologetic look toward Rose, but her mutinous look came right back as she advanced into Harry's personal space to stare him down. "So help me, if you hurt her, I will make you regret it, buster."

"I didn't. Chill out," he snapped.

Nina handed Sam's leash off to Rose, then put her hands on her hips. She faced off with Harry like an umpire with a belligerent ball player. "You have about fifteen seconds to tell me what's going on, Hank Rhodes, or whoever you are. 'Cause right now, I'm thinking I don't trust you any more than you're trusting us."

Harry gave Elsa a cornered look, but she was too jumbled to offer any advice. He glanced at Rose then, and at the solemn look on Rose's face, Elsa's heart broke for that too-old-for-her-years girl.

Rosalie pursed her lips, studied Nina, then gave Harry a nod. "Running hasn't gotten us anywhere, Harry. We have to try something else."

Harry scrubbed both hands through his hair. For a split second, Elsa glimpsed agony in his eyes, but he stifled it fast, then clenched his fists as if he wanted to hit someone. Elsa didn't doubt it.

"Fine," he snapped. "You want what's going on? My kid sister and I are on the top of a Mafia hit list, and we've run out of places to run. I can't feed her. I can't clothe her. God knows I can't parent her. The whole world's gone to shit, and this is all wrong as hell." He whirled around to stalk a few steps away, where he stood rigidly. His good hand came up to rub at his face, and he bowed his head.

Nina shot Elsa a look of alarm. Still in knots, Elsa gave her friend a helpless shrug. A long, silent stretch ambled by. "I'm sorry," Nina called to his back. "I didn't know."

He turned around with the fury back in his eyes. "Of course you didn't know. You shouldn't know. We should be miles from here by now."

"But you can't, because of your hand," Nina said. Elsa watched her teammate putting the pieces together, and Nina grew paler and paler. She reached out to Rose. "Oh, sweetheart."

Rose went to her. Nina hugged the girl and kissed the top of her head. Looking up from the circle of

Nina's arms, Rose said, "Harry, why can't we stay with them? They move around so much anyway, it'd be hard to track them. And the storms might keep...keep people away."

Elsa's already sore heart wrenched a little more. *They need a home even more than I did.*

The thought startled her...but it was true. She still missed her birth family, but once she'd arrived at Hope Creek, Elsa hadn't been alone anymore. She'd had a family and a home where she was welcome to put down roots, even though she'd chosen storm chasing instead.

Suddenly, her life began to look a little different. "She's right, Harry."

He glared at her. "Bullshit."

"No, she's right. The tornado warnings alone get everyone off the street, and sometimes there are evacuations. Would they risk their own exposure and safety to come after you by going into the path of a storm? We can protect you."

Doubt flitted through his pale-blue eyes. He angled his head and gave her a pleading look. "This is crazy."

Elsa's heart beat faster. Her power had always been a special gift to her, something valuable to be used in helping others, and never more so than now. "It's no crazier than what you've been doing. If they come after you, they'll have to face me."

Nina gave Harry a gentle smile, and in that moment, Elsa loved her more than she ever had. "Well, that settles it," Nina said. "You're the newest members of Team Pemberley."

Chapter Twelve

Harry finished the newspaper article with pain lancing through his gut. His stomach turned over again, and he was pretty sure in another minute, he was going to puke. He shifted his seat on the edge of the motel bed and dropped the paper into his lap.

"Malory said she was short on money," Rose said quietly. "She must have submitted it for cash."

"She had no right," Elsa said from where she stood behind him. Her voice shook.

Rose frowned. "We didn't tell her not to."

Harry passed a hand over his aching eyes. *Great. Add impending migraine to impending puke.* "We didn't know she'd blab to the press. I should have stuck with my gut." He groaned. Maybe sticking with his gut at this precise moment was a bad idea, too.

He sensed Elsa approaching him, and then she laid a hand on his shoulder. He stiffened. He couldn't afford to go soft, not now. Not ever again. This was what sparing a night for himself had gotten him.

"I'm going to go help Seth get ready to leave," Rose said. Harry couldn't even be bothered to give her a brotherly growl before she slipped out of the room.

The silence after she left was smothering. Harry stared at the paper in his lap and breathed through the stabbing sensation in his belly. One breath. Two. Three, four. The sick feeling lingered. He clenched his gut against the need to throw up.

The murmurs of Elsa's team filtered in from outside, indistinct. Nina shouted directions. A car door slammed, and someone asked a question.

"Say something," Elsa whispered at last.

He drew a breath, but it was another minute before he trusted himself to form words. "What's there to say?"

Her hand lifted away, and the warmth where it had been evaporated into the icy chill gripping the rest of his body. "Anything."

He gritted his teeth until it hurt. "I can't hide behind you. It's only going to get you killed, or your team."

"You can't just leave, either," she said, coming around the edge of the bed to kneel at his feet. She gripped his knees. "If my power isn't for protecting people—especially people I...I care about...then what's it for?"

The words almost spilled out. *You gotta get away from me.* But he made the mistake of looking into her eyes, and the words were lost before they left his lips. The pleading look on her face made his gut twist even worse. Her hands clenched on his knees, and then her cheeks colored. She leaned back a little, but her touch softened, even as she looked away.

Memories of her soft skin under his hands and his mouth blasted through him. He forgot about feeling sick. In his head, he heard the echo of her sigh when he touched her. He struggled to ignore the way his body responded, and forced an ice he didn't remotely feel into his tone. "I can't afford to care back."

Her breath hitched, and she removed her hands.

Her eyes sparked. At last, she met his gaze with a steely look of her own. "Fine," she said. "If this is the way you want to play it, fine. But I'll tell you something: those people are going to be looking for me and my team now, whether you leave or not, thanks to that article. So is it better to keep running for the rest of your life, or face them and have hope for an end to it? Think about it, Harry." She stood, and with a poise he had to admire, she ghosted out of the room and quietly closed the door.

Harry cursed under his breath, even though there was no one around to hear it. Finally, he grabbed his duffel and strode outside.

"Rhodes," Rory called on seeing him. "Give me a hand?"

Harry altered his course with a will. Anything to get his mind off worry, off Elsa, and onto a more immediate task, or he'd implode.

All Rory needed was an adjustment on some weather equipment, though, and Harry found himself chafing because the task wasn't complicated enough to occupy his mind. Tightening a loose bolt, he kept an ear on the chatter between Seth and Rose. The kid seemed to like teaching her about storm chasing. Harry heard enthusiasm in the young man's voice, and when Rose showered questions on him, he didn't balk.

He angled a curious look at his sister. She was smiling. Imminent disaster was breathing down their necks, and Rose was smiling. How the hell did she do that?

"Look alive, team!" cried Woz. He had a handheld radio and a map in one hand, and a backpack in the other. "Sounds like we got a potential mixer outside

Amarillo."

Elsa's team bolted to their vehicles as if someone had rung the starting bell for a horse race. "Rory," Elsa called, "get me data."

Rory reached out for the wrench, and Harry tossed it. The man snatched it from the air, then slapped it back into his toolkit. Gear disappeared into vehicles with clockwork precision. "Rose!" Harry shouted.

"She can go with me and Nina," Seth called. "In the back, Rose. Get Sam in, and buckle that harness."

Harry didn't get a chance to protest. "Harry, quick—come with me," said Elsa.

With a last glance toward Nina, Seth, Rose, and Sam—now getting swallowed by The Beast—Harry jogged toward Elsa and her wagon. "What about the Torellis?" he demanded as he tossed his duffel into the back seat.

They slid into the wagon together. "This is the best possible place to be," she said, all business as she started the engine. "They'd be stupid to come within miles of an active storm." She jerked the gear into reverse and pulled out of her space, then sped toward the lot entrance.

What about when she deactivated the storm? The confidence in her voice couldn't convince him, but no matter what they did, it was time to move. Staying in one place would get them killed for sure. He glanced out the rear window. The Beast and the van were tearing out of the lot close behind them.

Turning back around, he looked at Elsa. She was cool and focused. Too much so.

For God's sake, she was going to risk the lives of herself and her team for him. He opened his mouth.

"Don't even think it," she said, and that steel was back in her tone. "Don't tell me about how you want us to let you and Rose go. We're as much at risk as you, now, anyway."

"That's an excuse?"

Her cell rang. Frustrated, Harry stabbed the speaker button.

Rory's voice came over the line. "Stay west on Forty until we hit Thirty-Four. I'm seeing a definite hook echo in the weather pattern, fifty, sixty miles north of Amarillo. Looks like a baby nader, El."

"Get out your receiving blankets," she answered grimly, then stepped on the gas.

The line clicked off. Harry looked back to Elsa. "What's a nader?"

"A tornado, or about to be one." Her voice was calm.

He studied her, looking for some clue to what was going on in her head. She was amazing at keeping a clear head. More so than he was, even...but then, she made a habit of looking for trouble. She was driving *toward* the trouble, instead of trying to get away from it.

With a side order of trouble in her passenger seat.

He sighed. She had guts, that much he had to allow. "What can I do to help?"

"Road map in the glove compartment. Find Texas. We'll be on point until we get closer, and then we'll hand it over to The Beast."

"With my sister inside?"

Elsa smiled. "In a moving tornado bunker, which is more than we can say for my car and that sail of a weather van. They'll collect data, then determine if I need to kill the weather pattern. They'll be in constant contact, either by cell or CB." She pointed at a CB receiver tucked under the dash.

He pulled the map from the glove box. Rubbing a hand through his hair, he said, "I wish I could say your plan made me feel better."

She didn't respond, and in the pause, he had time to study her. What an ass he was. He'd never even acknowledged their night together since that first slip, good, bad, or indifferent. It was neither bad nor indifferent.

Most certainly not indifferent.

He fought with a knee-jerk reaction to touch her. What could it do but complicate an already huge mess? Still, his conscience sucker punched him. He tapped his sound fingers on the armrest, then subsided, watching her. "Thank you."

She nodded. "You and Rose will be safe...as safe as we can make you."

"Not for that."

Her lashes fluttered, and her cheeks took on that pinkish hue. She glanced toward him again, but didn't quite meet his gaze. Her lips parted, and then closed.

Shrugging, he added, "I was a dick this morning. I'm sorry. I should have...should have said something, I don't know."

"It's okay," she said at last.

"No, not really." Impatient with himself, he added, "Look, Elsa, you're pretty incredible."

"Please don't do that." Her voice trembled.

He eyed her, but her attention remained on the road. "Do what?"

When she spoke this time, her voice had gone hard,

but with an unmistakable note of hurt that surprised him with how much it bothered him. "Don't give me the 'It was great, but it's not going to happen again' speech. Because you know what? It *was* great, Harry. And I don't want you to spoil that with your lone wolf thing." She stared hard at the road as they drove, dry-eyed. Her hands clenched once on the wheel, and then she took a deep breath.

"How long has it been?" he asked quietly. "Since you..."

She barked a laugh. "I don't mess around with just anybody."

"Neither do I."

Her gaze shot to him then. Her expression read surprise.

Harry stifled a jab of insult. "Do you think I go around sleeping with every woman I meet? When would I have the time, first of all?" He curbed himself, and then heaved another sigh. "You've saved my ass more than once already, and you're willing to do it again. I just don't want you to get hurt because of me," he ended on a mutter. "I'm not good with that."

In the ensuing silence, the road noise sounded like a freight train rumbling down a bumpy track. Harry stared at the field flashing past outside his window under a leaden sky.

"I'll be careful," she said finally. "We all will, I promise...as careful as we can. Okay?"

The gentleness in her tone soothed his pride, but he didn't look. He knew she'd be watching him with those big, soft blue eyes. The mental image was bad enough. He wasn't sure he could take the real thing without caving. He drew a long, slow breath. "Yeah."

Silence again—less tense, but with an air of unfinished business about it. Harry stole a look.

Her gaze stayed on their route. Her long, pale-yellow braid cascaded down over the front of her shirt, but couldn't hide her slender neck or delicate collarbone. He thought about last night, when he'd kissed her there, and she'd sighed and nearly undone him.

No, he thought, their business was far from finished.

****

Malory Sternberg slapped the newspaper down on her desk. Freelancing an article for *The Oklahoman* hadn't gotten her much, but at least it had bought her groceries for the next few days.

Her home office was gorgeous—golden, quarter-sawn oak and stained glass, nothing like her cramped, sterile desklet at work.

The one to which her boss had demoted her.

She traced the headline of the newspaper, wondering if she'd be able to hold onto her beautiful house, now that her position and pay grade had gone downhill.

If it was a choice between writing two-bit articles to stay afloat, and looking down the barrel of the IRS, she'd do whatever it took. In an uncertain economy, the mercenary was king.

Her doorbell rang. Malory pushed aside her half-drained coffee, then got up to answer it.

The man at the door was as big as a refrigerator. She flinched back at seeing the livid scar running down the side of his face, but his crisp dress shirt and pressed slacks made her stop at shutting the door in his face.

"Can I help you?"

"Malory Sternberg?" His voice was only slightly less intimidating than his appearance.

"Yes."

"I came to talk to you about the article you wrote for *The Oklahoman*."

Hello, coincidence. "Are you with the paper?" she asked.

"No," he said, "more a fan of guitars. I understand the man you wrote about was in possession of an antique Gibson guitar, and I'm interested in buying it. Can you put me in touch with him?"

Malory hesitated. She might have been a lot of things, but hopelessly oblivious wasn't one of them. Fancy-Suit Scarface hadn't bothered to toss out his name before pumping her for information. "I'm sorry, he never mentioned where he was headed next."

"What about Miss Pemberley?" he asked.

She shifted her weight to one foot and remained in the crack of the doorway. "How about you give me your name and number, and I forward it on to her?"

The man smiled. A little chill skittered down Malory's back. She started to close the door.

The man on her doorstep plugged a big foot into the closing gap. Malory had no time to react—even a yelp of surprise—before he was pushing into her house with an enormous handgun in her face.

As he kicked the door shut behind him, she staggered back. Her dry throat produced no sound, even though she struggled to scream.

And her job was suddenly the very least important thing in all the world.

****

Elsa stared up at the clouds boiling in the sky outside Amarillo, Texas. High winds buffeted her car. She slowed, and as she pulled to the roadside, she picked up the CB. "Nina, you're a go. We'll keep it clear behind, in case you need to back off."

"You got it," came the response. Elsa hung the CB back on its hook.

As The Beast passed by, Harry stiffened in his seat.

"She'll be all right," Elsa assured him, even though she knew the words would probably have done as much good being whispered to a brick wall. She thought about her own little sister, a near-shadow in her memory. A pang burst in her chest, and she reached for Harry's arm.

He looked at her when she laid her hand on him, those pale-blue eyes full of worry, and she struggled for a smile. "I know it sounds odd that we're keeping her safe by putting her in the way of a possible tornado...but that's why you have me."

His arm stiffened ever so slightly under her touch. She sensed him drawing into himself—away from her—the same as he'd done that morning. A flash of their night came back to her, all skin and sighs and searing touches. She doubted it would happen again. Her smile wobbled a little, but stayed intact by main force of will. "Storms, I can handle."

He nodded, but turned his attention back to The Beast, which was now trundling forward ahead of them under that washing-machine churn of clouds.

Her cell rang. She picked it up, then hit the speaker. "Looks like it'll go live," reported Rory from the weather van behind them. "I've got a real solid model here."

"How close are we to town?" she asked.

"Under twenty and closing. Moving slow, but Amarillo's not sitting too comfortable right now."

"All right. We'll collect our data, and then I'll kill it. Honk when you're ready." She disconnected, then tucked her phone back under the dash.

When she reached for her door handle, Harry jerked to attention. "You're going out there in that?"

"Of course." She hesitated. "Want to come?"

"Seriously?" He peered out the windshield at the sky, which had picked up a gray-green tint. The wind shimmied her car on its tires and flattened the scrubby grasses. Now and then, there was the hiss of fine debris, sand and pebbles, being blown against the wagon's sides.

And then he surprised her. "Okay."

Her own delight surprised her even more. She had gone out into storms with her crew before—made a habit of it, really—but somehow, sharing it with Harry meant something different.

"Do you do this every tornado season?" he shouted over the wind as they climbed out of the car.

"Yep. We all meet up in Oklahoma, and spend each summer doing this," she yelled back. She shook out her hands and let her power flow. It crackled, then expanded, and as Harry joined her, he stepped unwittingly into the bubble of settled air around her.

His hair stopped whipping about, and the wind ceased tearing at his clothes. His brows rose, and with an adorable look of experimental concentration on his face, he dipped his good hand out of the bubble, where the wind still billowed about in every which direction. He drew his hand back in. "I'll be damned."

"Still think I can't help you?"

"Still think it's insane," he said, "but what choice do I have?"

Grinning, she answered, "You're perfectly safe. I do this with my crew."

"And they don't think it's insane?"

"Nina hates it," Elsa admitted, "but I think she's just being a mother hen." She slid her hand into his. A tiny, sorrowful pang made her hitch her breath. What would happen when Harry tired of rattling around the Midwest with her? When he gave up believing she could help him? She hated how much she liked the feel of holding his hand.

Back to the task, she ordered herself. She loosened her grip on her power, and the strength of it crackling underneath her skin filtered information about the storm back to her—wind speed, intensity, and most importantly, direction.

It was moving toward Amarillo, faster than she'd have liked. Right now, there was nothing in its way. They were far enough on the outskirts that there was still an open path, and no risk of damage or injury. "Come on, let's get closer."

As she tugged Harry's hand, he hung back, wariness etched plainly across his features.

"Five minutes," she urged. "I swear it'll be worth it."

He raised a brow at her. "How many times have you done this?"

"I've lost count."

He studied the whirling clouds. "They're dropping. Does that mean a tornado?"

"It might. As good as modern science is, and as

good as my power is, no one is able to predict a tornado yet. We can guess based on cues from air pressure and cloud patterns, but that's about it."

His pale-blue eyes flitted back and forth, searching the clouds as if they could tell him something more. "How close can you get? Have you been inside one?"

She laughed. "Not so far. Even I have my stopping point. As of now, the closest I've gotten was the day Rose saw me stop that twister by the farmhouse."

He remained silent a moment more, then nodded, tightening his grip on her hand. "Let's do it."

"Really?"

He gave her a grim leer, without much humor. "I'm getting good at cheating death."

Her answering smile faltered, but she saved it—mainly out of sheer stubbornness—and they started toward the storm.

As they walked, she pointed at the cloud shapes boiling in the sky, and explained what they were and how they interacted with the storm pattern now pushing in on Amarillo. The wind howled outside their protective bubble, plucking at her power like a child throwing a tantrum. "Mammatus clouds. I'm sensing a definite high-low pressure, pushing on the wind. It's not a guarantee," she reminded him, "but if we're lucky, we might see some action."

"You have a funny definition of luck." His words were skeptical, but he hadn't let go of her hand.

The hopeful spark inside her leapt higher, and she couldn't help letting it burn. It warmed her all over. Her power gave a reckless burst, pushing their protective bubble out farther.

Harry noticed the change. He turned his gaze back

to her to look her over in slow appraisal, betraying nothing. Finally, his grip on her hand loosened enough to let his fingers skate across her palm in what could only be a caress.

The spark flared, and a little shiver passed through her. He'd looked at her exactly that way last night. Her heartbeat pumped faster—nothing to do with the storm—and heat rushed after the shivers to pool low in her belly. She risked a step closer.

He closed the distance himself. "I'm an idiot." He touched her face. "I don't know how I thought it was gonna be possible to keep away from you. You're too damn amazing."

Her body betrayed her eagerness. She leaned her cheek into his hand, savoring the rough heat of his palm against her skin. His fingers slid over her cheekbone, then downward to stroke along her jaw. Elsa held her breath. Her power throbbed along her nerves, following the electric zing of desire pounding against her insides like a caged bird. Any more, and she thought she might blow apart.

He made a low, growly noise, then pressed himself against her. The hardness brushing her abdomen made it plain the attraction was nowhere near one-sided. She clutched at his shirt, greedy, and not caring who knew it.

Dipping his head, he brushed his lips against hers, the barest touch, and not at all enough. "I want you again," he murmured. "I shouldn't, but damn it, I do."

She thrilled to hear the words. Pulling him still closer, she kissed him fully. Harry wrapped his arms around her, and her insides jumbled together in a giddy, denial-happy mess. She told herself she didn't care what might happen later. Harry might decide he and Rose were safer if they moved on alone. But she had now with him, and now was enough.

It has to be, said the small voice inside her...because the idea of a life without Harry, now that she'd had a taste of it, just made her ache too much.

Chapter Thirteen

Not two minutes after Harry had done the idiot thing and kissed her, the storm boiled up to a point where Elsa had to stifle it. It was all over moments after it had begun...

...but not for him.

Watching the glow fade from her skin, and the storm settle into sporadic bursts that did no more than toy with her hair, he rubbed a hand over his tingling scalp.

He'd been asking himself for months on end what he was going to do about his life. He couldn't keep running forever. Now, staring at Elsa's back, at her mass of golden hair and slender waist and the all-too-mesmerizing curve of her hips, he didn't even want to. He was as trapped as an insect under glass, and he'd even seen it coming.

Dumbest move ever, in a long line of dumb moves. *To hell with it, Litch. She's got you, lock, stock, and barrel. At least until the Torellis catch up with you.*

As she came back to him, he reached out for her hand. Smiling a little, she took it. Glancing past him to The Beast, she gave a thumbs-up. Seth, Nina, and Rory were plastered against the glass, grinning back at her like a pack of loons.

They returned to their own car, and Harry noticed she was trembling. "You all right?"

"Just feeling drained, that's all."

"Give me the keys. I'll drive."

She relented without comment, which told him just how drained she was. He rounded the car to open her door for her. She gave him another wan smile and got in.

He closed the door, then walked around to the driver's side, gazing out at the flattened grass and torn-up earth the storm had left in its path. Elsa considered this her job, her mission. Not a traditional job, but she had a purpose, and one that benefited thousands of people.

His only purpose for the past eight or so months had been to keep moving, and keep out of the way of the Torellis. Even his parents had done something beneficial with their wealth and resources. Harry couldn't even touch the money he had.

But then, Elsa wasn't swimming in money, either. Not with a job like this. She made do.

In a flash of realization, Harry saw all the pieces of his fate clicking together. Elsa's team had computers and resources, and they stayed on the move. He might just be able to find a way to trap the tiger before it pounced, and help Elsa and her team at the same time.

He glanced up at the clearing sky. Apparently, God had been listening the whole time.

****

"You're very quiet," Elsa observed.

Harry had been driving silent since they got back into the car. Elsa sat in the passenger seat, wrapped in an old, plaid wool camping blanket. She studied his profile: like a Greek statue, without all the lack of expression. His face gave nothing away, but his eyes were a churning storm of deep thought.

A few seconds more, and then he finally opened his mouth. "I can't keep hiding behind you," he said. Before she could protest, he interrupted her. "Don't say I'm not, because I am. I think I might have a way of putting these guys on the defensive. Marco Torelli can't touch that money even to withdraw it and move it to another account, because he's worried it'll expose his account and all the nasty activities he's been buying with it. Same as I can't touch my own money without him finding me."

"Harry, where are you going with this?" she asked warily.

"Seth is good with broadcasting and audiovisuals. Rory's a computer genius. With your help, I can give this guy his worst nightmare, and he'll never know where it's coming from. I'm going to slip it to the press. Torelli might own some of the press, but he doesn't own *all* of them."

Elsa wasn't worried about her own team's safety. She could protect them with her power, if it came to that. Even with their arsenal of guns and goons, the Torellis would have no way of counteracting a force of nature.

But there was no denying the risk.

"Considering Miss Sternberg," she said, "I don't suggest beginning with *The Oklahoman*."

He glanced at her, eyebrows aloft. "I gotta be honest. I thought you'd think it was crazy."

"It is crazy, but you can't just keep running," she said. "Rory can scramble the message so there's no way to track the source. If we can't get it out to the press by that route, the team will help us broadcast the contents of that flash drive ourselves. Someone out there will help us fight them."

Harry turned his gaze on her as much as the road would allow. His stare was a lit match, and her longing for him rekindled. Finally, seeming to sense the tension in the atmosphere, he looked back to the road. "I have no way to pay you back for everything you've done for us...for me."

She warmed from the toes up, and not just because of his gratitude. She started to say something along the lines of *It's no big deal,* but the memory of his mouth on her skin came back to her, and stifled her response. For a few heavenly seconds, she was back in that hotel room, exploring his body as he explored hers. Feverish to the tips of her ears, she nodded and kept her gaze firmly forward.

Another several seconds went by. The air in the car crackled with tension, and she knew he sensed the turn of her thoughts. When he spoke, his voice was quiet and faintly hoarse. "Where to next?"

"Let's get some breakfast in Amarillo," she said. Her voice trembled a little, and she avoided looking at him.

All the rest of that day, they danced on eggshells around one another, never touching on anything more serious than a light joke or comment on the team's work. Elsa found herself relieved, to a point. Whenever she looked at him, it seemed those wheels were spinning in his head, searching for a way to make a clean break from the Torelli stranglehold. She wanted to reassure him, but she couldn't be sure a supportive touch of his arm would end there.

Breakfast was cheerful, almost buoyant. Rory had

gathered some excellent data, and Seth was near to bursting with the "wicked" footage he'd gotten of the storm. Rose beamed at him with an expression of utter infatuation. A little zing of fond empathy passed through Elsa at the sight. Once upon a time, she'd been in Rose's place—hopelessly in love with a boy from Sagerton, Montana...only that boy had been clueless about her affections.

Her smile faded. She'd never had what might be called a "real" youth. When her family died, she'd been sent off to foster care, left to the whim of which family might be willing to take her in.

When she, Cade, Morgan, and Ethan found themselves together at the Rathbone family home, they'd had a chance to grow up in a more stable environment.

But then came their powers.

Elsa remembered hurrying toward the mine behind the boys and her foster sister, not wanting to be left behind in their exploration. The boys bickered about the darkness inside the mine for a minute. Elsa remained at the entrance, wary of the inability to see inside, staring at the DANGER sign Ethan had kicked over when they entered. Boys were never afraid of anything, even when they should be.

The remembered *boom* blasted apart her recollections, and thrust her back into the present.

No, she thought, watching Rose's happy, glowing expression. Elsa had never had a childhood like that. After hiding her pain from the world, she'd had to hide her power, too. Rose shouldn't have to hide anything. She was a bright, beautiful girl with all the potential in the world.

Elsa glanced at Harry. And a family, too.

He caught her looking, and that tantalizing spark fired in his eyes again. Her insides tumbled over in a giddy somersault. Was it so wrong to hope for someone to come home to every night? To kiss in the mornings? To daydream with, just a little?

As soon as breakfast was over, they went back to business. Rory and Seth usually spent most of a day following a storm processing data and images. Elsa used the time to recover.

Among her foster family, she was the one who most often "punched" her gift, forcing it to its fullest extent to stop potentially damaging storms. Like any form of exertion, it tired her, but she found, to her surprise, that her power was stronger for it. She'd often wondered how far she could go before her ability failed. Then, in the face of a terrible new storm, she would realize with a dreadful chill that she hoped never to find out.

Watching Rose putter around The Beast's exterior with Seth, Elsa knew she couldn't go back and rewrite her childhood, no matter how she wanted to. But Rose was still a young girl, and even if it was only for one day, Elsa would help her have the time of her life.

****

"Absolutely not," Harry said. "An entire day in the city, after what happened in the paper?"

Sam must have sensed his agitation, because the Lab pushed his nose under Harry's hand. He ruffled the dog's ears automatically, then realized he'd done so.

Glancing at the dog, Harry gave an inward grunt of amusement. *I think we needed you more than you need us, mutt.*

Sam waved his tail and nosed at Harry's hand again. Scratching the Lab's head, Harry turned his stare back on Elsa, chock-full of worry.

"They're not going to look for us in a nail salon, Harry," she protested. She stood beside Rose, with an arm around her shoulders, the two of them together a wall of female solidarity. "I want this to be my birthday present to Rose. Nina and I will take good care of her, and you need a day off."

Rose said nothing, but that look of defiant hope was on her face again. She'd been wearing it more and more lately, now that she thought they had something to hope for. Harry begrudged it, resented it, and everything in between.

Mostly because he couldn't bring himself to buy into it, no matter how much he'd professed to having a plan.

Maybe the best protection for Rose now was to be away from him. The Torellis would look for him first. They might discount the threat of a thirteen-year-old kid as nothing. And if Rose had to be parted from him, her best possible protection was a woman with the power to call down storms.

He held Elsa's stare, simmering with irritation and worry...but the longer he looked, the more he saw the woman in his arms in every waking dream he'd had, in every spare millisecond since their night together.

His body prickled with awareness. He inhaled deeply, and then realized he was searching the air for her scent. He let the breath out in a rush. "Okay."

Rose squealed, then leaped across the room to crush him in a hug. "Thank you, thank you, thank you!"

Harry squeezed her back, his insides a mess. The

uneasiness had been a constant companion for so many months, he'd thought it a fact of life...but now, he had so much more to lose.

He glanced at Elsa, only a glance, because he didn't trust himself to let her go otherwise. "Be careful. Take your phone."

"Always am, always do," she said, sounding much more at ease than he.

Somewhere, he'd once heard a superstition that if you watched a person out of sight when they were leaving, you'd never see them again. As Elsa and Rose left his sight, he couldn't resist looking, superstition or not.

And if the back of his neck prickled wildly as he followed the departing swing of Elsa's braid with his eyes, well, maybe that was superstition, too.

****

This is going to be the best day *ever*," Rose said as she buckled her seat belt in the back of the wagon.

Elsa grinned at Nina, who sat in the passenger seat. "I think we could all use a little girl time, don't you?"

Nina, ever the party-crashing voice of reason, said, "Harry's right. We need to be extra careful, El."

With a playful scowl, Elsa demanded, "Is that why you came? Come on! Are you going to schoolmarm today, or are you gonna get your sassy-woman groove on with the rest of us?" She rapped the steering wheel in a go-get-'em gesture of encouragement.

Chuckling, Nina threw her hands up. "All right, you win. If these guys come in to the salon wanting a manicure and facial, though, I'm holding you responsible."

The undertone of concern in Nina's joke tugged at

Elsa's heart. Unable to keep the secret from her dearest friend, Elsa had confessed the story to Nina. Her team deserved to know what they'd gotten into, after all. And Nina, careful, worrywart Nina, had staunchly refused to let Harry and Rose leave.

Elsa reached across the seat to give her friend's hand a squeeze. "Thank you."

Nina smiled back.

Their first stop was a full-service beauty salon. Cade had never been grudging with the money he sent Elsa, and for once, she decided to use it for something frivolous. A spa day for a girl just turned thirteen was as good an excuse as any. When Rose saw the chandelier overhead and the marble flooring inside, her mouth opened in a big, round "O", and Elsa knew she'd hit the spot. "This is going to be so cool," the girl gushed.

Rose's enthusiasm was contagious. Laughing, Elsa approached the counter. "We want the works," she told the receptionist.

"Do you have an appointment?" the woman asked.

"No," Elsa said, then, tipping her head at Rose, leaned closer to whisper. "Her birthday just went by, and I want to treat her to everything you've got."

The receptionist glanced toward Rose, then smiled. "I think Lisanne is free. Let's get her set up in the back for a shampoo and rinse." With a bright smile, she beckoned to Rose.

With a little squeak of excitement, Rose hurried after the woman.

Nina sidled up to Elsa. "I have a little mad money, myself," she said. "I think if we're going to do the empowered-woman thing today, we ought to visit the clothing stores, too. I bet she'd love a new outfit."

Elsa gave Nina a grin. "And that's why I love you, Nina." She checked her own nails. "I guess it wouldn't hurt for me to have a slice of glamorous, too."

"Me, three."

They sat in the waiting area for the next available stylist. Elsa read two magazines without absorbing much of what was written in them. Every time she tried to focus on the words, she saw Harry's face instead. Smiling to herself, she picked up a family hairstyle catalog and paged through it, then realized she was comparing the men to Harry—an endeavor in which they failed to measure up.

A spa day. In the face of murderous men in pursuit of Harry and Rose. How silly it must have sounded to him...but if Elsa wanted a little time and breathing space to think about how she'd handle it when Harry disappeared on her—which he might still do—who could blame her for seizing this excuse to delay it?

The stylist called Nina, and after a while, Rose came back.

Glowing.

Elsa's mouth dropped open on an incoherent cry of delight.

Gone was the long brown ponytail Rose had worn that morning. In its place, she sported a shoulder-length style that framed her face perfectly in soft waves. She wore the faintest touches of blush, eye shadow, and lipstick. She held out her hands, and showed off a classy manicure in pink polish.

"You look so beautiful!" Elsa cried.

Rose pounced forward to squash Elsa into a hug. "You're the best, Elsa. Thank you so much."

"Come here," Elsa said. She pulled out her cell phone, then snapped a selfie, cheek-to-cheek with Rose. "That gorgeous 'do deserves some posterity, don't you think?"

After that shining success, Elsa was perfectly happy with a minor trimming of her hair. When they finished with the salon, the three headed for a mall to shop for a new outfit for Rose. At a boutique for teenagers, Rose found a selection of reasonably-priced outfits, no matter how Nina urged her to splurge. *Smart girl,* Elsa thought affectionately.

The twinge of pain when she thought about losing Rose hurt almost as bad as that plaguing her over Harry.

While she and Nina waited for Rose to come out of the changing room, Elsa checked the local news on her phone. In spite of her put-on poise that morning, she did worry—a little—about the Torellis. It couldn't hurt to keep an eye out.

Amarillo's major headlines covered yesterday's tornado, commenting on the city's good fortune in escaping it without a scratch. Nina, reading over Elsa's shoulder, looked up from the screen to give Elsa a wink.

Elsa chuckled, but even to her own ears, it sounded stilted. She wondered what tonight would bring. Would Harry want to be with her, or would the threat of Torelli pursuit pull him away again?

Her heart swooped, and she gave an inward sigh. In the two years she'd been chasing storms with Brian, Nina, Seth, and Rory, she hadn't wanted for anything. She'd been using her power to help people, with a team she loved.

But now that she'd had a taste of what could be, she feared anything less would never be enough.

She clicked on a video link to current coverage of the storm's aftermath, but didn't linger much on what the reporter said. Harry filled her thoughts. She imagined what his life must have been like before the Torellis entered it. Was he happy? Did he have someone special? He'd never mentioned. In fact, he rarely spoke of it. When he did, he talked as if that life had happened to another person entirely.

The television reporter said something about a related story. Elsa's attention jerked back to the screen.

"...a NOAA researcher, found by a neighbor in her home at about 7:30 this morning. The two had been set to carpool into work at the facility in Norman, Oklahoma. The neighbor discovered the door open, and found Sternberg on the floor with multiple gunshot wounds. She was taken to the regional hospital, where she was pronounced dead..."

A chill seized Elsa so hard, her teeth chattered. She lifted her stare to Nina, whose face had gone paper-white. They surged up as one from the seats by the changing rooms.

Rose came out wearing a new pair of jeans, fluffy socks, and a glittering, light blue T-shirt. "How do I look?"

Elsa struggled for composure as she sidled up to the girl. "You look absolutely beautiful, sweetheart, but we have to go. Don't bother changing out of the clothes. We'll take the tags off and buy them, just as you are."

Rose, too smart by half, sobered and asked, "Are they here in Amarillo?"

"I don't know, honey," Elsa said, "but there's a problem, and we've got to get back to the hotel right away."

"Harry?" she said at once. Panic flowed through her voice. "Tell me!"

"He's fine, as far as I know. We'll talk in the car. Not here."

As jubilant as their spree had been that morning, the mood now crashed through the floor. Elsa reeled with mental images of that poor murdered woman, worry over Harry and her team, and under that, a horrible, horrible guilt.

It's my fault. Malory Sternberg had been killed because Elsa had agreed that the woman could tag along with them, knowing Harry was a danger. Knowing that the more people who knew of Harry's presence with them, the more danger it would bring.

Nina seemed to sense her turmoil, because the older woman held Elsa's hand on the way to the car. Lurching under the weight of remorse, Elsa let her. She stumbled through the lengthening evening shadows on the way through the mall parking lot.

What kind of horrible person was she?

Nina drove, for which Elsa was thankful. Blindsided by self-reproach, she struggled to think straight. They sped back to the hotel as though the devil were riding their heels. When they raced up to their room, Elsa banged on Harry's door, breathless.

He jerked it open, and she bulleted inside with Nina and Rose right behind her.

"Malory Sternberg was shot, Harry," Rose blurted. "She's dead!"

Harry barely let the words leave his sister's mouth

before he was reaching for his duffel bag. A chill rippled through Elsa—partly dread, and partly the image of Harry walking out the door, never to be seen again. At least, not alive. She turned to Nina and Rose. "Give us a minute?"

Nina nodded. "Tell you what," she said, her gaze wise and thoughtful and so utterly lacking in rebuke that Elsa felt even worse. "I'll get her some dinner. You take your time." Grasping Rose's hand, she shepherded the worried girl from the room.

Trembling, Elsa closed the door behind them with a soft click. She rested her forehead against the cool wood, battling tears. She'd always thought her power was given to her with a purpose—to help others, to fix their problems as she'd been unable to fix her own as a little girl. Had she been so wrong? Were some things just unfixable, no matter what?

Was she forever destined to be on her own?

In the face of a woman's death, the selfishness of that thought horrified her. One tear spilled over to track hotly down her cheek. She let it fall.

She'd surrounded herself with her foster family as a girl. Later, when they left Hope Creek, she surrounded herself with her storm chasing team.

All because she was terrified to be alone.

"What have I done?" she murmured past a tightening throat.

"Nothing," Harry snapped, closer than she'd thought.

She turned to find him behind her, with his duffel on his shoulder and his guitar case in the other hand. "You gotta let me go, Elsa."

"This is all my fault."

He scowled. "Don't do that. Don't act like this has anything to do with you. This is all on *me*."

She caught her breath on a pained cry and reached out for him. "Please don't leave."

He sidestepped her reach. Anger flashed in his eyes. "I was wrong. The longer I stay, the more I chance hurting people." He dodged her again. His throat worked, and he gripped the strap of his guitar case so hard, his knuckles went white. When he brought his gaze up to hers, the agony there fisted a hand around her heart and crushed. "Especially you."

Elsa leaped forward, his censure be damned, and threw her arms around his neck. "I won't let you do this. I won't let you run again." Her tears spilled over, and she couldn't stop them. "I can't."

He stiffened in her arms. Afraid to see the determination that must be on his face, she hid her own against his shoulder.

Gently, he arched back. With one broad, warm hand, he tipped her face up so she had to look at him. The naked pain in his eyes sent fresh tears spilling down her cheeks.

An eternity of wordlessness passed between them. Elsa struggled for a decent breath, failed, tried again. "What are we going to do?" she whispered. "That woman... We have to tell the police what we know, Harry. They've got to know. Otherwise...it'll never be over."

Chapter Fourteen

It'll never be over, she'd said, but Harry heard what she meant by it, clear as day.

You'll never stop trying to leave me.

The look on her face chained him to the spot as iron and steel could never have done. Her body radiated a chill. He stepped closer, pressing against her, compelled to warm her. Straightening his arms, he let his duffel and the guitar slide to the floor.

Her arms slipped from his neck to his waist. "Please don't go. We'll figure this out. We have to figure this out."

The trembling in her voice brought him reaching for her face again. He cupped her cheek in his good hand, stroking away the wetness of her tears with his thumb.

She raised her gaze to his, her pleading blue eyes framed with damp lashes. A faint shudder traveled outward from his bones to his fingertips. More effective than any snare the Torellis could have devised, her need for him reached inside him and tied him to her by the very strings of his soul. The sensation stunned him with a wrenching tenderness, and a terrible, terrible fear for her life.

He touched his forehead to hers. "Elsa," he whispered, unable to say anything more because everything fought to be said at once.

Stifling a sob, she pulled him still closer, into a kiss. Harry returned the kiss willingly, freely, incapable of denying her. The more she wanted of him, the deeper he sank into a blissful abandonment of the desire to run. She pulled at his shirt. He tore it off over his head to fling it away. She tugged at his belt. He ripped the buckle free. She grasped at his zipper. He jerked it open. She touched him everywhere, and he gladly gave of himself. Anything, anything to stem that pain in her eyes, the loneliness that mirrored his own.

He kissed the tracks of tears on her face and breathed her in, savoring the way the clean scent of her washed away everything else. She tipped her chin upward. He pressed his lips to her throat, where her pulse beat madly under the tender skin.

With a muffled cry, Elsa arched against him. He drew her blouse upward, needing to touch her as she touched him. She reached for the hem, then slipped the shirt off to drop it beside his own.

Harry stroked her skin, painting swirls over her ribcage until she giggled through her tears. The sound eased the ache that resonated inside him at seeing her grief. Smiling a little, he pulled her against him. Her cool skin warmed against his chest. He stifled a groan. This wasn't to be rushed, and it wasn't about him.

They stood there like that, just holding each other. Harry pressed his face against her hair and breathed her in.

And then, gradually, he sensed it wasn't just about comfort anymore. The air thinned and heated and prickled, even for a man without her extraordinary power. He looked at her again, and found that heat echoed in her eyes.

She took his good hand in hers, then stepped backward toward the bed. "Lie down," she said.

He couldn't have disobeyed if he wanted. He raised a brow and gave her a skewed grin. "Yes, ma'am."

She shot his grin right back at him. He sat on the edge of the bed to admire the sight—gorgeous Elsa, platinum-blond Elsa, slim, curvaceous Elsa, smiling at him with the devil in her eye.

His Elsa.

His stomach clenched, and his erect cock twitched impatiently. He reached for her again.

She clapped a hand against his chest. "Down," she repeated.

He leaned back onto his elbows, watching her hungrily as she knelt beside the bed. When she tugged open the fly of his jeans to take him in her mouth, the hoarse groan he'd been holding back tore from his throat. He clenched his fists in the bedspread, shaking with eagerness even as she pinned him there with a heated look.

On fire, Harry threw back his head and gave himself over to the mind-bending feel of Elsa's mouth. With little more than the pressure of her hands, lips, and tongue, she owned him, body and soul. When she suckled him even harder, lightning bolts of pleasure blasted through him. With a huff of shock and need, he arched off the bed and bucked his hips.

Slipping her hand quickly upward over his belly, she pressed him back down.

Reaching, he panted, "Elsa, please. God. I gotta be inside you, honey."

With her mouth still around him, she gave him a look of wicked amusement. Sexy. As. Hell. Her nails dug into his belly, and he gave a low roar of frustrated desire. *No,* he ordered his lust. *This is her show. You stay fucking put.* But oh, God, he'd never done anything so hard in his life.

Swimming in euphoria, he almost didn't realize it when the first tremors foreshadowing an orgasm trickled down his nerve endings. *No no no no no!* his lust screamed.

Pushing her back, he hurtled off the bed, wild with need, then tore her pants down like an animal. Trapping her in his arms, he kissed her ferociously. When she matched him kiss for kiss, he snarled low in his throat and picked her up. Elsa circled his hips with her legs, and as he walked her over to perch her on the dresser, he drove into her with a howl of possessiveness.

Elsa moaned and dug her nails into his back. The sting made him buck harder. She trapped his lower lip in her teeth and ran her tongue along the edge, tasting of him. *A goddess,* he thought. She was no less than a goddess, sent to show him what heaven looked like, to torture him with glimpses of it when he knew he was bound only for hell.

She locked her feet together behind him, then drew his hips closer with her slender, muscular legs. Harry's arousal shot upward a few more notches. She wasn't one to shy from taking what she wanted. He kissed her like a man dying for lack of it. Her searching hands pushed the waistband of his pants downward. Harry paused only to shove them farther down, unwilling to let go of her for the barest second.

She broke the kiss to nuzzle in the hollow of his throat. "Harry," she gasped out, "oh, Harry, I'm going to—"

A flash of fire raced through Harry's veins. He crushed her against him and drove deep.

Elsa bit off a scream and clamped her legs around his back. He pistoned his hips, once, twice, again, again, again. Shuddering, she scored his back with her nails. Harry gave a hoarse shout as his release pounded through him like a bullet train. Breathless, he let the power of it roar down every nerve, that tantalizing, tormenting, too-fleeting feeling of being whole.

After that, only one thought remained to circulate in his obliterated consciousness: that hell on earth would certainly come to pass before he'd be able to let her go.

****

Shaking, Elsa rested her forehead against Harry's chest and tried to put all the scattered pieces of her senses back together. "Whoa," she whispered, spinning.

He chuckled. "Yeah, I'd say so." He tipped her chin up to kiss her, then circled her with his arms again to lift her against him. He turned toward the bed—and then toppled, hampered by his jeans, still bunched around his knees. She shrieked as they started to fall.

Harry spun around as they fell together on the bed, and then *smack*, the back of his head connected with the headboard.

Elsa landed hard on his chest. "Oh, my God, Harry, are you all right?" she cried.

He groaned loudly and rubbed at his scalp, blinking as if he were dazed. "That's gonna suck in the morning."

She patted at his face, worried, then kissed him. "Oh, Harry, jeez..."

He clapped his good hand over hers and gave her a

crooked smile. "Completely worth it."

She peered into his eyes, suspicious. He was always at his most lighthearted when he was feeling the most raw. "Are you sure?"

"Yep. Sure. Also sure I'm gonna need some pain relievers." She tried to get off him, but he clenched his arms tighter around her. "No. Stay. I like you here."

Everything that had happened before this rushed back to haunt her, and even though she smiled at him, her eyes welled with tears. She must have looked like an emotional madwoman.

Harry didn't even hesitate. Stroking her face, he stared straight into her eyes, then lifted his hands into the air in a half-hearted shrug. "You got me. I don't know where this crazy train's going, but it looks like I'm staying in the front seat with you."

Surprised, she elbowed up to peer harder at him.

He waved a finger in the air. "You. Me. Rose. Team Pemberley. We're all on it." The amusement in his eye faded, and with a breathless hitch, she glimpsed the real Harry. "I've got more to answer for than just my parents, now. We've got to stop them from hurting people. *I've* got to, whatever happens."

Warmth washed through her. She kissed him twice, brimming over with emotions she was too hopeful to name. "You're not doing it alone," she assured him, smiling away the last of her tears and letting determination fill all the spaces left behind. In the face of all that had happened, resolution only flowed through her all the stronger. Even her power simmered, as if it, too, were preparing for battle.

Through two years of storm chasing and all the dangers she'd endured with her team, she'd never faced a challenge that meant more to her. For the way he held her, for the look in his eyes, for the love of his little sister, she threw it all on the line, then and there.

Because a family was worth it.

Half an hour later, Elsa and Harry went to the room she shared with Nina and Rose. The girls had dogpiled on the bed with Sam and Seth, while Rory and Woz sat on the floor in front of the bed. Rory was watching the movie playing onscreen. Woz had tipped his head back against the edge of the bed and was snoring softly. The debris from a few recently attacked pizzas lay around the room. Sam's tail thumped the bedspread when he saw them.

Elsa noticed Harry stiffening at the sight of Rose and Seth sitting side-by-side with their legs touching, and talking in low voices. Then she noticed the textbook leaning against Seth's drawn-up knees. Mathematics.

Nina shot Harry a knowing, amused look. "I've been making them study."

Harry relaxed visibly and approached the bed to look over Seth's shoulder.

Rose glanced up at him. Her eyes, so much like Harry's, filled with concern and such a wise expression that Elsa's heart went out to the girl. "You okay?" Rose asked.

He nodded, but then Seth asked, "How do we catch these guys? What do we gotta do?"

"*Have to* do," Nina corrected, sounding irritable. Elsa almost smiled, but not quite.

Harry's good fist clenched convulsively. "You told them already?" he snapped at Nina.

"*I* told them," Rose said, her voice clear and

strong. "They need to know what's going on."

Woz snorted awake. He rubbed his eyes, then lumbered to his feet. "Oh, hey. Harry, or Hank, if you still want. Look, we want to help. We aren't letting you leave. Rose... She's this amazing whiz kid. She's better at computers than I am, and she knows more about current events than the reporters do. And you"—he looked a little awkward, which, for Woz, made his gangly frame seem that much more uncoordinated—"El really likes you, man. So, we're in."

She warmed to the affection in her teammate's voice, then transferred her watery, impossible-to-keep-back smile to Harry. "See?" she said.

Harry swiveled around, taking in all of the faces around the room. Every one of them stared back at him with a determination that reached inside her and squeezed.

With a sigh, Harry rubbed at his scalp. "My head hurts too much to argue," he mumbled.

Elsa's heart soared like an updraft. She grabbed Harry's hand and threaded her fingers through his.

He glanced at her. His incredible blue eyes held such a worried look, it almost broke her heart all over again, but then his shoulders relaxed a little.

Seth tossed aside the math book and clambered forward off the bed, nearly trampling Rory in his haste. "I know how we can use that flash drive. We can e-mail the contents to every newspaper in North America, and we'll scramble the IP address so it looks like it's coming from someplace in Canada. He'll think you got scared and left the country, right?"

Harry's eyes glazed over at Seth's excited speed-talk. To Seth, this was a puzzle, not a real, life-and-death situation. A little breath of chilly air tickled at the back of Elsa's neck.

"We're gonna set you up with some video, too, and scramble the source like the e-mails," Woz said. "You can do your thing, say what happened. They clap eyes on you, so there's no doubt it's you." Woz spread his hands. "Then, the thing goes viral, dude. No way to shut you up then. They aren't gonna silence the whole Internet."

Elsa saw the light leap up in Harry's eyes, the instant understanding of the possibilities, and a heart-wrenching hope. And when he looked to her, she thrilled to see that hope changing to a steely resolve.

She looked at each of her team members, and then Rose, brimming over with love.

She wasn't alone, and she would never be.

"You guys are amazing, you know that?" she said.

"Yep," Nina said. Her voice was bright, even though Elsa detected a note of concern. "Let's get some sleep tonight. Tomorrow, we start Operation: Litchfield."

****

Harry stared at the ceiling of his hotel room. After they'd wolfed down a few slices of pizza, Nina shooed him and Elsa right back to his room. After so many months of it, he ought to be getting used to not sleeping. He'd been restless all night, even though he'd had sex so good, his head should have exploded.

He shifted onto his side to gaze at Elsa's shadowy, sleeping figure beside him. Her hair and skin caught what little light there was in the room and glowed softly.

His throat tightened. Brave and beautiful and with

211

a heart as big as the world, this woman. How the hell did she do it, after everything she'd been through? The loss of her family. The arrival of a power she had neither expected nor wanted, something that would only give her the grief of hiding herself from the world?

What good had he done in God's eyes to earn this woman's notice? *Thank you,* he thought, skimming her side with his hand.

Strangely enough, even though he hardly slept, the arrival of morning found him reasonably alert. He rose from the bed before Elsa, trying to stay as quiet as possible. By the time he emerged from the shower, she was still asleep.

Gazing at her, he swallowed down an ache in his chest. That sunlit room in his mind's eye came back to him, filled now with the quiet of a drowsy Sunday morning, Elsa lost in slumber, and him, just watching her.

Worries assaulted him again. What if it all ended with the Torellis finding them and killing him, Rose, Elsa, even her entire team?

What if it didn't?

For more than eight months, he'd tried crushing any seed of hope under the weight of his responsibility for Rose. But even unheeded and neglected, that hope had stayed alive. The worries he'd carried all this time were familiar, almost rote. An old shoe he'd been reluctant to abandon.

Or maybe a ball and chain, dragging him down.

Maybe it's time, Litch. If this is the possibility, and the only alternative is to run forever, what are you waiting for?

Elsa stirred and opened her eyes. When she saw

him, a smile curved her lips. "What are you doing?"

He strode forward to slide a knee onto the edge of the bed. Leaning down, he kissed her. "Enjoying the view."

Her smile broadened into a grin. One slender hand slithered under the edge of the towel kilted around his hips.

Chuckling, he pulled back. "That's not gonna get us out of bed."

"And this is bad?"

Instant realization blasted through him like a charge of C4. He adored her, from her pale-blond head, to the tips of her painted toenails, to the sly-fox grin on her face, and most especially, the giving heart that beat under her exquisite breasts.

Oh, God, what if I lose her?

He lunged forward to kiss her again. She gave a little yelp of surprise, but snaked her arms around his neck. Harry threaded his hands into her hair, ignoring the injured finger, drowning his fears in the sensation of her.

Elsa met his kiss with equal enthusiasm, but when she pulled back at last, she searched his face. "Are you okay?"

He clenched his hands in the bed sheets. Pain speared through his injured fingers. He welcomed it this time—the electric shock that cleared his head. "As okay as I'm gonna be, as long as Marco Torelli's out there."

Elsa shifted, drawing aside the sheets, then sat up. The rising light picked out the svelte curves of her body. "It's going to be all right," she assured him.

He nodded gruffly, then reached for his clothes. Elsa stood with one last look at him before she went to the shower.

Harry jerked his clothes on with new hostility. Fate had a cruel way of giving him something, only to yank it back again. He didn't trust it for a second.

When they were dressed and ready to go, they met the team outside. Instead of finding them preparing for their next destination, however, Harry found Seth detaching The Beast's dashboard camera. "Been up since five," Seth told him. "Rose, grab the tripod from the back of the van, would you?"

"Sure," Harry's sister chirped. She set down the newspaper she'd been reading. Harry gave an inward smile. At least she'd been keeping up the habit.

Sam barked on seeing him. Tethered by his leash to the door handle of The Beast, he strained toward Harry, wagging.

He set his duffel and guitar case down, then patted the dog's head. "Up since five for what?"

"For your big debut, dude," Woz said, emerging from the van with an armful of cables.

Rory called from inside the van. "Feed's all set. Woz, where's that flash drive?"

Woz looked at Harry. "Moment of truth."

Harry turned his attention to his guitar case. With a sigh, he opened it, then pulled back a corner of the lining.

Sewn inside was the flash drive he'd been concealing for so many months. He peeled it out, then stared at it.

So much trouble for such a stupid little object.

But then he glanced up and saw Elsa, giving him that soft smile. *This is it,* he thought. He handed it over to Seth, who passed it on to Rory.

Seth pulled a sheet from the van, attached it to the side of the vehicle, and followed that up with a crate, arranged carefully front and center to the makeshift backdrop.

Harry sat down. Seth adjusted the camera on its tripod in front of him. "Rolling in five," he announced.

Harry clenched his good hand. He'd imagined what he would say for so long now that it was practically rehearsed. He stared at the blinking red light on the camera. Seth gave him the "go."

For a few seconds, Harry just sat there. He looked aside to Rose and Elsa, who gave him identical nods.

Harry turned back to the camera. "My name is Harrison Litchfield, Junior."

Chapter Fifteen

Marco Torelli hadn't had a day this good since his organization took control of an international bank chain. He'd just finished fishing the Internet for the Litchfield brats, and come up with the proverbial tournament bass. A blog on music featured a snippet on "Hank Rhodes" and his Gibson Les Paul, who'd been seen at a set in Colorado. The guitar had been seen afterward in Texas—exactly where that Sternberg bitch had been sniffing around with the storm chasers.

He sat back in his wing chair. His cell sat on the side table. He snatched it up to punch the speed dial, then waited until Vincent picked up. "Yeah," Vince said.

"We got him," Marco said, letting the satisfaction roll through his voice. "That sonofabitching, guitar-toting bastard is ours."

"You better turn on your television, Marco," Vince said, "'cause now, he's everybody's."

The first pang of alarm swished through Marco's blood. He snatched up the remote to flick the flat-screen on, then fought, swearing, through the channel guide to the local news.

Harry Junior's face greeted him. Marco wrestled with the volume, then turned it up.

Harry's voice rang through the living room. "...for the past eight and a half months, trying to protect what is left of my family from these men. The evidence I'm mentioning is now being made available to every major news facility in the United States, as well as to the FBI."

The man hesitated a moment, glancing downward. Then, he looked back at the camera. His pale-blue eyes seemed to stare right into Marco, who clenched his teeth. "Marco Torelli, I'm now speaking directly to you. I'm willing to stand in court to back this evidence up, and I challenge you to come forward. I'm done running." The camera clicked off.

For a few seconds, Marco just sat there, trying to soak it in. Had that little rich-kid *bastardo* just grown the balls to threaten him? *Him?* Marco found his tongue. "What the hell was that, Vincent?"

"The hits on the video are fucking crazy," Vincent said. "I've got Juno tracing it, but the source is scrambled. He can't tell where it's coming from."

"From the Midwest, you numbnut! You're there! Why the hell haven't you found this idiot and broken his fucking neck?"

"Hey, we're working on it. Some guy in a bar said he saw this sonofabitch playing that guitar."

"And while you're playing around, this sonofabitch had time to write me a video love note!" Marco shot out of his chair. Lucas rose to his feet beside him, with an expectant look and a wag of his tail in Marco's direction. "I'm coming there. I'll call you as soon as I get in, and you're picking me up. Since you can't get this punk, it's my turn, and so help me, Vincent, you're not gonna like me."

"Marco—" Vincent began, but Marco clicked his phone off.

Marco looked at the dog, then gave a derisive sniff. "That's the thing about me, Lucas. Why I stay on top. I ain't afraid of my own dirty work." Witnesses needed to be silenced, no question. Witnesses who'd deprived him of billions in offshore money needed a whole different kind of management. He stuffed his phone in his pocket, then strode out of the room with the dog on his heels, already picturing the many pleasurable ways he'd finish off the Litchfield loose ends, once and for all.

****

When Seth gave him the all-clear, Harry slumped with his elbows on his knees, and stared at the ground. Elsa started to worry he'd gone into some sort of shock.

Rory ducked out of the van, then handed Harry the flash drive. "All set, man. I made copies, but I don't think they're gonna be necessary anymore. I just e-mailed the file to twenty-five newspapers and all the major networks, with links to the video on YouTube."

"YouTube?" Harry repeated. His face was blank, like a victim of a severe storm whose house had just been flattened before his eyes.

Elsa hurried forward. "Give him a minute, Rory, okay?"

Rory blinked, then took at second look at Harry. "Yeah. Sure," he said. He disappeared inside the van again.

Crouching in front of Harry, she rested her hands on his knees. "We're going to get through this."

His breath exploded from his lungs in the mockery of a laugh. "If I didn't have a neon bull's eye on my back before, I sure as hell do now."

She squeezed his knee and gave him a sympathetic

look, unable to think of anything else to do or say.

Harry reached up to stroke her face. "So this is it."

"Yeah," she murmured, leaning into his touch. "But we're going to be with you. There won't be one second when you don't have a—"

"Bodyguard?" he finished for her, then gave another biting laugh. "Who's going to bodyguard all of you?"

A shadow fell across them. Elsa looked up to find Rose standing beside them. Sitting back, Elsa allowed the girl some room.

Harry took his little sister's hand. "We're in for it, Rosie," he said. The undercurrent of tension and protectiveness in his voice pulled at Elsa.

"We weren't going to be able to run from them forever," Rose said. Her hand shook a little in her brother's grasp. "If we can't stop them ourselves...at least others will be on to them now."

The pain in Harry's eyes intensified. "Kid, you haven't even lived, and you're talking like you're going to die."

Rose shook her head. With a smile that crushed Elsa's heart, she said, "I've seen the country. I know more about current events than I ever learned in class. I even got to go on a field trip with the coolest science team *ever*." She reached for Elsa's hand.

Elsa gave Rose's hand a squeeze. "Why don't you take Sam and Seth for a short walk, Rose? Just to the edge of the lot. I think your brother needs a little time."

With a nod, Rose took the dog and left. Harry watched her go. "Glad to see one of us is still optimistic."

"You should be, too," Elsa reminded him. "Yes,

you tweaked their noses, but now, you have a real chance at stopping them, Harry. All of that money? They can't touch it now."

"Okay, *two* of you are optimistic," he said.

"And why not?"

"Because it's not the money I give a crap about!" he burst out. "They're going to end us before the news even gets a chance to use what we sent them. And when they're done with us, they're gonna come after you and your team. It's not going to stop, Elsa. This was a huge mistake."

Rory's shouting from inside the van interrupted her response. "Ho-o-o-o-ly crap. Woz, get in here!"

Woz launched himself into the van. Curious, Elsa ducked around the back to look inside from the tailgate.

Woz and Rory were huddled in front of Rory's bank of computer equipment. "What is it?" Elsa asked.

Rory turned a flabbergasted look on her. "*It* is the mother of all supercells...and on my models, it's forming just outside Wichita. Like, obliterating half the state. This is going to be huge, El. If we stomp on it, we might make the storm before it's full-blown."

She levered herself into the van with one leap, then scanned the monitor. Her power plucked at her nerve endings on seeing the data alone.

Oh, no.

If there were a worst possible time for a storm this big, now was it. What if she drained her power, and had nothing left to protect Harry and Rose? Two people—two she cared for desperately—against thousands.

"We gotta go," Harry said.

She whirled around to find him standing behind her, looking past her at the computers. His expression held none of the worry she'd seen only moments ago. Now, that electric-blue gaze was calm, even resolute. "Harry, are you sure?"

He nodded. "We can't stop living, Elsa."

Her team passed a few anxious glances back and forth. Clearly, they worried now about Harry and Rose as much as she did. For that, she loved them all the more.

Rising on tiptoe, she kissed Harry's cheek. "Let's go, guys. Hitting the road in five."

Rose hurried back with the dog. Harry scooped his sister and Sam toward The Beast. Elsa rushed toward her car.

Harry beat her to the driver door. "Give me the keys."

"What, you're driving?"

"I'm not the walking storm radar. What happens if you need your hands free to punch it when we drive into this thing?"

A little prickle of nerves crawled through her belly. She'd never "punched it" on a storm that big. She didn't know if she could.

But now was not the time for nerves. She nodded and slid into the passenger seat.

Her cell rang, and she picked up without looking at the caller ID.

"Stay in contact. Save your battery and use the CB instead," Nina said before Elsa had a chance to answer. "We'll be behind you until we get visual on this thing, then The Beast will take point."

Elsa glanced at Harry. If he had any reservations about letting his little sister ride into what was coming, he didn't show them. No doubt it was preferable to a face-off with the Torellis.

She checked the clock on her cell. They had roughly a six-hour drive ahead of them. "We're going to be a while getting there. Let me know if you get tired. We'll switch off," she said.

"I'm fine," he responded, with that eagle-eye stare on the road.

"You don't look fine."

"I'm as fine as I'm going to get."

With a little sigh, she stared at the wallpaper on her cell: Nina and her, grinning against a backdrop of greenish sky. She glanced out the windshield at what was currently a powdery blue, dotted with fluffy clouds.

"How long do we have until this supercell thing hits Wichita?" Harry asked.

"Rory's models operate sometimes as much as twelve hours ahead. Sometimes we get there, and it's nothing."

"I don't think this is going to be one of those times," Harry said.

After a few minutes of silence, she couldn't stand it anymore. "Harry, say something. You've got to be going crazy right now."

He hitched a shoulder. "How would that help? I did what I did, and now that it's at twenty-five newspapers and YouTube, I can't exactly take it back."

"Do you want to?"

His jaw clenched. That laser stare remained on their route for a few seconds, then he glanced in the rearview mirror. "No. I want her safe, for good, and I want you safe, too."

Warmth filled her. "I will be. *We* will be."

"I don't have your confidence," he said.

His tension burbled on the air like the contents of a simmering pot, all the way to Kansas. Elsa's power answered it with fitful sparks that she stamped down with stubborn concentration. He wouldn't chase her off, not now.

The sky took on a greenish-gray hue as they approached Wichita. "Showtime," she murmured. "Hang back. Let The Beast go ahead."

He did, and all three vehicles lined up along the shoulder on the outskirts of the city.

"How do you want to handle it, El?" came Rory's voice over her CB. "It hasn't revved up yet—just high winds. I'm looking at hail, lightning, and hard rain on my models. Slow-moving, probably going to linger and make a big mess."

She glanced at Harry, who was watching The Beast like a man facing the gallows. "Get your numbers," she said finally, "and do it fast. I'm going to punch it before it gets worse."

"El, are you sure?"

She scanned the churning clouds. "If it gets bigger than this, I might not have the chance. I'd rather knock it down while I'm able."

"Copy that. I'll keep the line open in case you need us."

Her skin tingled all over. Elsa shivered, unwilling to admit even to herself that she might have met her match.

Could she stop it? Would she even make a dent?

With a resolute deep breath, she put her hand on the door handle.

Harry's attention snapped from the boiling sky onto her. "What are you doing?"

"I have to be in it to stop it," she reminded him.

"And what's wrong with leaning out the window like last time?"

"This is a little bit bigger than last time," she muttered, opening the door. She stepped into the weedy grass at the roadside, then shut the passenger door behind her.

Now that she was outside, the air swirled around her body, whipping her power into an irritable frenzy. She stamped her fears into the bottom of her belly.

Harry emerged from the car, hurrying around it to join her. "You can't do this. It's nuts, even for you."

"Do I have a choice?" She pointed toward the Wichita skyline. "Do *they* have a choice?" Stalking into the field by the road, she called on her power. When it sputtered, she shook out her hands and pushed her fears farther down.

Harry rushed after her. "What happens if this thing gets out of hand and we need to get out of here fast, Elsa?"

"Give me three minutes, and we'll find out if it's going to get out of hand." She glanced at him, and the worry on his face pierced her heart. "You should head back to the car, just in case."

"Like hell I will." The vehemence in his tone matched the look in his eyes. He stayed right beside her.

Elsa shook her hands again, then turned her gaze to the roiling cloudscape. Harry's presence edged into the sphere of her power, fizzing on its perimeter with a palpable reminder of his worry. She shifted her attention to the storm, but even as she let loose her power, his nearness blurred her focus with reminders of the nights she'd spent in his arms.

Heaven, those nights...and no matter what happened now, no one could take them away from her.

Concentrate! she ordered herself. Eventually, even Harry's nearness faded behind a years-long habit of putting her power at the forefront. Warily, she increased the stretch of the "sphere" that shivered, invisible but palpable, in the air around her. She tested the edges of the storm with her power, feeling out its breadth and width and intensity as carefully as any specialized radar.

She could handle this, she realized with a joyful skip of her heartbeat. The storm hadn't built to full strength, yet. It would be broad, but not so strong she couldn't at least take the edge off it with her ability.

But she'd better do it quick. With a deep breath, she expanded her power's reach.

Then Harry swore.

Her power snapped back into her body like a rubber band. On its heels came an icy chill. "What's wrong?"

"Elsa, get back to the car. Now!" He swooped an arm around her, then pushed her toward her vehicle without waiting for her response.

The sunny bronze of his skin had paled. Alarmed, she glanced down the road, in the direction of his piercing stare.

Trundling toward them from the city was a shiny black Cadillac.

"Christ help us," he snarled as he ran toward the car behind her. "He's found us already."

****

Elsa grabbed the keys from him, and Harry didn't

bother to argue. His mind had splintered into a hundred directions as soon as he saw that damned car. God knew he wouldn't be able to navigate.

Rose. Elsa. The entire team, besides—all in danger now, all because of him. The Torellis had found him faster than he ever would have believed. What had that entire almost-year been for? He'd only condemned more people.

What the hell made him think he had a chance against them?

At least, he thought grimly, someone else might have enough evidence to stop them now.

Inside the car, he snagged the CB off its hook. "Rory, Woz, we've got problems. That Caddy belongs to Vince Torelli. Get The Beast out of here."

The instant he said it, The Beast leaped ahead down the road. With his heart pounding double-time, Harry watched as it roared past the Caddy toward Wichita. The Caddy screeched to a halt in the middle of the road. The couple of cars approaching behind it peeled to a stop with horns blaring.

With an expression like wrought steel, Elsa stomped on the gas. Her car skidded away from the side of the road after The Beast.

"Don't follow!" Harry shouted. "Make a U-turn, now!"

She didn't need to be told twice. Her car swerved onto the opposite shoulder, then sped southward down the road.

Without asking, Harry knew she'd followed his train of thought. Alone, the bulletproof Beast would be safer from pursuit than they would.

As for their own safety, the window was closing

fast.

"El?" Rory called over the CB.

"Do it!" she called. "Nina, Rory, get us an access road, quick! We'll cut around the city."

The van roared after them, just ahead of the Caddy. Nina's voice came over the CB, impressive in its calm. "Let us by, El. We've got a side road that swings back southwest of here."

Elsa slowed long enough for the van to surge ahead of them, then pass by and race ahead. Harry glimpsed an expression of iron determination on Rory's face as they went by. "You're all going to get killed for me," he muttered.

"You're family," Elsa said.

He snapped his head around at her tone. She gripped the steering wheel so hard, her knuckles were bone-white against her skin. Her eyes sparked with a ferocity he'd never seen.

When he didn't say anything, she glanced at him. That ferocious look wrapped around him and sank into his bruised soul. "You're family," she repeated, "and we will fight for our family."

In her furious tone, he heard the echo of his own fiery resolve, which had burnt down during these many months, turning to bitter ash. The flame in his heart flickered, rekindled. He glanced in the side view mirror. The Caddy pursued them, a couple of cars back, like a serpent waiting on its chance to strike. Checking ahead, he saw the van bearing left onto a dirt road. Dust spewed up from its wheels on the still-dry path.

Harry checked the position of the Caddy again. Still with them, still a few lengths back. The Beast would now be stretching the distance between them.

Maybe. Just maybe.

Harry studied the sky, recognizing a worsening storm in the billowing clouds. If Elsa had a chance of stopping this before, that opportunity was long gone. "Elsa?"

"I know, I know." She veered around a pothole, still following the van. "Bigger problem."

A cluster of furniture-store warehouses loomed up on their right. "Stop here. Let me out."

"Are you kidding?" she cried.

Harry picked up the CB. "You guys keep going."

"Right," Rory responded. The van raced away.

Harry turned to argue with Elsa, but then the choice was torn out of their hands. The sky opened, and golf-ball-sized hail poured down.

She ground her teeth and careened the car into the field toward the warehouse. The terrain forced her to slow down, but it did the same for the still-pursuant Caddy. "I'm not letting you out of this car," she snarled. "He'll shoot you as soon as he gets the chance. That's if this hail doesn't knock you flat with a concussion first."

As they approached the warehouse, Harry lunged over the seat for a spare hardhat. "I'll take my chances." He snapped the hardhat on. Before Elsa could protest, he unbuckled his belt, opened his door, then hurled himself out of the vehicle.

The ground surged up at him, and he remembered at the last moment to tuck himself into a ball and protect his injured hand.

Slam. He rolled end over end like a tumbleweed, thankful for the scrubby grass that cushioned his fall. The moment he rolled to a stop in a patch of weeds, he sprang to his feet, and then bolted toward the warehouses.

The rev of an engine spurred him on faster. A glance behind him confirmed that both Elsa and the Caddy were following. Hail smacked down into the dirt all around him, pelting his back and helmet. Harry sprinted for the overhang of the nearest warehouse.

"Harry!" Elsa shouted, bringing her car around to where he stood. "Get back in the car!"

"No," he said, waving her on. "Get out of here, Elsa. Go get Rose and get out of here!"

Instead of listening—and some part of him had known she wouldn't, even as he urged her to go—she got out of the car. The hail bulleting against the side of the warehouse and bruising his body didn't even touch her.

"What the hell are you doing?" he demanded. "Get back in that car and go!"

"Not gonna happen," she said. She came to his side, and the hail pelting him gave way. She faced down the oncoming Cadillac with no trace of the fear gripping Harry's heart in a punishing crush.

Harry tore the hardhat off his head, then flung it in the dirt. He snatched her hand, then bolted around the side of the warehouse looking for a door. It was the weekend, so the parking lot was deserted except for a couple of lonely work trucks getting battered by the hailstorm. Gunshots rang out, and he flinched, but kept going.

"Harry, I can stop him," Elsa panted, running beside him.

"You gonna blast him with a tornado before he runs you down in that car?" he snapped. "You can't even call off the storm coming at us right now!"

She jerked on his hand, forcing him to stop as they reached a loading door. "I may not be able to stop it, but I can deflect it," she said.

The Caddy's engine roared, and for a second, that often-repeated dream filled Harry's vision—the one where he was running, running—always running, and never getting any farther away from the danger. The same fear clenched his gut. The same rust-and-iron taste filled his mouth.

He let go of Elsa long enough to try the loading door. It had been lowered, but not latched. He thanked what was obviously his last damned lucky star and jerked the door upward enough to drag Elsa inside, then slammed the door back down.

There was a screech of tires outside. Gripping Elsa's hand, he ran through pallets of boxed furniture.

No weapon to defend himself. Nothing to use as collateral. Now that he'd given up the contents of the flash drive, what possible reason could the Torellis have to keep him alive for one more second?

What reason would they have to leave Elsa unharmed?

He swore, half under his breath, and pulled her behind a tower of crates. "You've got to go, Elsa, please," he whispered.

"Not a chance. We started this together, Harry, and we'll end it that way, too."

Pained, he touched her face. "Please," he said again, willing his words to break through her stubbornness. "I'm not worth your life."

Her mouth fell open. The hurt in her eyes was unquestionable. "You don't get it, do you?" she murmured.

There was no time to answer. The screech of the loading door rang through the warehouse. "Harrison Litchfield!" shouted a man.

Not Vincent. Harry knew the Torellis' muscle by voice. He'd filed away everything he knew about the man for so long he could've written a biography on the subject.

No. The voice now ringing through the warehouse with vehement curses belonged to Marco Torelli.

Swallowing back bile, Harry closed his eyes. Too late. Too damn late.

"Harry." Elsa's voice cut through his despair like a red-hot sword.

He opened his eyes to find her glaring at him. Her hair lay loose around her shoulders like a pale-gold mane, and her eyes, impossibly blue, sparked with fury.

Good God, she was beautiful.

She put her cell phone into his hand. "We're going to make it, and we're going to use that storm," she murmured. "Call 911, and then get to the car."

"No. *No,*" he snarled, as loudly as he dared. He gripped her hand and stared desperately into her eyes.

And then, as he looked at her, everything fell into place. He wouldn't be leaving her, any more than she would leave him, because she was right. They belonged together, and had belonged together from the moment she walked into that bar. His run from the mob, her crazy power, the three-ring circus that had been their lives since they first met...

None of it mattered, because his whole life was in her eyes.

Keeping his gaze on her face, he raised her hand to

his lips, and kissed it, very, very gently. The stubborn look faded from her face, replaced by such a wondering look that Harry's heart wrenched in his chest.

"Litchfield!" Marco screamed again.

The threat in the man's voice hardly pierced Harry's awareness. He wanted to show Elsa everything about his life—everything he really was, instead of the broken-down blues singer he'd had to be all this time. He wanted to share the flash and flurry of society life in Los Angeles.

With a sudden, completely incongruous grin, Harry hit the talk button on Elsa's phone. "Come with me," he told her. "I have an idea."

Chapter Sixteen

Elsa hurried along behind Harry through the towering stacks of crates, and forklifts looming like steel monsters in the dim light. Moments before, Harry had worn the expression of a man on a walk to the electric chair. Now, the light in his eye was practically maniacal with determination.

Had the Torellis finally succeeded in driving him to madness?

They rounded the corner of a pallet reaching well over their heads. Elsa spied what Harry was aiming for—another loading door. Opening it would surely create such a screeching noise that the Torellis couldn't help being alerted to their position.

Harry didn't hesitate. He tugged her after him, his big frame surprisingly soundless as he crossed the floor in a scurry like a soldier across enemy territory.

Which it was.

A crash sounded through the warehouse as a crate went spilling over. "Where the hell are you, you rich-kid bastard?" screamed their pursuer. "I'm gonna rip your head off and make your kid sister watch! Don't think I won't catch her, Litchfield!"

She and Harry reached the loading door. Harry grasped the handle and waited. Alarmed, Elsa stared at him, but he only held a finger to his lips.

There was another crash, and Harry hoisted the

door as soon as it happened. The racket in the warehouse covered the screech of the rising door. He shooed Elsa out, then emerged himself. He lowered the door, and Elsa cringed at the squeal of the wheels on their tracks. Hail continued pelting down, rattling against the pavement as they sheltered under the overhang.

To Elsa's shock, he dialed a number on the cell. "Reggie? Yeah, it's me. Listen, I don't have time to talk. First person who gets to Wichita gets an exclusive interview. They can get my position using this cell number. Talk to you soon." He clicked off the cell.

"What was that?" Elsa murmured, afraid to speak any louder.

"That was my family publicist. She's smart. I bet she'll have someone here in seconds."

"Your family has a *publicist?*"

He grabbed her arm and hurried her toward her car, still sitting in the lot with its engine running. The automatic "weather bubble" Elsa had always been able to create formed around them, shielding them from the hail now pelting everything else.

When they got closer to her car, Elsa saw that the Torellis had shot out all four of her tires.

Harry's plan was clear enough—avoid capture or getting shot—until the media arrived. When they did, the Torellis would be at a loss to do anything, because any move they made would be on film, one way or another. She'd known these men were dangerous, and she'd agreed to help knowing that, but the sight of her car sitting on those blown-out tires threatened to steal away her confidence. She'd stopped tornadoes, yes, but bullets?

She let go of him to flex her fists. "How long do you need?"

The look that blazed in his eyes sent her heartbeat speeding. "As long as we can get," he answered. "Your keys, quick."

She tossed them, and using them, he popped her tailgate open, then scrambled inside for the tire iron.

While he was doing that, Elsa summoned her ability. It coursed through her body.

Now or never, she told herself. She stepped behind the relative safety of the car, then reached out into the atmosphere. Her skin tingled with the storm's increasing fury. Its strength sent flutters of doubt through her. With effort, she avoided looking at the blown-out tires. The air snapped with ferocity, a nebulous, teeth-gnashing monster of a tempest.

Maybe she didn't have to contain this storm. Maybe she could make it work *for* her and drive it toward the men trying to hurt Harry and Rose.

"Harry," she murmured, "stay here with me." She raised her hands, and at that moment, the loading door began rolling up.

The opening into the warehouse yawned like the mouth of a hellish beast. No one appeared. "Litchfield!" came a shout. "I got a Glock Nineteen here, with a loaded clip. You got—what, a weather girl and a chip on your shoulder?"

Marco and Vincent Torelli emerged from the warehouse. The leader of the Torelli mob gave them a crocodile grin as he pointed his handgun at them. Fear tugged at Elsa's nerves as Marco stalked out into the parking lot with the slow, deliberate motions of a man who thought he'd already won the standoff.

Elsa stared at the gun, transfixed. It absorbed her focus, taking up the whole world. For a moment, she forgot everything except the cold fact that death came from that tiny opening at the end of the barrel.

"You're an idiot, Litchfield," Marco said. He laughed and spread his hands, as if chastising a pal for a bad joke...but his next words were deadly serious as he and Vincent retrained their guns on Harry. "What's gonna stop us from drilling you both?"

Elsa's power crackled and spat, rushing through her, her only thought now to stop them from ending Harry's life. "I am," she said and, stretching out her power, sent the hailstorm flying at them.

The men cringed back from the onslaught. With grim satisfaction, she watched them retreat into the opening of the warehouse.

Harry tossed the useless tire iron onto the ground, then scrambled around inside the car. Wondering what he was doing, fearful the men would find a way around her power, she focused everything she had on sending as much of the nebulous hailstorm as possible at the men. They were too busy protecting themselves from it to notice her or aim at Harry, but how long would that last? Would the hail hold out, or would it cease as hailstorms so suddenly did, and leave her with nothing to stop them?

Harry emerged from her wagon with Woz's paintball gun and a fishing knife. "What are you going to do with those?" she protested.

"It may not look like much," he said, "but if it's all I've got, I'll aim for his eyes with it."

Endless seconds went by as Elsa stared at the open loading door. Her heartbeat sped frantically. She'd faced danger before, but never like this. *If Cade and Morgan and Ethan knew what I was doing right now...* She stamped the thought down, trying not to shake.

A prickling charge shuddered down the back of her neck.

Oh, no.

Elsa had no time to shout a warning. She barely had time to turn. Lightning split the darkening sky just as thunder crashed, leaving her ears ringing. Her skin fizzed with static. Wind swirled around them, rocking her car on its flat tires. Harry crouched against the car under its fury, even as Elsa hurried closer to him, using her natural shield to protect him from the storm. "We've got to get out of this," she said. "I don't know if I can keep it under control."

Anvil crawlers raced from cloud to cloud—rivers of lightning pouring across the sky, one right after another. The ominous rumble of thunder echoed in Elsa's bones. Looking up, she saw a circular swirl in the purple-black clouds. The wind howled around them. Rain poured down with the hail.

The bear's cage was going to settle right over them, with only her feeble power to protect them both from its fury.

And then the gunfire started up again.

*****

Harry knew that one way or another, he had to get Elsa out of there. He crouched behind the car with her, trying to avoid flying bullets that smacked into the corrugated-tin wall of the buildings behind them. He tried ducking around the front of Elsa's wagon to aim the paintball gun at eyes or faces, but gunshots forced him to retreat again. He clamped down on his nerves.

"If I don't make it, Elsa, I want you to take care of Rose."

"What?" she snapped. The still-shocking glow of her hands sputtered, then shone brightly again. She sent another spray of hail toward the warehouse.

"You heard me," he said, firing a shot with the paintball gun. A bitten-off swear word told him he'd hit one of the men. He had to get closer, he realized. Had to steal one of their weapons or disarm them, otherwise, this was only going to end with him and Elsa dead. He glanced at her, so beautiful, fighting so bravely, and his heart swooped at the mental image of her lying lifeless on the pavement.

Oh, God, anything but that. "Cover me," he said, and sprang up to run.

"What? Harry!" Elsa cried.

He kept running, aiming for the wall of the warehouse to the side of the open loading door. Gunshots blasted through the air. His breath scoured his throat, and his heartbeat pummeled against his ribs. Outside Elsa's protective sphere, the rain and hail pounded his body. Wind screamed in his ears.

Another volley of swearing reached him, and just as suddenly as it had resumed, the gunfire ceased again. He made it across the lot with his blood surging frantically. *Litch, you're out of your mind, you know that. Most of all, because you've been talking to yourself for the better part of a year.*

The wind roared, stealing his breath. Flattened against the side of the warehouse, Harry inched along toward the loading door with one eye on the sky. Any minute now, that circling mass of black clouds over their heads would stretch into a funnel that would blow them all to hell. He'd seen Rory and Woz talk about it often enough.

The hailstorm continued pounding the sides of the warehouse. The noise rang in his ears, almost as deafening as the gunshots had been. They never talked about that in the movies, how the abuse on a person's eardrums made a firefight even harder. He couldn't hear the movements of the Torellis, and though they probably couldn't hear him, he worried.

The revving of an engine over the racket of the storm brought his attention snapping up from the loading door.

The Beast careened into the parking lot. Dimly, muffled, Harry heard Elsa yell something, but the hulking weather tank skidded to a stop just short of the loading door. The driver's side doors opened. "Everybody in!" Nina called.

Elsa swore loudly and raised her hands as if to call down the storm itself.

Shouting at her to make a run for it, Harry bolted toward The Beast. He expected to be shot any second, but enraged barking filled the air under the shriek of the wind.

Teeth like daggers closed over Harry's left forearm. Agony speared him and tore a scream from his throat. He rounded on the Doberman attacking him, but the dog leaped at him and knocked him off his feet. Harry toppled over. He slammed to the pavement with his ears still ringing. The paintball gun clattered away.

A second black shape reeled through the air at them. Harry expected another Doberman, and teeth closing on his throat, but it was Sam. The Lab's bulk hurled against the Doberman, and the two dogs tumbled away in a snarling, snapping mass of black fur.

Ignoring his pain, Harry scrambled on his belly for the paintball gun. Lightning flashed like a strobe light, illuminating his waking nightmare. He couldn't hear. He couldn't see through the pelting rain. He was going to die here in the dirt, after everything he'd gone through.

There really was no protecting the people he loved.

He swung onto his feet in a fury and glared at The Beast. Why had they come back? What the hell was he doing this for, if not to keep Rose and Elsa's team safe?

He swiveled to shoot for the Doberman attacking Sam, but there was no telling the two dogs apart in that bundle of teeth and growls.

Marco Torelli emerged from the warehouse, aiming his gun. "Give it up!" he shouted over the screaming wind.

Harry froze where he stood. *This is it,* he thought. Time lost meaning. An eternity could have passed while he stood motionless, but he noticed nothing except the cold eyes of the man who'd stolen away his life.

A blur of motion finally caught his attention. Harry turned to find Elsa running at him with her hands poised as if to shove an armful of air at Marco. Her eyes blazed with anger. "Elsa, no!" he cried. He bolted toward her, trying to get between her and the gun.

A wall of wind knocked him back, and the world blew apart around him. Debris reeled through the air. Dimly, he realized Elsa had brought the force of the storm down on the Torellis.

Harry staggered toward the warehouse, aiming for Marco, who stumbled back under the force of the gale.

Even as his mind screamed a warning at the sight of Marco's gun, he advanced.

Someone grabbed him from behind, and an arm like iron locked around his neck.

Vincent.

Harry snatched at the man's hand. He had height on Vincent, but not as much muscle. The big man's arm choked off his air. In desperation, Harry lunged forward and bent, using his hips to drive Vincent off his feet and over his head. The man's bulky frame sailed over Harry and onto the pavement. The man's grip fell away.

Coughing, Harry aimed a kick for Vincent's face while looking frantically for the man's gun, but Vincent seemed to have lost it. Vincent rolled in time to avoid the kick. He snatched Harry's leg as it came down, and pulled Harry down with him.

End over end he rolled with the Torelli hitman. Harry heard someone shouting, muffled by the storm and his ringing ears, but he couldn't spare a look. Vincent's hands went for his throat again, and Harry flung his own up to grip the man's wrists. Pain roared through his injured hand at the contact. Doggedly, he shoved the sensation aside and used all of his weight to fling Vincent off him.

The man sprawled onto his back. Rose's livid face appeared overhead, and she stomped a foot down right between the man's legs.

Vincent howled and crumpled. Harry swung upright, intending to shoo her away, but with that same fierce look, she swung Elsa's tire iron at Vincent's face. Harry heard a crunch, and Vincent's nose gushed blood. "Back off!" she screamed.

With a moan, Vincent covered his face and rolled

into a ball away from them.

Holy crap, Harry thought, stunned for an instant. *Did my sister just do that?* He broke out of his fog to hurry her back to The Beast. "Go, let's go!"

"Not so fast, Litchfield!" Marco shouted above the shrieking wind and snarling dogs.

A high-pitched yelp snagged Harry's attention. Sam was lurching to his feet, ears back, hackles bristling. The Doberman cowered against the building with its tail between its legs.

"You son of a bitch!" Marco yowled. He raised his gun at Harry and cocked the trigger.

A whirlwind of dust and fine stones leaped up between them. Marco threw up an arm to protect his eyes, and Harry did the same. "Get to The Beast!" Elsa shouted.

He waved Rose back to the weather tank. "Sam!" he called over the noise of the storm.

The Lab trotted to his side, limping a little. Blood smeared his black fur. Harry opened his mouth to order the dog back to the vehicle, but a flash of motion caught his eye.

Marco raised his gun at Harry again.

Unarmed. Exposed. Point-blank. So this was how it would end. With everyone else he'd tried to protect, who'd defended him, still in danger after he was gone.

He curled his lip. *Hell, no.*

Harry gathered himself, then bolted straight for Marco, right through the whirl of Elsa's storm.

The wind rose to a scream. Harry saw the gun, but he didn't care.

There was a horrible rending sound, like sheet metal getting shredded, and the warehouse roof tore back like a peeled orange.

Marco's eyes bulged. His mouth fell open in a mask of horror. As Harry reached him, he lunged and tore the gun away, but Marco paid no attention. Harry stepped back, aiming the weapon.

"Harry, get out of there!" Elsa's voice sounded far away under the chaos and the savage, pounding echo of Harry's heartbeat in his ears.

Marco's mouth worked. He crossed himself. "What the hell is she?"

"Payback," Harry spat. "Get down. Face down, on your belly."

"Harry! Harry, get out! I can't control it anymore!"

The wind and rain roared into the warehouse. Studs buckled under its pressure, and the outer wall caved in. The rest of the roof shuddered, then gave way.

Harry abandoned his aim on Marco. In that space of endless seconds, he saw his choice. He could get out—he knew that. He could also leave this murderer under a pile of rubble and avenge his parents. He'd spent almost a year of his life trying to find ways to punish Marco Torelli.

Now that he had the man cold, Harry couldn't do it.

The warehouse wall groaned. Marco's gaze shifted to his dog. "Lucas!" he called, running toward the Doberman cringing on the pavement just outside the door.

Debris pelted Harry's exposed skin. Shielding his face, he hurried away from the building...

Into a whirlwind storm that sucked the air from his lungs.

Marco knelt over his dog. Vincent, still holding his

nose, lay beside The Beast, which had remained in the lot. Nina laid on the horn, and through the bulletproof windshield, Harry saw her waving frantically for him to get to the vehicle.

Several feet away, Elsa stood with her hands in the air. Everywhere he saw skin, she glowed. She yelled to him, but over the noise, he couldn't hear her anymore.

Metal screeched again. Harry looked up.

And up. And up. He opened his mouth in shock.

The supercell had evolved into a tornado growling overhead, a horrific pillar of destruction that tore at the rest of the warehouse. A sheet of metal the size of The Beast slid off the buckled roof.

Toward him.

Adrenaline crashed through him. Harry bolted, but the sheet of metal was too big, and coming too fast.

A flash of blond hair caught his eye, a second before Elsa reached his side. She threw her arms up. Brilliant, white light surged outward around her, then sputtered. The shell of her protective sphere collapsed, and debris pelted against him. Harry shut his eyes, but the image of Elsa's terrified, tear-streaked face burned through him.

She has no juice left. She can't hold this back.

Harry flung himself over her body and tackled her down to the pavement against the side of The Beast. The scream of the wind and rending of metal filled his ears. Something crashed into his back. His head slammed against the side of the weather tank. He saw stars, and then, nothing at all.

****

"Harry? Harry, wake up! Please!" Fighting to stem her sobs, Elsa cradled Harry's head. Sirens flashed around her. People crowded in, a bedlam of emergency responders and onlookers and people with cell phone cameras and God knew what else. Their voices muddled together in a meaningless babble.

"Look at that piece of the roof..."

"—barely missed everybody—"

"—either the best luck on earth, or—"

"—poor dog. Someone get him to a vet."

Through a blur of tears, Elsa searched the crowd, feeling like a child all over again, with strangers all around and an awful, immeasurable grief in her heart.

She barely paid attention as a police cruiser took Marco and Vincent Torelli away. Someone gathered up the injured Doberman, then loaded it into a vehicle bound for the veterinarian.

A girl's voice, raised in fury, broke through Elsa's fog. "Get out of the way! That's my brother!" Rosalie shouldered her way between the gathered people with a force that belied her petite size. "Elsa! Are you okay?"

She stared at Rose, unable to do more than clench her fist convulsively in Harry's shirt.

Barking filled the air, and an instant later, Sam burst through the throng. Into the gap he'd created came Rory, Woz, Seth, and Nina. When Nina knelt beside her and laid a comforting hand on Elsa's back, Elsa stifled a moan of relief.

They were here. Her family, all around, all of them safe.

Except...

She looked back down at Harry, at the blood matting his dark hair. "A doctor," she croaked, still clutching his shirt. "Someone get a doctor."

Sam shoved his way toward them, then pushed his

nose right into Harry's face. Whining, the dog licked Harry's chin.

"Ugh. Ow. God, get off, dog!" Harry flung an arm over his face.

Joy burst through Elsa's chest. "Harry!"

He lowered his arm enough to fend off Sam's frenzied attentions. He bit off a groan when the dog bumped his splinted hand, then turned to Elsa. "Are you all right?"

"Me?" she cried. "Have you seen *you*?"

He levered himself to a sitting position, ignoring her team's protests. "Marco. Vincent."

"The police just took them away."

His gaze snapped to her face. Disbelief registered in those clear blue eyes—disbelief, and heartbreaking hope.

Elsa nodded. "They're gone, Harry."

His breath whooshed out. He looked at each of them, and finally, his gaze landed on his sister. "Rosie."

She launched herself at him to hug him around the neck. Seeing the girl cry on Harry's shoulder, Elsa swallowed hard.

"Harrison!" a voice shouted. "Harrison Litchfield!"

The crowd parted to reveal a tall, suit-clad woman with long, light brown hair and a microphone. Behind her was an army of cameras.

Harry gave Elsa a rueful look. "Reggie works fast."

The jostling crowd gave way. Emergency medical technicians approached them, but the newswoman got there first. "Harrison Litchfield," she repeated. "Carlene Salinger, News Channel Three." When the med techs urged her back, she held out her microphone. "Everyone's been wondering where you've been,

Mister Litchfield."

Harry's lip twitched in a smirk. He jerked his chin, indicating he wanted room to get up. Her team moved back. Rose grabbed Sam's collar and tugged him with her.

"Are you sure?" Elsa faltered. "Harry."

"I'm all right."

Her breath hitched. She bit down on her lip.

His gaze softened. He gathered his legs underneath him. Rising, he took her hand and pulled her up with him. "It's okay now." His voice was rough for a minute, then he repeated it more strongly, as if he were just now coming to believe it, himself. "It's okay." He slid an arm around her and touched his forehead to hers. "I'm not gonna leave you," he murmured.

Her tears started afresh, but now, they were joyful ones. "I love you, Harry."

"I love you, too, Elsa Pemberley. I don't even have words for how much I love you. You gave me my life back." He kissed her. Dimly, she registered the flash of cameras, but Harry only drew back enough to stroke her cheek. "I can't think of a better way to spend it than by thanking you for it every hour of every day, for the rest of my life...if you'll have me."

Words spilled away. Elsa stared at him. Everything but his face ceased to matter for a long, long time.

"What are you waiting for?" Nina yowled.

Her whole team started yelling at her, all at once, punctuated by Rose's encouraging, "Say it, say it!"

Elsa came back down to earth just long enough to give Harry a vigorous, tearful nod. "Yes. Yes!"

The delighted look on his face left no room for doubt that this was right. And there in front of the rescue workers, the news crew, her team, his sister—everybody—he kissed her again.

A muffled ringing reached her ears. With another rueful look, Harry drew her cell phone out of his back pocket and then handed it over.

Beaming, Elsa checked the caller ID.

Ethan.

Wiping away her tears, she answered it. "Hello?"

"Tell me you're in one piece right now," Ethan growled.

She stifled a laugh. "Hi to you, too."

There was a pause. Elsa could almost hear her foster brother listening to the chaos of the sirens and chatter around her. One of the medical technicians reached Harry and questioned him about his injuries. Ethan sighed loudly. "Cade is going to have a stroke over this, El."

"Not if you don't tell him."

"How am I not going to tell him, when he can probably switch on his TV and see you right now? I'm looking at you, and it looks like you fought with a combine harvester and lost."

"TV? Oh, my God." She glanced up at the flashing cameras, the newswoman with her microphone, the video camera with its red light. She worried for an instant that her power might surface, triggered by nerves, but for once, it remained obediently silent.

"Just answer me one thing," Ethan said. "You're okay?"

Elsa reached for Harry's hand. She grinned at her teammates, then Rose, then at Harry again, with such love in her heart it must have been plainly written on her face. Harry pulled her close and tucked his arm around her.

Elsa turned her attention back to her cell. "Ethan," she assured him, "I have never been better. Talk soon." She clicked off the cell amid his protests, then shoved it into the pocket of her jeans.

The crowds could wait. The cameras could wait. Even her minor cuts and bruises were unimportant. All of it paled beside the knowledge that she finally had everything she'd ever wanted, right here beside her, and even on the other end of a disgruntled phone conversation.

Blood ties didn't matter. Distance didn't, either. Only one thing mattered. Only one thing bound people together as a family, whether they were related or not.

Love.

A word about the author...

Nicki Greenwood graduated SUNY Morrisville with a degree in Natural Resources. She found her passion in writing stories of romantic adventure and combines that with her love of the environment. Her works have won several awards, including the Rebecca Eddy Memorial Contest. Her first book, *EARTH,* debuted in 2010 through The Wild Rose Press, Inc.

Nicki lives in upstate New York with her husband, son, and assorted pets. When she's not writing, she enjoys the arts, gardening, interior decorating, and trips to the local Renaissance Faire.

http://www.nickigreenwood.com